To

Ken,

th ... ch

for all your help and support.

Regards

Virginia (Mary)

About the Author

Virginia Sidley was born in Longparish, a small village in Hampshire, in 1941. She married and with her husband of fifty four years, lived in Singapore, Dubai, Zambia, Botswana and South Africa, before settling in the beautiful Devon village of Winkleigh.

Recently widowed, this is Virginia's first novel.

For the two lovely men I was lucky enough to share my life with. My beloved husband Dick, who passed away in April 2015, and my late dad as this was partly his story.

Virginia Sidley

DOWN ARGENTINA WAY

AUSTIN MACAULEY
PUBLISHERS LTD.

A CIP catalogue record for this title is available from the British Library.

ISBN 9781786122230 (Paperback)
ISBN 9781786122247 (Hardback)
ISBN 9781786122254 (eBook)

www.austinmacauley.com

First Published (2016)
Austin Macauley Publishers Ltd.
25 Canada Square
Canary Wharf
London
E14 5LQ

Acknowledgments

Many thanks to my friends in Argentina, Betty Descalzo and her late lovely husband Jorge, and to the Blake family at Estancia Killik Aike, who gave me access to their library and farm records, helping me build a picture of what life was like in the 1920s and 1930s.

To my fellow writer Glennis Horne, who told me I could do it. My tutor at Writer News School, Elizabeth Ashworth, who helped and encouraged me.

To my friend Ken Howarth, who showed infinite patience helping me to put the book into digital format.

Last but by no means least to my publisher Austin Macauley and their team of professionals who lead me through the complex process between writing and the reality of seeing the completed novel in print, a huge thank you.

Chapter 1

Please tell me Laura Anne where have you been all day.
Since you went on that journey down Argentina way.

He was restless having been cooped up aboard ship. He couldn't wait to leave the docks behind him. May, 1937, his favourite time of year in England, the green buds on the trees peeping through, the bluebell woods, newborn creatures, everything fresh and new, and hopefully a new beginning for him too.

It was a very different Tommy who disembarked at Southampton to the one that had sailed from Liverpool some twelve years earlier.

This was a fit, lean well-muscled Tommy who at thirty-two years old who stepped onto the dockside, his handsome craggy face weathered from his outdoor life in the Argentine. His limp was barely discernible. His moneybelt fitted snugly round his slim waist.

He had no idea of what he was going to do for work. He'd left Estancia Montalban with no thought to the future. He just wanted to put as much distance as he could between himself and Catriona.

His first priority on his arrival in Reading was to go to his bank. Tommy stared around, taking in everything, the hustle and bustle of the traffic, motor cars, delivery vans, buses and taxis, people rushing back and forth like a colony of ants. When he'd left England motor traffic had been minimal. The noise struck him, the tooting of horns, the squeal of tyres, a cacophony of sound, the smell of oil and exhaust fumes.

The slight deafness in his left ear, normally not a problem, seemed magnified. He supposed he'd get used to it.

He found his way to the railway station to find he was in luck. There was a train going to Reading in twenty minutes. Once settled comfortably on the train, he watched the countryside roll by. He'd forgotten how many different shades of green there were. No wonder they called it 'England's green and pleasant land' he mused.

He thought about his brothers: Georgie, who he'd kept in touch with, and Matthew, who'd never answered his letters, but Georgie had kept him informed of Matthew's whereabouts. The twins were twenty-eight now, both of them married. Matthew had married Alice Metcalf from the village and was now a postman in Bournemouth. Georgie had married a girl from Reading, and they had two daughters. Georgie lived in Swallowfield, while still working with their father as assistant gamekeeper, still on Lord Pendleberry's estate.

He wondered about his father. He'd written home every Christmas, but George had never replied. His father had married Maude exactly three months after his mother's death - his 'fancy woman' as Tommy had always thought of her. The last three years he'd received a reply but from Maude. She had taken it upon herself to try to heal the breach between Tommy and his father. She had written that she hoped, that if he ever came home, he'd be willing to let the past be just that, and that their wish was that he would come and visit them.

He wondered how much Maude really knew about the past. The sadistic and cruel beatings for minor misdemeanours, nothing more than childish pranks. The open hostility his father had always shown to him, that had made him ask his mother at six years old, 'Why does Daddy hate me so?'

The horrendous incident, just six weeks before his tenth birthday when his beloved dog, Podge, was shot by his father. George had ordered Tommy to tie the dog up to the garden gate and then told him to take a couple of steps away. By the time the time George had slipped a couple of cartridges into his twelve bore and brought the gun up, the realisation of his father's intention hit him.

Both barrels exploded, momentarily drowning out his screams, his screams continuing long after the sounds of the explosion had died away. He felt the warm mixture of blood and brains splatter onto his face.

He closed his eyes trying to erase the memory that had given him nightmares for so many years. He didn't doubt Maude's sincerity - just her interpretation of his father's wishes. Well, he'd see, he might even put it to the test.

He looked forward to seeing Amelia Nelson. First as his schoolteacher she had gone on to become his mentor, eventually a close and valued friend. Throughout his years at Melchet Court, to his departure to the Argentine, their letters spanned seventeen years. What had begun as a teacher-pupil relationship had over the years blossomed into a deep and abiding friendship.

He fingered his mother's ring which he still wore on a heavy silver chain around his neck. He never took it off - it had become part of him. His mother's words came back to him when she'd given it to him. She said she'd hoped he'd find someone to give it to one day. He hoped so too. He thought of Catriona and just as quickly blocked her from his mind. He'd made his decision and he'd promised himself there would be no going back, no regrets.

The train screeched to a halt, billowing white smoke, into Reading station. He came back to earth with a jolt.

His first stop was the bank where, much to his surprise, his three hundred and ten pounds from 1925 had grown into a decent sum. What was even more surprising was that his pesos converted to a staggering five thousand and seventy pounds giving him a grand total of five thousand six hundred and thirty pounds, and that was without the money he'd changed in Southampton, which was sufficient to see him over the next couple of months and buy him a respectable wardrobe.

On leaving the bank his next stop was the barber for the luxury of a shampoo, shave and a haircut. His hair was unfashionably long, his clothes ill-fitting and he realised he must look like a tramp.

He sat in the barber's chair luxuriating in the warm, scented foaming soap and gave himself up totally to the sensuous pleasure of being shaved.

'Can you recommend an outfitters where I can get kitted out?' he asked through the foam.

'Why yes, certainly, sir. If you'd like to buy off-the-peg there's a Burtons just around the corner - very good quality but if you're looking for tailor made,' he paused, the pause implying that he couldn't imagine where Tommy could possibly find the money for a tailor, 'then there's Nathaniel Silver's just off London Road in Church Street.'

'Thanks,' Tommy grinned, 'Silver's sounds O.K.' He enjoyed the look of surprise that came over the man's face and, even more, the expression as Tommy tipped him generously 'Thank you, sir,' he said in amazement, his lantern jaw dropping open.

He made his way to Church Street and Nathaniel Silver's shop. There he purchased, underwear, jumpers, two pairs of off the peg trousers, along with various other items, he was measured for two tailor made three piece suits, which would be ready for a fitting the following week, and finally he was persuaded to purchase a camel overcoat, which Mr. Silver assured him was the very latest word in overcoats this year. He drew the line when Mr. Silver suggested the whole ensemble required a soft brimmed trilby to set it off. Tommy resisted. He didn't want to look like a tailor's dummy.

He killed some time looking round the shops as he'd discovered the next bus to Swallowfield didn't leave until three thirty. On passing the Red Lion Hotel he was assailed by a variety of delicious aromas. Realising he was hungry we went in recalling the many times he and Gareth had talked about home on the nights they'd been sleeping over at an out-station. They usually discussed what they wouldn't do for a plate of roast beef and Yorkshire puddings, a good home-made steak and kidney pie, as they tucked into their adequate but uninteresting rations.

Lunch over he made his way to the bus depot. Half an hour later he alighted from the bus at The Huntsman pub in Swallowfield looking quite the gentleman in his new clothes. Arriving at Rose Cottage, he strode up the once well-known pathway that he'd seen in his mind's eye, once he'd made the decision to return to England. He was surprised at the emotions he felt as his feet trod the familiar path - he felt as if he'd come home. He raised his hand to the brass knocker, but it never reached there. The door opened and Amelia stood there, a gentle smile of welcome lighting up her dear familiar face.

'Thomas, how wonderful to see you. I have so looked forward to today.'

'So have I Amelia,' he said dropping his packages and holding out his arms. He hugged her, reluctant to let her go as if afraid she'd disappear.

'Come in Thomas. Welcome home. Your room is ready. My goodness,' she added, taking a step back to get a better look, 'but just look at you - you've become so handsome. I still can't believe you're actually here at last.'

'You look a sight for sore eyes. You don't look any different to when I saw you last,' he smiled.

'Why thank you Thomas. I see you've learnt the art of pleasing a lady. I half expected to see you return with a Spanish bride,' she laughed.

'No not for me,' he said slowly, a shadow crossing his face momentarily.

Amelia recognised a shutting down of emotions, a concealing of his thoughts and feelings, something Tommy had been very adept at. She wondered what had happened. Obviously a man of his age must have had some involvement with women over the years. Never one to pry, Amelia couldn't help but feel just that little bit curious.

After a hearty supper and a bottle of good red wine Tommy had brought - something he'd learned to appreciate from Mr. Grimes, the butler from his Melchet Court days as a trainee footman, they chatted relaxed and totally at ease in each other's company, until Tommy mentioned his letters from Maude.

'Do you know her Amelia?' he asked curiously. 'What's she like?'

'Yes I do, and quite honestly I think you might be surprised to find that you'd like her. She's a very down to earth kind of woman and rumour has it that she rules the roost in the Lawrence household,' she said, a faint smile appearing at the corner of her mouth. 'Her and your father go to whist drives at the village hall and always attend the church socials, and the summer fête, and come to that any other village activities.'

'Well that's a turn up for the book. The old man could never be persuaded to go anywhere with my mother, let alone a church social.' He shook his head. 'He's succumbed to petticoat government has he? I must admit I'm curious about her. She invited me to visit, but I'm not sure that I want to. You know the relationship between us, past history and all that. What do you think Amelia?'

'Well your father is getting older Thomas, and as we get older we do sometimes regret some of the things we've done in life, and often some of the things we didn't do too. Don't you think,' she went on, 'that like your stepmother suggests, it might be time to put the past behind you?'

Tommy looked shocked, 'Good God Amelia! I never thought of her as being my stepmother - only as my father's "fancy piece", and it's not a thought I'm entirely comfortable with I might add.'

'Well now, that's what she is Thomas, whether you like it or not, and,' she went on tartly, 'I hardly think it's gentlemanly of you to refer to the woman your father has been married to for twelve years as his 'fancy piece'. You don't even know the woman. Maude Appleton was a perfectly respectable widow when she married your father. I know you resent her taking your mother's place as it were, but be fair - it takes two people to make a relationship work. I know how much you loved your mother, but you can't hold Maude or your father responsible for your mother's death. It was an illness,' she finished on a gentler note.

'So what you're trying to tell me Amelia is yes you think I should visit them,' he asked wryly.

'Yes that's exactly what I'm saying,' she nodded vigorously.

'O.K. tomorrow I'm going to see Georgie and meet his family, so I'll take a walk up to East Lodge after. Now that's settled, how about you allowing me to take you to dinner tomorrow evening? I'll order a taxi in the morning and we'll go to the Red Lion in town. I had lunch there today, it was excellent,' he smiled.

'Good heavens, that's very extravagant Thomas,' she looked pleased, 'but you should be taking out some nice young lady of your own age, although I must admit it sounds very nice.'

'Well, you'll have to find me suitable young ladies Amelia, because I wouldn't even begin to know where to start looking.'

With your looks you won't have to look too far Amelia thought to herself.

They sat till midnight catching up on events. Tommy described his life in the Argentine until he rose saying, 'Will you please excuse me Amelia? I think I'll just go outside for a last cigarette before I turn in.'

'I told you many years ago when your mother died, you were to regard this as your home, and a man should be able to smoke in his own home if he wants to - please feel free,' she said rising and bringing him a heavy glass ashtray from the sideboard.

'Thank you Amelia,' he said softly, both of them being aware it was not just for the ashtray that he was thanking her.

Chapter 2

Tommy was tired but sleep evaded him. He'd told Amelia he'd go to visit his father and Maude, but he was already half regretting it. Putting the past behind him was easier said than done. There was nothing Amelia didn't know about his childhood. Why would she agree with Maude?

The memories flooded back; the beating at six years old with his father's leather belt with the big brass buckle cutting into the soft tender flesh of his buttocks, drawing blood. The incident with his dog shot supposedly for killing a couple of pheasants, which Tommy knew deep down was another sadistic act of cruelty inflicted on him by a father who hated him.

He also remembered that fateful evening a month before his fifteenth birthday, two years after he had started working with his father, at the shoot organised by his father as Lord Pendleberry's gamekeeper was over. It had been a long day. Supper was over, the twins tucked up in bed and an air of Christmas about the house with the smell of plum puddings cooking. Tommy had sat at the kitchen table reading while his mother was turned a collar on one of his father's shirts while George himself seemed to be dozing in his chair.

Tommy looked up. 'Mum, I was loading for Mr. Bingham today and he asked me if I enjoyed my work. He then said had I ever thought of doing anything else. I wasn't sure what he meant but then he said his sister was looking for someone my age to start as a footman and to be trained as a butler. What does a butler do, Mum?'

His mother was about to launch into an explanation of a butler's duties when his father spoke.

'Well that's very nice I must say. Lord Pendleberry employs you at good money for two years and you, you ungrateful little whipper-snapper, have got the bloody cheek to ask one of his shooting guests for a job.'

'I didn't ask anyone for a job, Dad. Mr. Bingham was just talking to me between drives.' Tommy said staring hard at his father. Why, he wondered did he deliberately misunderstand what he said and grasp every opportunity to be unpleasant and quarrelsome?

'Are you going to sit there and bloody well tell me that Mr. Bingham would be interested in you, you little liar?' he glowered.

'No Dad,' Tommy jumped up sending the chair flying with a clatter, 'I'm not a liar. Why do you always try and put me in the wrong? It happened like I said.'

'Don't you stand there and argue with me. Pick up that chair and shut up. You're not big enough to argue with me yet. I can still give you a good hiding and don't you forget it!' he shouted.

'No Dad you can't,' Tommy's lips tightened and the blood drained from his face.

'Can't what? Huh you wouldn't be threatening me would you boy, because you're making a big mistake if you are,' he said, in turn rising from his chair.

His mother put down her sewing and stepped in between them.

'That's enough now...,' she began when his father swept her roughly out of the way causing her to fall against the range burning her arm as she did so.

Something in Tommy snapped, a white rage took over. For fifteen years he'd suffered physical and mental abuse from this man. He knew this moment was inevitable. It was almost as if his whole life had been building up to this climax.

He lunged forward catching his father with first a fist in the face followed by one to the stomach, which temporarily winded him.

Tommy stood there, his arms hanging slackly at his sides suddenly aware of the enormity of what he'd done. His rage, quick to flare at the sight of his mother being pushed, was already subsiding.

His father straightened up, a murderous expression on his face, 'You little bastard. You'll pay for that,' he gasped and grabbing the front of Tommy's shirt in one swift movement he brought his head forward sharply. Tommy heard the crack and felt the searing hot pain as his nose smashed with the impact of the head butt.

His mother screamed, 'Please George! No please don't!' as the blood from Tommy's nose sprayed through the air leaving dark spots on the green tablecloth.

Tommy couldn't see for the tears in his eyes from the blow. He lashed out wildly, fists flailing into fresh air. His father had no such impediment, and he rhythmically started to beat Tommy, relentless blow after sickening blow until he dropped to the floor. He was gasping and struggling to rise when his father delivered his first almighty kick, his hobnail boot making a dull thud as it connected with his stomach. He kicked him once more as his mother threw herself down beside Tommy's inert body.

'No more George, you'll kill him,' she pleaded.

'I hope that'll teach him a lesson. That's just a taste of what's to come if he ever argues with me again,' he snarled.

His mother and the barely conscious Tommy heard the door slam as his father strode off into the cold winter's night.

She helped Tommy sit up, his back against the wing chair. He groaned as he clutched his body. His face was covered in blood.

The latch rattling on the stairs door made Tommy open his eyes. The door opened to reveal Matthew standing shivering in his nightshirt.

'Mummy what's happened to Tommy?' he asked, his chin already starting to quiver.

'He's hurt,' she replied. 'Quickly Matthew, you've got to be a brave boy. Go and get dressed. You'll have to run to the village for Dr. Anderson.'

'No Mum,' Tommy whispered through lips that were already starting to swell. 'No Doctor! What can you tell him?'

'Yes, Tommy we must,' she insisted. 'Go on Matthew, get dressed quickly and wrap up warmly.'

'I'll run all the way, Mum. Is Tommy going to be all right?' the eleven year old Matthew asked anxiously.

'I hope so Matthew. Oh God I hope so,' she said 'Although it'll be no thanks to your father if he's not.'

She did her best to make Tommy comfortable stopping him when he tried to speak. He wanted to reassure her. He wanted to know if she was all right, but everything was in a haze as he drifted in and out of consciousness.

At the sound of Dr. Anderson's pony and trap, his mother went to the front door and sent Matthew straight back upstairs to bed with the promise that she'd bring him up a hot cup of cocoa later. She ushered the doctor into the warm kitchen where Tommy lay propped up against the chair.

'Now then Mrs Lawrence, what's going on?' he asked briskly. 'I couldn't make any sense out of that young man of yours.'

'Tommy and his father were out after poachers, doctor, and they got separated in the dark. The poachers got to Tommy and beat him up,' she lied smoothly.

The doctor cleaned Tommy up discovering the broken nose, cut over one eye requiring four stitches and several broken ribs.

'Not a lot to be done, I'll bind the ribs up tight, the nose'll mend itself, maybe a bit crooked, and the cuts and bruises and swellings will all disappear in a couple of weeks, but you'll live,' he ended cheerfully. 'And that's a nasty burn you've got on your arm, Mrs. Lawrence, I'll give you something to put on that.'

She paid him his five shillings fee and thanked him for coming out on such a night as she saw him to the door. His final instructions were to keep the patient in bed quietly on a light diet and plenty of fluids for a few days.

She went quickly upstairs to see to Matthew who was already fast asleep. Coming back down she helped Tommy to his feet getting him upstairs and into bed. She fussed getting hot water bottles and an extra quilt. Dr. Anderson had administered a dose of laudanum which was taking effect, lessening the pain but making Tommy feel decidedly woozy.

She finally came into the bedroom. Turning the key in the door, she prepared to settle down in the old armchair in the corner of Tommy's room. Tommy lay breathing shallowly, his eyes closed, but he wasn't asleep. He groaned and she rushed to the bedside. He opened his eyes, a wave of humiliation and despair washed over him.

'It's alright Tommy. In a couple of days, when you feel well enough, you'll go to your grandmother's. Then I'm going to get in touch with Mr. Bingham about that job. I've saved thirty one pounds of your money over the last two years. Your father will never hurt you again. Do you understand?' she finished gently.

He nodded. He wanted to thank her, but his mouth felt full of cotton wool. In fact he was surrounded by cotton wool floating on clouds of the soft white fluffy stuff. He let himself be enveloped in it as he drifted into a drug induced sleep.

Two days before Christmas Tommy made the slow and painful journey to his grandmother's. The whole village was talking about the dreadful beating Tommy Lawrence had suffered at the hands of poachers. He remained at his grandmother's through the New Year. Miss Nelson visited as did Dr. Anderson, his mother, and his brothers, but no one saw George Lawrence either enter or leave the Shaw's cottage during that time.

George didn't ask Martha how Tommy was, and in turn, she didn't volunteer any information.

As promised by Martha, the New Year found Tommy on his way to Melchet Court, the home of Mr. Bingham's sister, which was to be Tommy's home for the next five years.

The following morning Tommy rose early, barely five thirty, and made his way quietly downstairs careful not to disturb Amelia. He let himself out of the house and started to walk.

His thoughts were concentrated on his forthcoming visits. He knew it was stupid, but he felt nervous of meeting Georgie and his family. When Tommy had left England, Georgie had been a raw sixteen year old - now he was a married man with a family. What would they talk about? Would they have anything in common or would it be like two strangers meeting for the first time? Writing a couple of letters a year wasn't the ideal way to keep in touch. His correspondence with Amelia had been a different kind of relationship, built up and nurtured over the years.

A few hours later found him on the step of number one Breech cottages. The little garden was neat and well-kept with pansies growing in the border. He took a deep breath and knocked firmly on the door. A few moments later and Georgie opened the door. The two of them stood awkwardly neither knowing quite what to say.

'Tommy,' the man in the doorway said - it was almost a question, 'I can't believe it's you ... Come in.' He then stepped back to admit Tommy into the tiny dark hallway, which with the two of them standing in, looked about to burst at the seams.

'Come down to the kitchen. Sylvia's there and the kids are playing in the back garden,' he said leading the way down a narrow passage which led into a surprisingly bright cheerful room with red and white check gingham curtains and matching cloth covering the table. The window sills were crammed with pots of brilliant red geraniums. The kettle was singing merrily on an old black lead range. The woman at the earthenware kitchen sink turned at their entrance, hastily drying her hands on her apron and self-consciously reaching up to pat her fluffy blonde hair. She smiled shyly at Tommy.

'Sit down Tommy. Sylv, make us a cup of tea. You'd like some wouldn't you our Tommy?' And with that familiar form of address, all trace of nervousness vanished.

The children were called in and introductions over, Tommy produced the carefully chosen gifts from Buenos Aires for them all. After many *oohs* and *thank yous* the girls returned to their play and Sylvia excused herself and left the brothers to catch up on the past. The conversation flowed easily. Georgie was eager to hear all about Argentina and Tommy was equally eager to hear about Georgie's life. Lunchtime came and Tommy sat down with his brother and his family to a meal of pot roasted brisket surrounded by succulent baby carrots, potatoes and onions.

Tommy thought briefly about his childhood when he had last sat down for a meal as part of a family. The ominous silences, his father stern and forbidding at the head of the table – so different from this occasion in his brother's house. The laughing and chattering of the children, the conversation of the adults, the so obvious ease they felt with each other. He felt a pang of envy for his young brother's undisguised happiness and contentment with his family.

After lunch Tommy said reluctantly, 'Well I suppose if I'm going to visit East Lodge I'd better be making tracks. Thank you for the meal Sylvia. It was lovely.'

'You're welcome Tommy, it was so nice to meet you at last,' she said with genuine pleasure.

'I'll see you out Tommy,' Georgie said rising from his chair. 'Won't be long Sylvia then we'll take the girls to fly their kite down on the common.'

Once outside Tommy said, 'You've got a lovely family Georgie. You're very lucky. Look after them.'

'Yeah, I know. Now that you're back you must come and see us often. What are you going to do next?' he asked.

'Oh I suppose I shall have to start looking for a job soon. I've got a bit of cash put by, but I don't want to touch it if I can help it.'

I'm glad you're going to see the old man and Maude Tommy. He's mellowed you know, Maude's doing I'm sure. I think he's got his regrets regarding you, although you know him. He doesn't say much.'

Tommy grunted, 'We'll see.'

Tommy took an interminable age to reach East Lodge. Normally a brisk ten minute walk, he took a full half hour. As he rounded the last bend the memories rushed back. The last time he'd seen the house had been the day his mother had died, and the last time he'd seen his father had been the day of her funeral.

With his hand resting on the gate, he hesitated. He was filled with an overwhelming desire to turn and run. Come on, he told himself, you're thirty two years old. Why in the hell do you still feel intimidated at the thoughts of seeing the old man again after all these years?

He shook his head, opened the gate and walked determinedly up to the front door where he knocked boldly and waited.

Chapter 3

He didn't have to wait long - the door opened to reveal a short, grey haired motherly figure wearing a bright floral print dress. She cocked her head to one side, birdlike, and studied him before speaking.

'Hello, you must be Tommy, or do you prefer Thomas?' she asked briskly.

'Yes Ma'am, you're right about who I am, and I prefer Tommy. I take it you're...,' he hesitated unsure of what to call her. Mrs. Lawrence sounded stiff and formal and Maude sounded too familiar for someone he'd only just met.

'Please call me Maude, and do come in. Your father is in the back garden. We'd heard you'd arrived yesterday,' she smiled and went on. 'Well you know how news travels in the village.'

'I'm sure it does, although I only got to Amelia's late in the afternoon. How is Dad?' he asked.

'He keeps well enough for a man of his age - hard work and good country living never does anybody any harm. Listen, why don't you go out to the garden and say hello while I put the kettle on. I'll call you when I've made some tea.'

'Thanks,' Tommy said heading for the back door. He would willingly have forfeited the tea. He'd forgotten just how much tea the English consumed. Yes, the Englishman's panacea - a good cup of tea cures all ills. He'd grown accustomed to mate, a herbal concoction peculiar to the

Argentine, or coffee and actually found tea a bit insipid for his taste. He found his father digging over a patch ready for planting.

'Hello Dad,' the words stuck in his throat.

George looked up and, wiping the sweat from his forehead with the back of his hand, he said, 'Mmmm, you're back then. How have you been?'

Tommy was shaken at how much older George looked, shrunken and smaller in every way, than Tommy's memory of him. Tommy was now the bigger, taller man of the two. 'Okay thanks, and you Dad, how about you?'

'We're all right. I keep busy and Maude and I manage. Did she let you in?' he jerked his head in the direction of the house.

'Yes,' Tommy said fishing in his pockets for his cigarettes. 'She seems okay Dad,' he finished awkwardly not knowing quite what else to say.

'Mmm, she's all right, I'spose. Talks too much like most women. That's why I come out here for a bit of peace and quiet,' he grinned wolfishly.

Just then Maude's voice could be heard calling from the back door.

'George? George tea's made.'

'Better go and have it - never hear the end of it if it goes cold,' he muttered.

Tommy couldn't believe the metamorphosis that his father had undergone from the bullying, domineering character to a henpecked husband whose wife obviously wore the trousers. As they approached the kitchen door Maude's voice came out, 'Take your boots off dear, before you come in.'

Tommy suppressed a grin at George having to remove his boots before he was allowed into the house.

Once ensconced in the parlour with tea and home-made fruit cake, Maude asked, 'Are you back for good now Tommy?'

'I'm not sure. I guess so. I'll start looking for work next week.'

'So Argentina didn't work out then?' George said with the hint of a sneer in his voice.

'What do you mean that it didn't work out? I've just spent twelve years there and felt in need of a change. That's all,' Tommy retorted sharply.

'So I s'pose you'll be looking for work round here then. What sort of job do you reckon you'll be going after? A farm labourer or try your hand at being an under keeper, the same way I started?'

'Not necessarily round here, and no to both suggestions. I thought after managing an *estancia,* that's like a huge farm,' he said by way of an explanation seeing the puzzled look on his father's face. 'I might try to be a bit more ambitious and apply for a farm bailiff or farm manager's post.'

'Humph a manager no less, you always had ideas above your station,' he snorted. 'Your mother and that schoolmarm woman encouraged you.'

Here we go again Tommy thought, leopards don't change their spots. Why did he ever imagine that things might be different? He felt his anger rising. It was as if he was back to being a fifteen year old, taking yet another reprimand from this joyless, morose man that was his father. But he wasn't fifteen any more and he didn't have to listen to disparaging remarks about his mother and Amelia.

'Before you go any farther down that road, my mother and that "school marm", whose name as you well know happens to be Amelia Nelson, only ever wanted me to be the best I could be, and if that in your narrow-minded, bigoted way means I've got ideas above my station, as you so succinctly put it, then so be it.'

Tommy was inwardly seething. Manners dictated that he should show courtesy to Maude, but it was time for him to curtail his visit before the situation got totally out of hand. He was about to rise from his chair when Maude intervened.

'Shame on you George, the lad's quite right. What's wrong with trying to better yourself? He looks as if he's done pretty well for himself so far, and you should be proud. Don't be so hard on him.'

'Humph maybe, so what's Argentina like then? What do they farm on these fancy *estancias*?' he asked grudgingly.

'All sorts, but where I was in Patagonia, it's mainly sheep. The country's pretty barren, so there's no crops but constant winds, hard winters, thousands and thousands of acres with nothing but sheep, no towns, no villages, but somehow it has a fascination all of its own,' he enthused.

Since the situation defused by Maude, Tommy stayed a while longer, talking mainly about Argentina, before finally taking his leave. He felt as if he and his father had reached an uneasy truce. He thanked Maude for the tea and fruit cake.

'Well it was nice to meet you at last. Take no notice of your father. It's just his way. I hope you're going to come and visit us again, and I really do mean it. It wasn't so bad was it?' she asked her eyes twinkling.

He found himself returning her smile. 'No, it wasn't so bad Maude, mainly thanks to your intervention, and yes, I'll come again.'

Later that same evening Tommy and Amelia sat over coffee and petit fours, having enjoyed the Red Lion's excellent cuisine. The opulence of their surroundings enveloped them like a warm cloud with carpets so rich and thick that you sank into them and the crystal and silver sparkling like early morning dew. Even the staff talked in muted tones usually reserved for church congregations.

'I'm so glad you made a kind of peace with your father Thomas. You know it's only when you have no family that you realise just how important they are.' Her hand strayed to caress the silver brooch, a gift from Tommy, pinned to the lapel of her light woollen dress. 'I'm sure your dear mother would have approved of you making the first move.'

'Yes I'm sure she would Amelia, but you know I can't begin to tell you how much he still intimidates me. I'm a grown man and I still feel inferior in his presence. Why Amelia? He's done nothing special with his life. Why should I be bending over backwards for his approval? Why should I even care?'

'Force of habit Thomas. As a child you constantly sought his approval, and it wasn't forthcoming, and so you're still looking for it. You've grown into a fine young man - stop doubting yourself. You left here a young inexperienced boy and you've come back a man of the world. For what it's worth, I'm very proud of you.'

His eyes held hers steadily. 'Thank you Amelia, your opinion is worth a great deal to me. Now, changing the subject, can I ask you a very personal question?'

'Yes?' she nodded raising her eyebrows quizzically.

'How come you've never married? I know it's really no concern of mine, but over the years I've often wondered.'

She sighed softly, 'Probably because no one has ever asked me. After my parents died I was so busy trying to make ends meet and by then I was in my mid-twenties and was already considered to be an old maid.'

'That's a shame Amelia. I'm sorry. I didn't mean to pry.'

'No that's quite alright, but now I have a personal question for you too.'

He laughed. 'Well fire away, you've got me in a corner now. You answered my question I can hardly refuse to answer yours, can I?' He was relaxed with the atmosphere, and the wine drunk over dinner, but a wary look came into his eyes.

'It's the same question Thomas. Most men of your age are married and settled down with families. Has there been anyone or, should I say is there anyone?'

Tommy closed his eyes momentarily - it was a mannerism he'd adopted over the years to hide either embarrassment or emotions he didn't want to share.

As Tommy looked up his eyes were full of pain. Why hadn't he seen his coming, someone was bound to ask sooner or later, he supposed he should be grateful that it was Amelia, who could be trusted with any secrets he might divulge.

'Yes there was someone Amelia, but it's over. It didn't work out. It was a disaster and her name was Catriona Ramirez. Yes,' he nodded, 'that's right, the *estancia* owner's daughter. It was a situation I should never have got myself into. I was old enough to know better even if she wasn't. I'm already wondering if I did the right thing in leaving.'

'Is there no going back? Nothing you can do?' she urged seeing the misery reflected in his eyes.

'No, it's better this way - that's what you always told me Amelia - and I'm sure in this case it's the right way.'

She reached across the table and patted his hand. 'Now I'm the one who's sorry I asked Thomas. You'll find someone else. It's so much easier for a man. And now let's think of the future and tell me what kind of work you think you're going to look for.'

'Well something in the farming line. I guess that's what I know best, and what I'm cut out for. As I told Dad I'm hoping to get a job as a farm manager or farm bailiff if possible. If not then perhaps I could get a place in an Agriculture College. I've got a little money put by. Mind you I'd feel pretty stupid a man of my age going back to school,' he grinned weakly.

'Nonsense, it's very commendable and there's nothing wrong with adult education. You were always a model pupil. I'm sure you'll get a job anyway Thomas, as you've excellent references from both of your jobs in the Argentine and by that alone they can see you've had twelve years' experience.'

'Mmm,' he shook his head doubtfully. 'I'm not sure that my experience on an *estancia* in Patagonia qualifies me to run a farm in rural England.'

'Well you won't know till you try will you?' she said decisively.

Over the following week Tommy applied for three positions: one in Hampshire, another in Wales and the third in Northumbria and then he sat back and waited for replies.

Meanwhile he dug Amelia's small back garden, planted flowers, and that done, he painted the interior of the cottage.

He then found time heavy on his hands. He'd heard nothing regarding his job applications. He wasn't accustomed to much leisure time and after being home for two weeks, boredom was nipping at his heels.

It was a dull overcast day, with the air heavy and oppressive like a thick wet blanket, that he found himself in Reading, not for any specific reason other than to pass away another day. By midday the thunder was rumbling and the first heavy drops of rain plopped down. Within minutes the heavens opened. Everyone took cover rushing into shops, or the handiest doorway. Tommy raced for the nearest door which turned out to be a pub called The Greyhound.

In those few steps he was soaked. His hair blacker than ever when wet was plastered to his head. His shirt clung to him and his shoes squelched with his every step. He stood just inside the door and shook himself, dog fashion, droplets spraying everywhere. He blinked the water out of his eyes and was startled to see a young woman standing behind the bar watching him.

She was quite the most beautiful young woman he'd ever seen. Her skin was fresh and creamy, her shoulder length hair a thick lustrous gold curtain, high cheekbones accentuating the most striking hyacinth blue eyes. He knew he was staring, but he couldn't stop.

'Hello,' she smiled revealing small even white teeth, 'You look like a drowned rat. Can I get you anything?'

He found himself grinning foolishly. 'Umm, yes I suppose so,' he hesitated since never very fond of beer, he wasn't sure of what else to order. 'I'll have a brandy and soda please.'

'That's called a horse's neck. Did you know that?'

'What is?' he said vaguely, unable to take his eyes off her face.

'A brandy and soda. Is my lipstick smudged?' she asked pertly.

'Oh no, I'm sorry. I didn't mean to stare, but you're very pretty, but then I suppose you get told that all the time,' he finished lamely. 'Thanks,' he said as she put his drink in from of him.

'Are you new round here then? I don't think I've seen you before. I'm sure I would have remembered you.'

'No probably not. I'm living in Swallowfield at the moment I've just come back from the Argentine. Do you live round here? By the way my name's Tommy Lawrence. What's yours?' he asked feeling somehow gauche.

'Emma Butler, and yes, I live right here in The Greyhound. My aunt and uncle own it. I don't work here normally,' she went on, 'it's just that my aunt had a dentist's appointment and as I'm on a week's holiday from my job, I'm helping out. Where did you say you'd just come back from, Argentina? Sounds exciting. What did you do there?'

He was aware of Emma Butler watching him as he talked, but he was totally unaware that women found him attractive with his smoky grey eyes, the small scar over his left eyebrow and his slightly crooked nose only adding to his attraction. His shirt still damp clinging to his shoulders, defining his every muscle, coming down to a flat stomach. She eyed him appreciatively without a trace of shyness. To Tommy there was something in her bold look reminiscent of Catriona - not that there was any physical resemblance. Emma was a golden vision, where Catriona had been a dark, sultry beauty with masses of tumbling black curls. He could feel and smell them now against his face, silken sandalwood. How many times had he fallen asleep, his face buried in her hair after a night of passionate but forbidden lovemaking? Her face swam before him.

The sound of Emma's voice brought him back to the present.

'What did you say?' he drained his glass.

'I said that sounds a very exciting life you've led. Won't you find it a bit dull round here? You're looking for work you say. Well it would be a pity if you had to move from the area to get it,' she smiled coquettishly, 'before you've even got round to making some new friends.'

'Yes but perhaps I'll get a job in Hampshire I applied for. Who knows, and that's not far from here. I wonder, I was thinking of going to the cinema this afternoon to pass the time. Perhaps you'd like to come with me, or as the rain seems to have stopped, maybe you'd rather go for a walk?' he suggested.

'It's closing time in about quarter of an hour. I'll just tell my uncle I'm going for a walk with a friend. I know we're not really friends, but who knows maybe we will be soon.'

He watched her walk through to the other bar. A small trim figure, her hips swinging jauntily. He noted her shapely legs. He hoped her prediction would turn out to be right and they would become friends.

Lying in bed later that night he thought briefly about Emma Butler. Almost against his will he found himself attracted to her. The last thing he needed was any involvement of any kind with a woman, it was just too soon.

He lay awake listening to the wind getting up, mulling over his time in England so far. Everyone, Amelia, his brother Georgie, his father and Maude and now Emma Butler all eager to hear about his time in the Argentine. His conversation with Amelia the other evening about Catriona had disturbed him and had given him doubts. He was struggling to put it all behind him. Twelve years of his life had been spent there and Catriona had been a part of his life for four years. It wasn't as easy to shrug it all off try as he might.

As the wind increased in its ferocity, he was taken back to his arrival as a raw twenty year old.

He had spent three weeks on a ship of the *Blue Star Line* to Buenos Aires followed by six days on a steamer to Rio Gallegos. During the last night, the wind had blown a howling gale and Tommy had expected the old tub to crack up. It creaked and groaned like an arthritic old man, its engines throbbing monotonously above the noise of the gale.

Sometime around four o' clock in the morning the wind started to die a little, and then, and only then did Tommy take off his boots and finally lay on his bunk allowing himself the luxury of closing his eyes. When he woke, the wind had stopped completely and dawn was cracking through the fast breaking clouds. He finally saw the land. Nothing he had heard or imagined had prepared him for what lay before him.

It was a flat arid landscape with scrubby bushes dotted intermittently, no trees, and it seemed to stretch forever. Rio Gallegos itself, a small colourless town, was only really in existence for its port facilities.

Where were the green rolling hills he'd dreamed of? The thoroughbred horses Mr. Bingham had talked of? His heart sank. It was nothing like he'd thought. Was he really going to spend the next three years of his life in this bleak and desolate country?

Chapter 4

He was given little time to wonder any further, for as he walked down the gangplank of the old steamer, a burly figure with a bushy red beard streaked with white, as if someone had taken a paint brush and tried to change the colour, approached him.

'You must be Lawrence.'

It was more of a statement than a question.

Tommy nodded, 'Yes I'm Tommy Lawrence.' He held out his hand.

'Aye, well we've no time to hang about,' Red Beard said, ignoring Tommy's outstretched hand. 'Follow me.'

Tommy followed wondering who the man was. He'd made no attempt to introduce himself. Did he own the *estancia*? Was he one of the Cartwrights? Surely not. He wore rough working clothes.

Red Beard led the way to a huge cart where oxen were harnessed. Tommy had never seen an ox cart. In England horses pulled carts. Red Beard climbed onto the driver's seat motioning for Tommy to climb up alongside. Tommy threw his small trunk onto the back of the cart which was already laden with goods and clambered up beside him.

'Is it far to the *estancia*?' Tommy asked.

'Aye,' Red Beard grunted.

Tommy thought to himself however far it turned out to be, it would seem like twice the distance if the journey was to be made in silence.

He tried again, 'How far?'

'About thirty miles,' he glanced at Tommy as he went on dryly, 'and before you ask, it'll take us about eight hours.'

Encouraged by this burst of speech, he asked again.

'What did you say your name was, and do you own the *estancia*?'

With this the old man threw back his head to reveal a mouthful of tobacco stained teeth. He guffawed and finally spluttered, 'Do I own the *estancia*? That's rich boy. Do I look like I own an *estancia*?'

Tommy found himself grinning foolishly in reply.

'I don't know. I don't know what an *estancia* owner looks like,' he parried, 'and you still haven't told me what your name is.'

'Everyone calls me Old Jock,' he answered. 'Tell me boy, what do you think of Patagonia?' he waved a hand encompassing the landscape.

'Well,' Tommy started hesitantly, 'it's not quite what I visualised. I knew a man in England that lived in Argentina, and he used to talk about the green hills and the pampas, and the beautiful thoroughbred horses, and well somehow it doesn't fit in with his description,' he ended apologetically.

The old man looked at him and shook his head. 'Ah but he didn't live in Patagonia. He must have been from somewhere like Santa Fe by the sound of it. That's cattle and thoroughbred country. This is sheep country boy, and that's all it's bloody well fit for. '

Tommy sighed. It didn't sound too promising, but still it was different and it was a new life, and that, above all things was what he'd wanted. Who knows he might even grow to like the country given time.

They stopped for lunch. Old Jock producing a loaf of bread and a leg of boiled mutton, to be washed down with two bottles of cold sweet tea. He tore the loaf in half handing one of the pieces to Tommy. He brought out a knife and cut off a hunk of meat. Nodding his head in the direction of the leg of mutton, he said gruffly, 'Help yourself boy.'

Tommy's eyes were as big as saucers. The piece of meat was big enough to feed his whole family - not once but several times - he thought wryly, and along with that thought, the realisation that he didn't really have a family anymore.

Tommy learned from Old Jock, who eventually became quite expansive on the subject of Patagonia, that it was occupied by people of very diverse origins. There were the English – mainly in the far south, the Spanish, Italians, Scots even a few Swiss and Germans, and the Welsh who'd settled in the Chubut valley. He told of the indigenous people, most of whom had long since vanished - some succumbing to diseases brought by the settlers, other dying in long ago battles, the remainder integrated into the newcomers' world, the only traces being in the features of some of the people.

Tommy listened, occasionally asking a question but generally content to listen. He remembered how fascinated he'd been as a child listening to Miss Nelson telling the class about faraway places and their people, but this was no lesson, this was for real and he was here.

As the journey continued the plains sprouted some small hills, but there was no sign of habitation. A few sheep appeared on the sides of the hills. Suddenly Tommy, who had started to feel drowsy, sat bolt upright and pointed.

'What in the hell is that?' he gasped.

Tommy was pointing to a small group of the strangest looking animals he'd ever seen. They were a light tan in colour, something like a red deer, but with long necks, huge eyes and slender bodies.

'Guanacos, boy. There's some say they make mighty good eating, although I can't say as I've ever tried 'em.' he cackled, revealing his stained teeth like so many brown weather-worn tombstones.

They saw several grey foxes, or *zorros* as Old Jock called them, and plenty of hares.

'They look like the hares we have in England, except much bigger,' Tommy remarked, 'right down to the black tips on their ears'.

'Calls 'em Belgian hares here tho' don't s'pose anyone knows where they come from,' said Jock.

'Is it true that the *estancia* is one hundred and eighty thousand hectares? I can't imagine anything that big. It's huge. That's about four hundred and fifty thousand acres, incredible.'

'You'll realise how big it is when you have to bring the sheep twice a year for shearing and dipping. Hope you like sitting in the saddle for days on end,' Old Jock finished.

Tommy shrugged, 'I don't really know. I've never ridden a horse.'

This resulted in the old man bursting forth with another one of his hearty guffaws.

'What's so funny?'

Jock shook his head disbelievingly. 'They send you young fellas out here filling your heads full of nonsense and don't tell you that most of your next three years will be spent in the saddle.'

'Well it can't be that hard to ride a horse,' Tommy said confidently, 'anyway I'm sure they'll teach me won't they?'

Tommy thought the old man was going to have apoplexy. He wheezed and choked until the tears trickled down the crevices in his ruddy cheeks, disappearing without a trace into his streaky beard. Eventually he managed to get his breath back.

'Oh yes I'm sure they will,' he nodded. 'They'll tell you to choose a horse, and you'd better just hope that the *domador* has done his job well.'

'What's a *domador*?' Tommy asked.

'That's a horse breaker boy, and some is better than others as you'll find out.'

The wind had been blowing incessantly for the last four hours and Tommy wondered if this was a permanent feature of the climate. He yawned. Due to the storm last night he hadn't got much sleep. He hoped that they must be nearing the end of their journey since they'd been on the road for nearly eight and a half hours now.

The old man must have seen the fatigue on Tommy's face.

'Nearly there boy. Just over that next hill and you'll be able to see the homestead,' he said reassuringly.

A few minutes later they topped the rise and Tommy saw spread out before him the welcome sight of buildings, buildings with smoke rising from the chimneys. He heard dogs barking and voices carried on the wind. So this was El Carranches.

El Carranches lay at the bottom of a deep gulch, the tidal river entering from the north, opening out into a huge basin, surrounded by a high level plain. The beach was a hundred yards from the big house. The whole scene was bathed in a rosy golden glow of the setting sun.

Tommy noticed there were a few trees dotted around and contraptions that looked similar to pictures he'd seen of windmills in Holland.

'What are those things Jock? Are they windmills?'

'Well not quite, they're wind pumps that pump the water up for the homestead. They're all over the *estancia* to fill the troughs for the sheep. That's another job you'll have to do, learn to check the pumps every so often.'

It seemed to Tommy at the moment that there were an awful lot of things he was going to have to learn.

The ox cart stopped outside the cookhouse where several men were gathered. There were a pack of dogs lying close by, one with a litter of puppies. Tommy recognised them as border collies.

'Henry, take these boxes into the cookhouse,' Old Jock indicated three large boxes. 'The rest I'll take down to the stores before it gets dark.'

Tommy alighted from the cart, his body stiff and aching. While the man called Henry was off loading the boxes, Old Jock was talking to one of the other men. After a few minutes he turned to Tommy.

'Go with Rees here. He'll look after you.'

'I'm Gareth Rees,' the young man stepping forward said.

'Tommy Lawrence,' he replied.

Gareth was a few inches shorter than Tommy, but broader. A lock of fair hair flopped across his forehead. Tommy guessed him to be a few years older than himself, with an accent Tommy had never heard before.

'Right boyo, let's get you fixed up with a bed and somewhere to stow your gear. Come with me to the bunkhouse.'

The bunkhouse was a long low building containing eighteen beds all with lockers.

'This'll be your bed, and this is your locker. When you've unpacked your trunk you can stow it under your bed.' He grinned a cheeky lopsided grin. 'How's this for first class accommodation?' he asked sitting down on the bed next to Tommy's, which was his.

'How many people work on the *estancia*?' Tommy asked. He'd never slept in a room with other people. His whole life he'd had the luxury of a room of his own, no matter how small. It felt strange to know he'd be sharing with seventeen others.

'There's eighteen of us in the bunkhouse, then there's Mr. Manners - he's the manager, he lives with his wife and family in a cottage. Then there's Jack Crooks, he's the foreman, he has a room just off the stores, and Old Jock and the cook have two small rooms off the end of the cookhouse.

'So that's twenty two workers.'

'Well, maybe sixteen workers and half dozen shirkers more like but you get them wherever you are,' laughed Gareth. 'Up the end there,' he said leading the way, 'through this door we've got washing facilities, six shower cubicles, and, take a tip, first up in the morning gets the best of the hot water. If you finish unpacking your trunk it'll be time for grub.'

Tommy took his half dozen precious books and put carefully into his locker.

'Do you like reading then?' Gareth asked.

Tommy nodded. 'Oh yes, whenever I get the chance, but I don't suppose there'll be much opportunity will there?' he asked ruefully.

'Oh you're in for a big surprise. We have our own club room, a small library, workshops and our stores where we can buy anything our hearts' desire - well almost,' he chuckled, 'and you thought you were leaving civilisation behind you. Don't you believe it.'

The *estancias* all had stores where most things could be purchased. This ranged from cigarettes, chocolate, soap and other toiletries to clothes which could be mail ordered from England. This took four months for them to arrive. Given the amount of things on offer, money earned on the *estancia*, was destined to go back into the *estancia*'s coffers.

Trunk stowed Tommy washed up, they made their way to the cook-house. The steamy warmth hit them as they entered. The smell of roasting meat made Tommy realise he was hungry.

'Don't worry about getting to know people tonight. You can start in the morning. I'll just tell everyone who you are. Hey fellas, this is Tommy Lawrence!' he shouted above the clatter of dishes.

A few waved a hand, some smiled, but all looked friendly. The food was every bit as good as it smelled. Following the meat and vegetables was steamed treacle pudding served with thick creamy custard.

Tommy sat after supper feeling full and drowsy. The cook-house was warm and smoky as the men lit up their pipes and cigarettes. His eyes were getting heavier with every passing minute until eventually Gareth nudged him.

'C'mon boyo, tomorrow's another day. You look all in.'

'Mmm I guess I am,' Tommy yawned.

He fell asleep to the metallic cranking noise of the wind pump which could be heard above the ever present wind.

The following morning he woke to the sound of his bed fellows, several of whom were snoring raucously, others stirring restlessly, as if sensing even in sleep that it was nearing the time to rise. Tommy glanced at Gareth's bed only to find it was already empty. He remembered Gareth's advice of last night regarding the hot water. He slipped from his bed moving noiselessly, so as not to disturb the men sleeping around him and made his way to the showers.

Of the six cubicles three were occupied. The six showers had bat wing doors and crudely made stands with large enamel bowls with a small mirror above each for shaving purposes. Tommy was surprised at how modern the facilities were, more so than at Melchet Court, where he had been employed as a footman on leaving home, until his departure for the Argentine.

A musical voice from the shower unit said, 'Good morning, you took my advice then boyo, and got in early.' A well soaped Gareth Rees grinned at him over the top of one of the bat wing doors, only the upper part of his body and from the knees down were visible.

Tommy nodded, 'Yes, what time do we start work?'

'Breakfast is at quarter past seven, and after that the foreman will allocate who he wants to be doing what.'

The water was hot and Tommy gave himself up to the luxury of the red hot needles hitting his body. He was showered and shaved and back at his locker a towel wrapped round his waist within seven minutes. By this time people were up and moving, grumbling, clearing their throats, and shouting at one another to hurry up with the showers. Tommy put on a warm woollen shirt and was about to button it when Gareth spoke.

'You'll need more than just that to keep you warm out there. Haven't you got any long johns?' he asked eyeing Tommy in shirt and underpants.

Tommy shook his head, 'No I'll be okay.' He hurriedly put on his thick tweed trousers, heavy wool socks and stout boots.

'We've just got time before breakfast for you to go and choose a horse.'

'Okay,' said Tommy shrugging into his heavy jacket. In the cold light of morning without the glow from the setting sun of the previous evening, El Carranches didn't look so appealing. Apart from the main house, which was a solid double storeyed red brick construction, the rest of the buildings were all low single storey with ugly corrugated tin roofs.

The moment he stepped outside he realised what Gareth had meant. A raw biting wind was still blowing, cutting through the layers of clothing.

They reached the barn and Gareth took a saddle and thrust it at Tommy, taking another one for himself. There were several fenced paddocks beyond the barns, each of which had a dozen or so horses in. Gareth stood at the fence and whistled. The horses raised their heads but didn't move, on his second whistle one mare trotted over, the others then followed.

'Take your pick boyo,' he invited, 'any one you fancy except the dun coloured one she's mine.'

'I'll take that one,' Tommy said pointing to the chestnut mare that had come when Gareth whistled.

Gareth laughed, 'You can't take her she's the bell mare.'

'What's the bell mare?'

Gareth explained that the bell mare or *madrina* (godmother) was the leader of the group of horses who were devoted to her. The group was referred to as a *trupilla* and riding horses in Patagonia were broken to run in *trupillas*. The bell mare would come at your call and the others would always follow, but no one ever rode the bell mare.

'Okay that one then,' Tommy said pointing to a black horse with a white blaze. 'I suppose one horse is pretty much the same as another aren't they?' he asked.

'You've never ridden before have you Tommy?' he asked quietly.

Tommy shook his head.

'Listen, your life may one day depend upon your horse, so no, one horse is not pretty much the same as another.' He went on, 'God you're going to be sore, but we'll take things as easy as we can but old Crooks wants his pound of flesh. Listen to me, I'll help you all I can, this will be your horse, get to know him well. Before you get on him, pet him, touch him all over his neck, his body. Talk to him - they know voices – and he'll sniff you and get to know your smell. You have to have absolute trust in each other. On a lighter note be gentle him and caress him the way you would a woman, because you're going to spend a lot of time with him.'

Tommy put out a tentative hand and rested it lightly on his neck. He twitched his muscles but stood still accepting the caress.

'C'mon boy.' Tommy whispered, his hand moving slowly as he repeated over and over, 'Good boy.'

'The *domador* that's been the last few times is a Swiss bloke,' Gareth remarked, 'and he's good. He knows his stuff. His horses will stand where you leave them if you let the reins drag and will never buck you off when you mount. We'll saddle up now. I'll show you how while there's no one about, and we'll leave them tied to the rail while we go and get breakfast. And just remember, after me, this horse is the best friend you're going to have.' He finished jokingly.

Tommy grinned back, neither man realising at the time how strong a friendship they were to form. Their lives to be intertwined in away neither of them could ever imagine.

Chapter 5

Tommy studied his freshly shaved face in the bathroom mirror - he'd do. He patted on aftershave, sucking in his breath as it stung his face. He was ready. He went downstairs to find Amelia sitting at the table reading the paper. She looked up as he entered the room.

Sliding her glasses down her nose, she peered over the top, 'My goodness Thomas, you do look smart. May I ask where are you taking this lucky young lady?'

He grinned, 'Some fancy new supper club. It's just opened apparently. The Golden Slipper. Emma says everyone's raving about it. I might not come home tonight Amelia. The club is open with late night dancing, so I might stay over at the Red Lion.'

This was the third time he was seeing Emma in the nine days since he'd met her.

'Where or when did you ever find the time to learn to dance?'

He chuckled infectiously, 'Amelia I'll have you know I'm a very good dancer - Gareth was my teacher, he taught me to waltz, quickstep and foxtrot, and of course the local ladies taught me to tango. However there's one small snag, I've had little opportunity to put much of it into practice, but,' he said a wicked grin coming over his face as he reached out and switched on Amelia's old radio and twiddling the knobs until he found some music, 'we'll soon remedy that.' Holding out his hand, he asked, 'May I have the pleasure Madam?'

'Oh please Thomas, it's been donkey's years, I haven't danced since I was a young girl.'

'All the more reason,' he replied, pulling her gently to her feet then twirled her round. They danced around the tiny kitchen. Tommy skilfully guiding them between the sink and the table until eventually Amelia cried out breathlessly, 'Oh please Thomas stop, no more have pity on an old lady.' She sank gratefully back into her chair saying, 'I take back everything I said about not knowing how you ever found the time to dance, either Gareth was a wonderful teacher, or you were a wonderful pupil, I'm not sure which.'

'Well I never knew when I might need to sweep a lady off her feet, so I concentrated real hard, and now having swept one off her feet, I'd better get cracking and see if I can manage to do the same again tonight.'

Later that same evening after supper Tommy asked Emma if she'd like to dance with the warning he hoped he wouldn't tread on her toes.

'I'd love to Tommy, and don't worry I'll take that risk.'

Tommy took her in his arms. The top of her head just came up to his chin. Her perfume filled his nostrils, a light flowery smell with a tang of citrus. She moved closer within the circle of his arms, pressing herself against him. His arms tightened around her. They danced for several minutes until he eased himself back from her. He willed himself to go slow, Emma was no Catriona. This was only the third time they'd been out together. Thoughts of Catriona invaded his mind. He felt a burning aching desire flow over him - whether for Catriona or the woman he held in his arms - he didn't know. Just then to his relief the music stopped. They went back to the table where Tommy downed the remains of his drink in one long swallow.

She looked at him through her lashes and asked suddenly, 'Are you married Tommy, or have you ever been married?'

He was startled, 'Good Lord no. Whatever makes you ask?'

'Well I don't know, it's just that a man of your age, well I don't actually know how old you are, but Auntie Annie said to make sure you weren't a married man,' she finished.

'I'm thirty two Emma, and no I promise you I'm not married, I have never been married and am totally a free agent. There weren't too many ladies where I've been for the last twelve years. Will that satisfy your Auntie Annie?'

'I'm glad there weren't many otherwise you'd have been snapped up and I'd never have met you would I?' she said.

'And what about you Emma, any husbands or boyfriends lurking in the background that I should know about?'

She laughed, 'Don't be silly Tommy, husbands indeed, and as for boyfriends there's been a few, but no one special... so far.' She tossed her head, 'I'm still looking for Mr. Right. Can we dance some more Tommy? I love dancing.'

Back on the small intimate dance floor he took her into his arms again. She tilted her face up to his she asked, 'Would you like to kiss me Tommy?'

He hooted with laughter, replying lightly, 'Of course I would. Who wouldn't? But not here.'

'I don't see what's so funny,' she pouted.

'I'm sorry Emma, I shouldn't have laughed. I'll take everything you say seriously in future, I promise.'

'You're still laughing at me, and if you don't want to kiss me there are plenty of others that would like to,' she said huffily.

They left the Golden Slipper at about one o'clock, the doorman calling for a taxi. In the taxi Emma said in a small voice reaching for his hand, 'I'm sorry if I made you cross

Tommy. My Auntie Annie says I'm terribly spoilt, and I am childish and sulky if things don't go my way.'

He smiled into the darkness. Tommy thought Auntie Annie was probably right.

Tommy paid off the taxi saying he'd walk the few blocks back to the Red Lion.

In the porch-way of the pub Emma fumbled for her door key. Having found it she turned to Tommy who was leaning against the porch column.

'Thank you very much for a lovely evening,' and standing on tiptoe, she kissed his cheek.

'Would you like to ask me again?' he asked pulling her gently towards him into the thick velvet shadows, so that her body rested against his. He bent his head and kissed her slowly. Her lips were soft and sweet tasting as they parted under his own.

'Oh Tommy,' she breathed softly as he lowered his hands to her hips. Her arms came up around his neck running her fingers through his hair, pressing herself even closer.

It was Emma who finally broke away saying, 'No Tommy we mustn't, I've got to go in now.'

'Hell's teeth!' he groaned feelingly, 'Do you know what you're doing to me?'

She giggled, 'Of course I know - I'm not a child.' she turned quickly and unlocked the door.

'Wait,' he said grabbing her wrist. 'When am I going to see you again? I've got my interview in Hampshire on Monday. I should be back for early evening. I'll call for you at sevenish Okay?'

She nodded. 'Oh yes lovely, best of luck,' and with one swift movement she kissed him briefly on the lips, and slipped quickly through the door with a whispered, 'goodnight.'

Back in his room at the Red Lion he lit a cigarette and thought about Emma. Despite his years, his experience with women had been limited. There had been Miriam, the wild gypsy girl throughout that long hot summer, sneaking out at nights, during his time at Melchet Court. Then there had been those forbidden years with Catriona. Emma was different, childlike, innocent, yet strangely seductive. He knew she'd been as eager as he was. She'd been more than responsive to his kisses in the dark porch way, and this only served to whet his appetite for more.

Tommy arrived back at Rose Cottage midmorning on Sunday. 'I didn't expect you till lunchtime Thomas, but now you're here I'll make some coffee and you can tell me all about the supper club,' Amelia greeted him.

'I wanted to have a quiet day. You haven't forgotten I've got an interview tomorrow at Belmont Park with Mr. Stewart-Shenley, have you Amelia?'

'Oh good gracious! So you have. It had completely slipped my mind. What time will you get back do you think?'

'I shan't be back till late. I'll take my key if that's all right with you. I'm seeing Emma on Monday evening.'

She raised he eyebrows, 'Again Thomas, well she must be quite some young lady. Tell me all about her, all I know is her name. What does she do for a living, how old is she, where does she live and what does she look like? I was always taught as a child that if you didn't ask questions, you'd never learn anything.'

'Well that's no beating about the bush. Okay... here we go, she's twenty three, small and dainty (holding out his hand at approximately his chin level) slim with beautiful blonde hair, blue eyes and a great pair of legs,' he grinned. 'She works for a firm of solicitors as a typist, and she lives with her Uncle Frank and Auntie Annie at The Greyhound pub in Cross Street. They own it. Her parents were killed in an accident three years ago, and she's no brothers or sisters. Is there anything else you'd like to know, or have I missed anything out?' he asked laughingly.

Amelia laughed with him, 'Oh dear you make me sound like a nosy old woman, but yes there is one more thing. When am I going to have the pleasure of meeting her?'

'Soon I hope, but I don't want to rush her after all meeting you will be like meeting my family as far as she's concerned. She's already half afraid of meeting you, as soon as I said you were a school teacher.'

'Silly girl, does she think school teachers bite then?'

'No, but then she said she couldn't imagine being friends with any of her teachers. I told her maybe she wasn't as lucky as I was,' he said giving her a spontaneous hug. 'I suppose eventually I shall have to think about letting her meet my real family, Georgie and Sylvia are no problem, or Maude for that matter. It's just the old man, but still I'll cross that bridge if and when I come to it. It's early days yet.'

Monday morning brought two letters, one from the job in Wales, saying the position had already been filled, and the other from Northumbria setting a date for an interview to be held at the Grosvenor Hotel in London.

But today his appointment with Mr. Stewart-Shenly was foremost in his mind.

Belmont Park was a magnificent estate situated about eight miles from Winchester. Much to his surprise Mr. O.B. Stewart-Shenley, the owner, turned out to be Mrs. Stewart-Shenley.

Olivia Belle Stewart-Shenley was a gracious, dignified striking looking woman of about sixty. Her white hair was drawn back in an elegant chignon. She was nearly as tall as Tommy, which would have made her at least six foot, and her eyes were a startling shade of violet. She must have been a beauty in her day Tommy thought. She was knowledgeable and well versed in the running of the estate, which she had run herself since the death of her second husband, she explained. She was twice widowed with one grown up son, who'd shown no interest in the estate, beyond the income it provided to fund his playboy lifestyle.

Mrs. Stewart-Shenley showed an interest in Tommy's years in Argentina, and on reading his references from Mr. Manners at El Carranches, and from Señor Ramirez asked him why he'd left. He said it was for personal reasons which he didn't elaborate on. She asked pertinent questions about his ideas on the running of the estate, any improvements he may be able to suggest, and took time to show him round part of the thirty thousand acres, including the home farm and part of the woodland area. It was mixed farming with a good shoot.

He explained that his knowledge of crops and cattle was not extensive and had been assured that the head cowman was a man with many years of experience, and what she was really looking for was someone to co-ordinate all aspects of the estate. There would be two hunters at his disposal, or if he would prefer, a utility vehicle to get around the estate.

The chauffeur, Edward, who had met him in the Daimler at Winchester station at ten thirty that morning returned him in time to catch the four thirty back to Reading.

He'd come away from his interview feeling reasonably satisfied with the way he'd acquitted himself. He had no qualms about working for a woman and had been amused at the explanation of her use of the 'Mr.' title in many of her business dealings. On parting she'd shaken his hand and assured him she would be in touch.

On his arrival in Reading he made his way straight to The Greyhound to wait for Emma. At exactly seven o' clock she came looking radiant in a pale sage green dress, the skirt falling softly to her calves.

‘Hello,’ she greeted him, kissing him swiftly on the cheek, ‘I’ve got a surprise for you. You haven’t eaten yet have you?’

‘No I haven’t and I’m starving. I thought perhaps we could grab a bite somewhere and then go for a walk.’

‘Well I had a better idea. It’s Monday evening and my aunt and uncle’s night off, which is why Norman’s doing the bar, it’s always quiet on Mondays - and here’s the surprise, I’ve cooked supper. Come along upstairs, it’s nearly ready.’

He allowed himself to be led upstairs to the living quarters. The table was laid in the dining area.

Emma brought supper through almost immediately saying, ‘Come to the table Tommy, I’ve filched a bottle of Uncle Frank’s best claret.’

Emma was a good cook. She had a light touch with pastry, and Tommy ate a hearty portion of her chicken and ham pie, over which they talked about the job interview and speculated on his chances of being offered the job.

Emma giggled, ‘Well if it’s a lady employer and she’s a widow, she’s bound to give you the job - a good looking single man.’

‘Emma the lady in question is about sixty, and her son must be about my age.’

‘That doesn’t make you any the less attractive.’

‘Well I understood the position to be that of a farm manager, not resident gigolo, although I must admit she’s still a very attractive woman.’

After supper he told Emma about his forthcoming interview in London.

‘Ooh Tommy you lucky thing, I’ve never been to London.’

‘Well can’t you take a day’s holiday, or be ill that day and come to London with me?’ he suggested.

'Mmm maybe, that would be nice,' she said wistfully.

'Where have your aunt and uncle gone on their evening off?' he asked casually.

'Oh they've gone to spend the night with Auntie Annie's sister, so they won't be back till tomorrow. We have the place to ourselves to do as we like,' she finished coyly.

'They have lovely spacious living quarters,' said Tommy skilfully changing the subject.

'Would you like to have a look round while they're not here?'

He didn't particularly want to, but could see she was keen to show him round.

She gave him a tour with the last room being her bedroom. She stood in the doorway while Tommy looked over her shoulder.

'Yes, very nice.' he murmured.

She took his hand and tugged gently, 'Come in and see properly.'

What happened next seemed inevitable to Tommy. He reached out for her, kissing her. She returned his kisses hot-eyed and eager. He drew back for a moment and looked into her eyes.

'Are you sure this is what you want?' he asked.

'Yes Tommy I'm sure.'

He closed the door softly behind him. In the gathering dusk the room was suffused with an eerie light as the street lamps on. He made love to her slowly and gently, holding himself back as long as he could. It ended for both of them in a long shuddering climax with Emma crying out his name.

They lay quietly in each other's arms in the rosy afterglow of lovemaking until Tommy spoke.

'That was your first time wasn't it Emma? I hope it wasn't too painful.'

'Yes it was the first time, and no, apart from at first, it didn't hurt so much. It was lovely Tommy. Can we do it again?' she said softly, nibbling at his ear.

'Soon Emma, but meanwhile there are other things we could do that you might enjoy,' he whispered as he leant over and proceeded to demonstrate.

The following week Tommy kept his appointment in London. He persuaded Emma to take a day's holiday from work. The interview was conducted by a Mr. Hunt, a distant relative of some sort to Sir Archibald Grayson, the owner of the estates.

He was a large, bluff man, sandy haired and red faced, with a network of little blue veins running across his bulbous nose. The interview was short, Mr. Hunt asking Tommy very few questions, and only briefly scanning his references. He talked mainly about the wildness and beauty of Northumbria. The interview lasted barely forty five minutes.

Tommy joined Emma in the hotel lounge where he'd settled her with a pot of tea. She looked surprised to see him so soon,

'Gosh you weren't long. I thought you'd be ages yet. How'd it go?'

He shrugged, 'Your guess is as good as mine, I'm none the wiser than when I walked in there. All I know is his parting words were, "I'm sure you'd fit in well. We'll be in touch."'

'Oh don't worry Tommy. I'm sure you'll get offered both jobs and you'll be stuck for choice,' she comforted.

He laughed ruefully, 'Thanks for your undying faith, but seriously Emma I was hoping to have heard something from Mrs. Stewart-Shenley by now. Still what will be will be I suppose. Anyway, come, we've got the rest of the day to ourselves, and as you've never been to London before, where would you like to start? Madame Tussauds, Buckingham Palace, and Kew Gardens - you just name it - I'm at your disposal. When I worked at Melchet Court we used to come up to London, the whole household, for several weeks at a time.'

They crammed everything in, stopping briefly at a Lyons Corner House for lunch, until finally they found themselves in Hyde Park catching their breath. Tommy lying full length, the jacket of his suit folded carefully beside him.

'I shall miss you Tommy if you get the job in Northumbria. I hope you get the one in Hampshire, then we'll still be able to see each other won't we?'

'I've already missed you. We haven't had much chance to be alone,' he said opening his eyes.

'What do you mean? We're alone now except for passers-by.'

He sat up and turning to her in fond exasperation. 'You know what I mean Emma - it's been more than a week,' he whispered leaning forward and nuzzling her neck.

'I know Tommy,' she said kissing him lingeringly, 'but it's so difficult. We've nowhere to go, only the pub on a Monday evening, and that's only if my aunt and uncle go out, and you don't live on your own, which doesn't help.'

'I know, but if I get that job in Hampshire there's a house with it, you could come down and visit me on weekends. How does that sound - a whole weekend?' he said suggestively giving her an exaggerated leer.

'Wonderful Tommy,' she sighed, 'only I'm afraid my aunt and uncle might have something to say on that subject, me coming to stay with a single man on my own.'

'God! Emma, you're not a kid. You're twenty three years old. It's time you pleased yourself.'

'That's easy for you to say,' she said crossly. 'You don't seem to realise that it's my reputation that's getting muddied, not yours. A man can go to bed with as many women as he likes, and everyone thinks he's quite a lad. When a single woman goes with just one man, then she classed as loose, or fast.'

'I'm sorry Emma I'm perhaps not used to the way of things here. Are people talking about you?'

'No, don't be silly. Nobody is talking about me, not yet. I haven't exactly advertised the fact that I've slept with you,' she gave him a penetrating look. 'You do care for me don't you Tommy?'

He looked downwards, eventually raising his eyes to meet hers he said, 'Of course I care very much, and you Emma, what about you?'

Kneeling she moved closer and winding her arms around his neck, she leant her cheek against his, her breath warm on his face, she whispered, 'Oh yes Tommy I care. I love you Tommy. That's why I feel not quite right about us ... you know. I was brought up to believe that if you were a nice girl you didn't sleep around. Aunt Annie says a man loses respect for you once he's got what he wanted.'

'Do you feel bad because we've made love, and we're not married or engaged? Do you think what we've done is just us sleeping around and do you feel bad about it?'

'No, not bad. I loved what we did, but I felt guilty afterwards. Do you still respect me Tommy?'

'Yes of course I do. I know I was the first, maybe if I hadn't been I might have felt differently.'

Her arms were still around his neck. He put his hand up and stroked her cheek. She leaned into him and kissed him deeply teasing him with the tip of her tongue. He returned her kiss, eventually pulling back his head he said, 'Hey that's enough, unless you really want to ruin your reputation and do it in front of all the passers-by. Come,' he said gently pulling her to her feet, 'we'd better head for Waterloo. Our train goes at six.'

Chapter 6

The morning after Tommy's interview in London, he rose early as was normal for him. He prepared the coffee percolator and moved it across on the range. Amelia came downstairs at seven to the aroma of fresh coffee.

'Mmm Thomas that smells wonderful. I'll just pop some toast in.' She busied herself with laying the table. That done she sat down and continued, 'Right, now tell me all about your interview yesterday. How do you think it went?'

'I'm sorry I was very late in last night Amelia. I hope I didn't wake you. It was a nice night so I walked home from Reading. I thought the exercise would do me good and give me some thinking time. As for the interview, I don't really know what to think. I don't hold out much hope for that job. I'm not altogether happy about the one in Hampshire either,' he went on. 'I would've thought I'd have heard something by now if they'd been interested.'

'It's early days yet Thomas. The interview was only eight days ago.'

He nodded, 'Yes I suppose so. It just seems longer. By the way Amelia, changing the subject rather, two things I want to ask you, first of all can I bring Emma to meet you on Saturday?'

'Why of course you can. I shall be delighted. And the second thing?'

'Mmm, yeah I did didn't I? It's a bit delicate Amelia,' he reddened, obviously embarrassed. 'I don't quite know how to put it, although I suppose there's only one way,' he said plunging straight in. 'What's the general attitude towards young women who have... um, well, that sleep with someone before they're married?' he finished lamely, wishing he'd never started this conversation.

Amelia hid a smile, 'Well it's not really done Thomas, although minds may have broadened since I was young. Things haven't changed that much. Nice girls are supposed to save themselves for marriage. According to society, it shows a distinct lack of control and morals. I presume your question is purely rhetorical?' she said innocently.

He burst out laughing, 'Oh Amelia, I can see you don't presume anything of the kind. You know exactly why I'm asking. I'm serious Amelia. I never intended for this to happen, but it has. I don't want to jeopardise Emma's reputation, and I suppose things like that never crossed my mind. It's my fault. I'm that much older than she is, and I should have been the one to exercise a bit of self-control. I didn't really think too much about it until Emma brought the subject up.'

She smiled, 'Like I say Thomas, in all seriousness it's all too easy for a woman to get a name for herself. It really is rather silly - such double standards, for a man to do the same thing makes him experienced and exciting.'

'Mmm, Emma said the same thing, or words to that effect.'

The following morning brought the news that Tommy had been hoping for, the eagerly awaited letter from Mrs. Stewart-Shenley, offering Tommy the job as estate manager with the grand salary of forty pounds per month, plus a free cottage, the starting date to be the first of July, if that suited him.

He grabbed Amelia hugging and kissing her.

‘I can’t believe it Amelia. I’ve got the job! Oh Amelia, what a relief. I just hope I don’t let Mrs. Stewart-Shenley down, and that I haven’t bitten off more than I can chew.’

‘Of course you won’t let them down,’ she assured him. ‘You’re a very capable young man Thomas. Give yourself credit. They’re lucky to be getting you. I’m so pleased for you. I know how badly you wanted this.’

By Saturday when he went to call for Emma, he’d just about taken in his good fortune at getting the job. There were a few things to be sorted out. He’d need furniture; he’d been shown the cottage at his interview, which consisted of a kitchen, a sitting room, with an added on bathroom downstairs, two bedrooms and a third very small room upstairs. He’d written to Mrs. Stewart-Shenley accepting her offer and agreeing on the start date. Next, what about Emma? That was a dilemma. He wasn’t sure he wanted to get married at this stage. After all he’d only known Emma a few short weeks and, on such a brief acquaintance he thought marriage might be too big a commitment. Would he lose her if he went to Hampshire without her? She’d already intimated that she didn’t think it was a good idea as a single woman for her to come and stay with him at the weekends. He certainly wouldn’t be able to get to Reading very often. She had told him she loved him, and he’d told her the truth when he said he cared for her, but that wasn’t the same as loving someone. He wasn’t sure he was ready to love again.

He arrived at The Greyhound by lunchtime. Greeting Annie behind the bar, he asked if Emma was ready, as they were going to catch the two o’clock bus back to Swallowfield.

‘I don’t know Tommy. Go on upstairs and hurry her up. She’ll be late for her own funeral that one will.’

‘Thanks Mrs. Butler, you’re sure you don’t mind?

‘Of course not, just go on up.’

Tommy went up the stairs two at a time calling, 'Emma, Emma where are you? I've got the job...'

The door to Emma's bedroom was open as Tommy crossed the landing. Emma sat at her dressing table and she was wearing a delicate cream coloured camisole with matching lace trimmed French knickers.

She clapped her hands, 'Oh Tommy, I'm so thrilled for you. Oh that's wonderful news.'

Tommy grinned. 'Yes I can hardly believe my luck.'

Emma suddenly looked self-conscious sitting there in only her underwear.

Tommy grinned, 'You look nice Emma. Did you choose that outfit with me in mind?'

'Don't be cheeky, and no, I didn't. Auntie Annie says you must always wear nice clean underwear in case you have an accident and get taken to hospital.'

'Well you look very nice whoever it was chosen for - me or the ambulance man. In fact,' he went on all amusement gone from his face to be replaced by a look of pure unadulterated desire, 'you look very sexy.'

She rose from the stool, 'Yes well I think I'd better put my dress on now.'

'What's the rush? The bus only leaves at two and it's only one o'clock.'

He came and stood behind her, his arms snaking round her waist as he whispered into the back of her neck, 'Your aunt and uncle are really busy downstairs. We've got at least half an hour to ourselves - time for a quickie.'

She wriggled round to face him, slipping her hand into his shirt as she did so. He lowered his mouth to hers and groaned, 'It's been so long Emma.'

'Close the door Tommy.'

They ran the last fifty yards to just jump on the Swallowfield bus as it was pulling out of the depot. 'Made it by the skin of your teeth. You must have been caught up in what you were doing,' the conductor said with a smile.

They stifled their laughter as Tommy said poker-faced, 'Yes we were rather pre-occupied I'm afraid, and forgot to keep our eye on the clock.'

'Oh Tommy.' Emma became helpless with giggles. A moment later she turned to him suddenly serious, 'I'm so nervous of meeting your Miss Nelson.'

'Rubbish Emma. You'll like Amelia, and I'm sure you'll become friends,' he said confidently.

They alighted at the bus stop and walked slowly through the village holding hands.

'Where did you get that ring that you wear around your neck Tommy?' Emma asked curiously. 'I meant to ask you before. Is it from some old girlfriend in Argentina?'

'No, it's not. It belonged to my mother. It's silver and amethysts and I bought the chain in Argentina because I was always afraid I'd lose the ring if I didn't wear it. Why?'

'I just wondered. It's beautiful. Did you have a girlfriend in Argentina?' she asked.

'Yes,' he said shortly, 'there was someone.' His mouth set in a grim line.

Emma stopped walking, pulling Tommy up short. He turned his head to look at her. She squeezed his hand in hers, 'I'm sorry Tommy. I didn't mean to be nosy.'

She looked so earnest that he relaxed a little.

'It's okay Emma.' He squeezed her hand back, but his expression forbade any further discussion.

'Here we are. This is Rose Cottage,' he said stopping in front of a picturesque thatched cottage.

'Oh it's lovely Tommy - just like a picture from a box of chocolates.'

Tommy opened the door ushering Emma inside.

'Amelia,' he called, 'We're here.'

'Through here Thomas.'

Once again Tommy opened a door and motioned Emma in. Amelia rose from her comfortable wing backed chair to greet them. She smiled graciously as she held out her hand to Emma.

'Hello Emma, it's so nice to meet you. You're exactly as Thomas described you.'

For a moment Emma just stared, until at last she managed to stammer, 'Hello.'

Amelia Nelson was not your average picture of a village schoolteacher. Her looks belied the twenty four year age gap between her and Tommy. At fifty-six, looking nearer forty, her soft brown hair showing no signs of grey, her penetrating hazel eyes that looked as if they'd miss nothing. Her cream linen dress showing impeccable taste, revealing a trim shapely figure. She wore her precious silver brooch from Argentina on the lapel of her dress.

'It was such a lovely afternoon I thought we could have tea in the garden,' Amelia said. 'Thomas will you carry the tray out for me please. Come Emma let's go outside.'

The table was laid with a dainty white lace cloth with matching napkins, all under the shade of a copper beech tree, its leaves shimmering in the afternoon sun. Tea consisted of a plate with a variety of tiny sandwiches, a Victoria sponge and a plate of home-made shortbread, all accompanied by a pot of tea for two, and a small pot of coffee for Tommy.

Amelia complimented Emma on her pretty summer dress, then turned the conversation to Tommy's life in the Argentine, coming round to his future with his new job about to start in Hampshire.

Tommy noticed that Emma was unusually quiet and put it down to shyness. The afternoon passed pleasantly enough until Emma mentioned that she'd have to be going if she was to catch the six thirty bus back to Reading, as she'd promised her aunt she'd help in The Greyhound tonight.

After thanking Amelia for a lovely tea. Tommy walked her to the bus stop, commenting on how quiet she'd been.

'Perhaps I didn't know what to say - she didn't look much like I'd imagined. I sort of had an image of a plump matronly person, wearing glasses and having ink stained fingers. She wasn't a bit like that. She looked very sophisticated, and I think I was a little over-awed,' she admitted.

Tommy looked amused, 'No Amelia's none of the things you imagined. She's a gem though.'

Later that evening Tommy and Amelia sat quietly both engrossed in their books when suddenly Tommy put his book down.

'Well what did you think of her Amelia?'

'She's very pretty Thomas, and seems very well brought up.'

'You're not very forthcoming, that's not like you. Did you like her or not?' he asked his eyes not leaving her face.

Amelia hesitated, but only for a moment, 'Goodness me Thomas, you're very intense. She seemed very nice, but three hours in someone's company doesn't qualify me to give a character reference.'

'Sorry Amelia, you're right. I suppose I am wound up, I so badly wanted you to like her. And then I'm wondering, what's the next move as far as she and I are concerned, with me going to Hampshire.

'Listen Thomas, at this moment you wouldn't notice if Emma had horns and a tail, so a word of advice - give yourself time. Don't rush into anything you may have cause to regret later. Emma seems a nice girl, but she's still very young.'

The following weekend fast approaching, Amelia asked Tommy what his plans were for organising furniture, pointing out he only had three weeks before he started his job.

'Yes I'd better get cracking hadn't I? Wouldn't you like to come with me, and help me choose Amelia?'

'I'd love to Thomas, but wouldn't you rather ask Emma? I'm sure she has very good taste and maybe more modern ideas than myself.'

'I'm sure she has good taste too, but no, I'd like you to come with me, that is if you'd like to.'

'It'll be my pleasure. I shall enjoy that, thank you.' she beamed.

So that was how they found themselves at midday on Saturday at The Greyhound, furniture having been selected and paid for at Thompsons Furniture Emporium in Reading, with delivery to be taken care of by their Winchester branch.

It was at Tommy's suggestion they call and ask Emma to join them for lunch at the Red Lion.

'It will give you chance to meet Emma's aunt and uncle.'

Introductions made Annie asked Amelia if she'd care to join her in a glass of sherry, saying to Tommy, 'I don't think Emma's expecting you till this evening is she Tommy?'

'No, we're going to the cinema, but Amelia and I have been shopping and are going to the Red Lion for lunch, so I thought we could see if Emma would like to come with us.'

'That's nice of you. She's upstairs so go on up. It's all right. Miss Nelson and I are quite happy with our sherry, aren't we?' she smiled at Amelia.

'Of course, and please, my friends call me Amelia.'

'Please excuse me ladies. I won't be long.' Tommy headed for the door.

Ten minutes later he returned with Emma.

'Oh,' she said looking surprised, 'You never said Amelia was with you.'

'Yes, we've been shopping, then decided to go for lunch.'

Over an excellent lunch the conversation turned to Tommy's job.

'What's the cottage like Tommy?' Emma asked.

'Well it's only small, but it's more than adequate for my needs. I don't need anything too big, me being a bachelor...'

'Well you might not always be a bachelor might you?' Emma interrupted, 'Bachelors have been known to get married.'

'It's still plenty big enough, in a lovely spot too, super views, a ten minute walk to the stables at Belmont House and about a quarter of a mile to the main road where you can catch a bus to Winchester.'

'What are you going to do about furniture?' Emma wanted to know. 'You'll have to buy some won't you?'

'That's what we've been doing this morning, it's all organised,' Tommy answered.

For a moment there was silence. When Emma spoke it was in a tight little voice, '"We", who's "we"?'

'Amelia and I of course. I suggested she come with me to help me choose, as I know she has such good taste.'

There was another pause during which Tommy looked up and glancing from Amelia to Emma, sensed the atmosphere.

The rest of the lunch passed fairly quietly with Amelia only asking Tommy when he was going to show Emma the cottage.

Emma throughout was uncharacteristically silent, and on finishing lunch lost no time in pleading a headache.

Tommy rose offering to walk her back to The Greyhound, but she waved him back down, 'No please you and Amelia stay and have coffee. I'll see you tonight at seven Tommy.'

'Are you sure you want to go out this evening? I hope your headache will be gone,' he said.

She gave him a long look, 'Oh I'm sure it will. Goodbye Amelia, nice to see you again.'

On her departure Tommy said, 'What a shame. That headache came on rather suddenly wouldn't you say?'

'Maybe it was something she ate, or perhaps the weather as it is a bit thundery. Don't you think you should have insisted on walking her home Thomas?'

Tommy looked at her levelly, a grim set to his mouth, 'No Amelia I don't. Emma behaved badly - headache or not. She could have waited another half hour. She knows we have to walk past The Greyhound to get to the bus station.'

Amelia remained silent.

Tommy thought he knew the cause of Emma's headache and decided he'd deal with it later.

That evening, strolling hand in hand on their way back from the cinema. Tommy suddenly changed course and headed down Market Street.

'Where are we going Tommy?'

'The park,' he answered, letting go of her hand and placing his arm around her shoulders, he pulled her close.

'There are things we have to talk about Emma.'

The moonlight was brilliant, lighting up the park, its eerie silver beams casting black velvety shadows under the trees. They reached a bench under the first chestnut tree and Tommy steered her towards it. Sitting down he turned to her,

‘Before we talk about anything more serious Emma, what was all that headache business about at lunch? Do you have a problem with Amelia?’

She looked taken aback, but recovered swiftly and with a shake of her head she answered, ‘No, of course not Tommy. She seems very sweet, although I’m not sure she approves of me.’

‘Why, what makes you think that?’

‘I don’t know - nothing specific - just a feeling I have. I know how much she loves you, perhaps she doesn’t think I’m good enough for you.’

‘Rubbish. Amelia’s not like that and she doesn’t judge. She likes you fine so you’re imagining things,’ he said shortly. ‘She’s a very important part of my life Emma, and if you’re going to become a part of it too, then you’re going to have to accept that and make the effort to get along with her.’

Emma didn’t look at Tommy, but fumbled in her purse for her handkerchief. She gave a muffled sob.

‘Please don’t,’ he said putting his arms around her. ‘Don’t cry Emma.’

She clung to him. Her sobbing intensified. He kissed her wet cheeks whispering, ‘Please Emma, don’t cry.’

She stopped sobbing and turned her face to him kissing him. Eventually Tommy broke away saying, ‘Hey, I brought you here to talk. At this rate we’re not going to get much talking done.’

‘It’s all right Tommy. If you’re going to lecture me go ahead and let’s get it over with.’

I’m sorry, I didn’t mean to lecture. It’s just that it’s very important to me - you and Amelia getting on I mean. Amelia has always been there for me, my whole life, since I was six years old. The day my mother died Amelia offered me a home, and I love Amelia like a mother, but she's more than that, she's my friend.'

'It's all right Tommy. I'll try a little harder, but I feel intimidated by her.'

She snuggled closer into his arms.

'What are we going to do Emma, about me moving down to Hampshire? How often will I see you? I know you're not happy about spending weekends down there with me. I won't be able to come up here very often, but I don't want to lose you Emma,' and as he whispered those last words softly into her hair, he realised it was true.

He didn't want to lose her. He was tired of being on his own for as long as he could remember. His brothers were both married - even his father had someone.

'What do you say to us getting engaged before I move, and then it wouldn't be so bad for you to come down and visit me - your legitimate fiancé?'

'I don't know Tommy. Are you asking me to marry you or are you just offering me an engagement ring so that I'll come down to Hampshire and share your bed at the weekends?' she asked.

'Yes darlin', I guess I am asking you to marry me. We'll get married before Christmas I promise... Well what do you say? '

'Oh yes Tommy, if you're sure it's what you want,' she breathed, 'but I don't want you to feel pressurised. Are you really sure?'

She had a childlike quality that appealed to him, that made him want to care for her, to shield her from life's pitfalls. She made him laugh. She was bubbly and vivacious, brimming over with an infectious enthusiasm for life, and she so obviously adored him.

Her body was close to his, he could smell her heady perfume. How could he hesitate to assure her that he didn't feel pressurised.

'Yes I'm certain that's what I want,' he said as he bent his head to lose himself in her kisses.

Just three months after he'd proposed, on a sunny autumn day in September Tommy and Emma were married. A small ceremony with just Annie and Frank, Annie's sister Ivy, Tommy's father and Maude, Georgie and Sylvia, with Tommy's small nieces as bridesmaids, and of course Amelia present.

Christmas nineteen thirty seven, he'd been home eight months - a married man settled and in a steady job. He'd settled into his job quickly. He got on well with Mrs. Stewart-Shenley. He could be seen every day riding round the estate on either the powerful grey gelding or the bad tempered black stallion aptly named Satan. Both horses had been put at his disposal. By the time his marriage took place he'd got to know most of the estate workers and their families who, in turn had grown accustomed to seeing his familiar figure riding round the estate. It felt good to be in the saddle again evoking memories of the Argentine.

Chapter 7

His first day immediately after breakfast, the foreman Jack Crooks, allocated the men their work for the day.

'You'll be Lawrence I suppose,' he said his eyes alighting on Tommy. 'Listen up, for now I'm going to put you with Rees for a few weeks until you get to know the ropes. Mr. Manners will see you later.'

Jack Crooks was a man of about fifty, his skin pitted like orange peel, with mean shifty little eyes. He didn't sound mean, but Tommy's gut feeling told him it wouldn't pay to get on the wrong side of him. Something about him struck a chord in Tommy's mind, something he couldn't quite put his finger on - his father maybe - no, now he was being ridiculous.

'Yes sir,' Tommy nodded.

'C'mon then, we'd better get cracking if we're going across to the north side and start bringing some sheep down before the snow starts.'

'Will it snow soon?' Tommy asked as they made their way to where the horses were saddled up and ready to go.

'Well it's mid-May now and it usually snows by the end of the month. Anyway let's report in to the cookhouse, pick up our food, and let them know where we're going. Crooks knows where we're going, but always make sure that someone else knows as well,' he explained. 'Never go off without at least two people knowing where you're heading, then at night when they do their headcount they know where to start looking for you if you don't pitch up.'

The next few weeks were hard. By the end of the first week Tommy's legs were stiff and sore in spite of the horse liniment Gareth had given him to rub in. His muscles burned and cramped during the night.

The bitter icy winds gave him itchy chilblains on his knuckles. The cold crept into his bones despite his borrowed long johns which were too short, Gareth being the shorter of the two. He'd ordered some for himself, and to replace Gareth's, and more warm clothing from Barbour & Sons through the *estancia*'s flourishing mail order business. These would take about six to eight weeks to arrive, meanwhile he'd have to manage.

'You'll get used to it boyo,' Gareth laughed.

And he did. As the weeks passed he found himself not just getting used to the work, but actually enjoying it. Even the country didn't seem so hostile and desolate. He even started to enjoy riding Blaze, who'd snicker a greeting, and trot over to the fence when he heard Tommy's voice.

One afternoon on their way in from a long day of fence mending Gareth said, 'I'm just going down to the kennels to have a look at my bitch Jess, she's about to whelp. Do you want to come?'

The row of kennels with runs had room for about a dozen dogs, the kennels were empty with the exception of Gareth's.

'Hello girl,' he said softly. 'When are you going to have your babies?' He opened the run gate and Jess came out wagging her tail and whining with pleasure. Gareth bent down and patted her affectionately.

'I thought she might have had them today,' he said turning to Tommy. 'Do you know anything about dogs?'

'A bit,' said Tommy modestly. 'My father always kept working dogs.'

‘Oh, what sort of dogs? What does your father do?’

‘Gamekeeper. Spaniels,’ he replied shortly, elaborating no further.

‘Well, when do you think my Jess here is going to drop her litter?’

Tommy bent down, held out his hand for the dog to smell, once she smelled him he fondled her ears and gently felt her swollen abdomen.

‘I reckon not for another twenty four hours or so yet.’

‘Rubbish! It’ll be tonight. Care to make a small bet Boyo?’

‘I’m not a betting man,’ Tommy replied.

‘If that bitch goes another twenty four hours then I’ll give you the pick of the litter - free.’ Gareth grinned pushing a lock of hair out of his eyes. ‘And let me see, if I’m right then you buy me a bottle of whisky from the stores. How’s that?’

‘Well like I said I’m not a betting man, but maybe now is a good time as any to start on such a sure thing. You’re on.’

‘That’s the spirit Boyo. You might as well get into the swing of things and betting is a part of our way of life here, gambling, cards and racing our horses. Do you play cards?’

Tommy shook his head. He thought about his nest egg in the bank in England. He remembered when he left home at fifteen how he wished he’d had money and that he could have taken his mother away with him. He vowed to himself that his three years in Argentina would add to his savings. He felt the need for security and to Tommy, money and security were one and the same thing. The job was not highly paid, but food and accommodation as part of the conditions of employment, there didn’t seem to be anything much to spend your money on. He was reluctant to risk any of his precious wages, even if he did win his sure bet with Gareth.

He did indeed win his bet with Gareth, and through it acquired Bella, who as soon as she was old enough to be weaned went everywhere with Tommy during daylight hours, riding in front of Tommy across Blaze's neck. Despite winning Bella he never became a dedicated gambler like many of the men. Tommy had even seen them betting on where a fly was going to land next.

He'd chosen well with his horse Blaze, and he had won several of the Sunday races, much to Gareth's delight, who never failed to place a bet on his friend. He became popular with the men, with his youthful unassuming ways and his willingness to work.

There was one however, who was neither impressed by Tommy's popularity, nor happy with his race wins - Jack Crooks. The foreman had a good mare called Goldie who, until Blaze had entered onto the scene, had repeatedly won races.

After winning a race one Sunday on Blaze, Jack Crooks turned to Tommy and said sourly, 'Don' t get too cocky about winning a couple of races, that doesn't make you anything special.

'Leave off Jack,' Old Jock chipped in, 'I'm happy for him to win, as I'd put my money on him.' He guffawed, rubbing his hands with glee.

'What was all that about, what have I done?' Tommy asked Gareth later.

Oh take no notice of him Boyo, nobody else does. For someone who'd never ridden a horse until six weeks ago, you're turning into a darn good horseman. You're doing okay, and as long as you keep winning, Old Jock and I are more than happy with you.'

Letters from Amelia arrived regularly - his father had married his widow lady, his brothers were fine, news of Amelia's happenings at school, and the inevitable questions about what Tommy's new life entailed. He looked forward to her letters replying promptly, telling her of his having won Bella, his learning to drive one of the newly acquired vehicles, of his winning a couple of races on Blaze.

The months rolled by turning into years, and one day it was brought home to Tommy by a casual remark of Gareth's that only nine months remained of Tommy's three year contract.

'Roll on the next nine months. My leave's due about the same time as you. I'd just got back when you'd first arrived.' he commented.

'Will you go home?' Tommy enquired, thinking they might travel together, 'And will you sign up for another three years before you leave?'

'Home Boyo, where's home? I've got my father and my little sister Megan, and although I feel a bit guilty about Megan sometimes, you know me leaving her to cope after my mother died, I've long since stopped thinking of Wales as home. No Tommy, it's Buenos Aires for me for two or three weeks, and by then I shall be ready to start work again. My Dad's okay but I don't think he's ever forgiven me for not following in his footsteps and becoming a doctor.'

Once a month there would be a social held for the men. Light refreshments were served, there would be music and dancing, and Mrs. Manners would play the piano. The first hour would be attended by Mr. Simon Cartwright and his wife from the big house, one of the rare occasions they would actually be seen, after which they would retire, leaving the men to relax.

Tommy was always too self-conscious to dance as the men would partner one another Gareth had no such qualms.

'C'mon Boyo, it's just dancing. You don't have to marry your partners,' he laughed.

'I don't really know how to dance,' Tommy mumbled blushing to the roots of his hair.

Gareth roared, 'Neither do half this mob. Who do you think taught them to dance? Why me and Mrs. Manners, isn't that so Ma'am?' he went on not waiting for an answer. 'I always knew those classes my mother sent me to would be useful one day. I should be charging for lessons.'

Mrs. Manners laughed along with him, 'You're incorrigible Gareth, but yes Tommy, Gareth is a very good dancer.'

So it was that Tommy learnt to dance - his initial embarrassment soon wore off. When Mrs. Manners was not playing the piano, the records would come out and someone would be elected to wind up the gramophone. Mrs. Manners would dance with her husband, and occasionally with Gareth, and sometimes one of the other men would buck up courage and ask her to partner them. She never refused, and to see her and Gareth whirling round to the sounds of a scratchy Strauss waltz was a sight to see. One such evening Tommy finally found himself asking for a dance.

'Why thank you Tommy, I'd be delighted. I was beginning to think you'd never ask me.'

Tommy took her nervously in his arms and hoped he wouldn't disgrace himself by trampling over her toes. He needn't have worried - he'd learned his lessons well. Despite being a plump motherly figure, Mrs. Manners was as light as a feather, and he found himself thoroughly enjoying the experience.

It was during one of these social evenings that Jack Crooks, who had been casting baleful looks at Tommy throughout the evening that the trouble started.

Tommy had just danced with Mrs. Manners and had returned her to her chair. He walked over to the makeshift bar, where beer and soft drinks were served, and had ordered himself a lemonade when a voice came from behind him.

'That's right. You stay nice and sober so's you can ask the boss's wife to dance again, nancy boy.'

Tommy swung round, 'I'm staying sober because I don't like the taste of beer, that's all. And, as for asking the lady to dance again, I wouldn't dream of monopolising her.'

'Humph,' Crooks sneered. 'Dancing with the manager's wife won't get you a promotion so you're wasting your time anyway.'

'Look Jack, I'm looking for nothing. There's nothing for me to be promoted to.'

'Hey you,' Crooks raised his voice belligerently, 'I'm Mr. Crooks to you.' He leant forward and gripped Tommy's forearm in a vice like grip.

Tommy blanched. Here comes trouble and not of his making, but he was ready for it. He felt it had been simmering long enough and was about ready to come to a head.

'Mr. Crooks, take your hands off me - now,' he said quietly.

He sensed what was coming next and moved slightly to one side causing Jack Crooks to stumble as he swung at Tommy. Tommy could smell the alcohol and knew it was something stronger than beer Crooks had been drinking.

The next thing Tommy knew he was halfway down the room being swung round in the dance by Gareth, but not before heard Old Jock say, 'C'mon Jack, leave the lad alone. Mr. Manners is watching - just pretend you slipped. What is it with you? You've never liked that lad. What's he ever done to you?'

'He's after my job, that's what. He'd not been here more than a few weeks and Manners was saying, put Lawrence onto that, let Lawrence learn to do that, creepin' little sod – he's after my job I tell you.'

'Don't be so daft man that's the grog talking.'

The incident with Crooks occurred in July. Tommy had nine months left of his contract to run. He discussed it with

Gareth. How could he sign on for another three years given the situation with Crooks?

Gareth tried to convince him otherwise. 'Miserable sod, but you don't have to live in his pocket Boyo.'

Tommy knew this, but he did have to work under him and was reluctant to commit himself.

It was about a month after the social that Mr. Manners stopped Tommy as he was riding in from a day of checking fences.

'Tommy you've learnt to drive the Ford truck haven't you?' he went on without waiting for a reply. 'We've sold two stud rams to Señor Ramirez over at Estancia Montalban. I want you to deliver them. They're in a pen next to the big barn, so get someone to help you load them up in the morning, and then set off straight after breakfast. See Jack Crooks for the keys, I couldn't find him earlier, tell him it's on my orders.'

Tommy found Jack Crooks and asked for the keys, telling him of Mr. Manners' instructions.

'Really, and how come Mr. Manners sent for you direct and not for me may I ask - been arse creeping again have you?' his mean piggy eyes narrowed.

'No, and he didn't send for me, he just stopped me as I rode in. I'm not looking for an argument, so just give me the keys ready for the morning please.'

'You mealy-mouthed little sod, you'd better watch yourself or you might find you'll get your comeuppance one dark night.'

'If you're threatening me then take a word of advice - don't. I'm not looking for any trouble, just trying to do my job. What's your problem with me anyway?'

'I don't like some jumped up kid creeping round the bosses behind my back, trying to get my job, and you needn't bother to deny it,' he snarled.

Tommy shrugged and held out his hand, 'The keys please, nothing I say is going to convince you I don't want your job, so I've got nothing more to say.'

The journey would take several hours on the rocky roads which were little more than tracks. Mr. Manners had organised for Tommy to stay overnight as the trip would be virtually impossible in the dark, and the hours of daylight weren't very long at that time of year.

The following day he found his way to Estancia Montalban. Señor Ramirez was one of the few *criollas* of Spanish descent to own an *estancia* in that area, as they were mainly English settlers.

He was a tall silver haired man of regal bearing with a gentle manner. His family consisted of his wife and daughter who had come to them late in life and was petted and spoiled by everyone on the *estancia* as Tommy was to learn.

It was during his overnight stay that Tommy met the fifteen year old Catriona who, even at that tender age, showed signs of the wilful, beautiful young woman she was to become. Tommy was twenty three years old.

Tommy was invited to dine with the family that evening. He was embarrassed, and said he would be happy to eat in the cook-house, but Señor Ramirez insisted.

'We get so few visitors, and it will give my wife and daughter a chance to show off their English, of which they're very proud, but get little opportunity to use.'

After washing, and changing his shirt, he ran his fingers through his hair and went through to join the family for the evening meal.

The meal turned out to be a paella, a typically Spanish dish which Tommy had never heard of, it turned out to be a rice dish, with chicken and a spicy sausage, called chorizo, flavoured with garlic and saffron, tastes that Tommy had never experienced, but tucked into with relish. This was followed by a deliciously light fluffy soufflé of chocolate and oranges.

The conversation began with Señor Ramirez discussing sheep, mainly the breeding programmes at his *estancia*, and at El Carranches, until Catriona interrupted with, 'Papa this is so boring, please let us talk to our guest about England. Mamma and I would like to know about London wouldn't we, Mamma? Do you come from London Señor Tomas?' she said fluttering her eyelashes at him.

'No, I don't,' he replied somewhat amused by her flirtatious manner, 'but I know London very well. I used to spend several months of the year in London.'

She clapped her hands, suddenly childlike, 'Oh please tell us, have you seen Buckingham Palace, where the king and queen live?'

The next hour passed quickly with both Señora Ramirez and Catriona wanting to talk about London.

At nine o'clock he thanked Señor and Señora Ramirez for their hospitality and begged to be excused, as he had an early start in the morning.

While saying goodnight to the ladies, Catriona said looking up at him through her sooty lashes, 'Will we see you again Señor Tomas?'

'Catriona,' her mother said sharply, 'It's time for bed. It was so nice to meet you Señor Lawrence, and do have a safe journey tomorrow.

Back at El Carranchies Tommy was faced with a dilemma. He and Gareth had talked about Tommy signing another contract several times, and he desperately wanted to, but couldn't decide. Jack Crooks still being the stumbling block.

Eventually six weeks before his contract was due to expire, William Manners sent for him.

‘Now then Tommy, what’s it to be, would you like another contract? I am aware of the antagonism Crooks has shown towards you in the past but I have spoken to him, and Crooks is a good foreman, and is not a fool, and I have been given his assurance that things will not escalate, and that the two of you can work together without any further aggravation. So where do you stand, the contract is here if you want to sign.’ He passed the document across to Tommy, who hesitated for only a second before picking up the pen and signing for another three years.

Tommy wrote to Amelia to tell her he was disappointed not to be coming home, but would take long leave at the end of his next three years. He told her of his being able to drive a motor vehicle, of his trip to the Ramirez *estancia*, and of his forthcoming leave to be taken in Buenos Aires with his friend Gareth.

Gareth and Tommy set off in high spirits for Buenos Aires. Gareth knew his way around the city. It was a big sprawling place built along the Rio de la Plata and it was a busy city by day and positively ablaze by night. A dynamic place with street cafés, parks and boulevards lined with shops, hotels, restaurants and tango bars, an inevitable feature of the city’s nightlife. The harbour district of La Boca, where the roots of the tango were born, was one of Tommy’s favourite places.

Tommy’s first visit to a tango club was a revelation. People would pair up with perfect strangers at the sound of the music beginning. He found the rhythm and motion of the dance the most sensual of experiences. At first he was too shy to join in, and was content to sit and watch, but after watching Gareth, who had no such inhibitions, he soon threw caution to the wind, and joined in.

One afternoon when they’d stopped to sit on a park bench, Tommy commented, ‘I can’t believe how different this is, it’s lush and green. It’s how I imagined Argentina would be.’

Gareth laughed, 'Yes, I suppose you were a bit taken aback to say the least. Arriving at Rio Gallegos, followed by a nine hour journey by ox cart isn't exactly awe-inspiring. What do you reckon now tho' Tommy. You've had three years here. Do you think you'll make your life here?'

'Gosh! I dunno Gareth,' he said thoughtfully. 'I suppose I haven't thought that far ahead. I've got a bit of money saved. I wanted to leave England and now that's happened I didn't really plan any further. Anyway I've signed another contract now, so that's the next three years mapped out.'

After two weeks in Buenos Aires it was Gareth who said one day out of the blue, 'I think I've had enough of city life. I miss the quiet, the open spaces and the solitude. I miss being in the saddle. It gives me a |feeling of peace Boyo, do you understand what I'm saying? But we can stay for a bit longer if you want Tommy,' he added hastily, 'seeing as it's your first time in the city.'

Gareth felt like an elder brother to Tommy. They knew one another as well as two people ever can. They lived together, worked together, they'd learnt to trust each other, to respect one another's privacy, when to hold their tongues, and when to speak. There were many special friendships formed between men of totally different backgrounds, due to the circumstances under which they worked and lived. Tommy knew Gareth was good for him. He was irrepressible, full of good humour, and was well read with a keen mind. He taught Tommy how to play chess, to read the stars, as well as teaching him how to dance, something he'd often tease Tommy about.

He nodded, 'I understand completely Gareth and yes, I'm ready to go home. We're not city boys. Let's go and get started on our next three years.'

Little did he realise that due to circumstances, he wouldn't complete his next three year contract.

Chapter 8

Sunday morning Tommy woke up to the rattle of tea cups and the smell of toast.

'Wake up Tommy, I've brought you tea and toast.'

'What time is it?' he groaned.

'It's nearly eight o' clock,' Emma said pouring two cups of tea. She put them on the bedside tables.

'Come back to bed,' he said patting the bed invitingly.

'I am,' she replied, slipping off her nightdress and sliding in beside him.

She put out a hand and stroked his chest, leaning over to kiss him. Her hair fell a golden curtain as he took her head between his hands, kissing her slowly. He lay with half closed eyes, caressing her until he knew she was ready, rolling her gently onto her back, their positions reversed. Her legs came up around his waist and they began the age old rhythm, ending with a shuddering climax for both of them.

They lay sleepily sated, with Emma's head on his shoulder. 'You're gorgeous, do you know that?' he asked huskily.

She took his hand and placed it on her slightly rounded stomach.

'Tommy,' she whispered, 'I've got something to tell you. I hope you're going to be pleased - I'm pregnant.'

His eyes sprang open. 'You mean we're going to have a baby?' He was now fully awake.

'You're not cross, are you? Please don't be.'

'No, of course I'm not cross Emma. Why ever would I be?'

'I didn't know whether you wanted babies or not. We never really talked about it. I'm scared Tommy.'

'Shh, don't be scared. There's nothing to be afraid of you silly girl,' he soothed, 'and of course I want babies with you Emma, - that's a big part of being married, having a loving family.'

They quietly until Emma said, 'The tea's gone cold Tommy. Shall I make some more?'

'No,' he laughed. 'How can you think about tea at a time like this? When's the baby due?'

'July. We'll need a cot and a pram and so many things,' she sighed.

'That's okay, we'll get everything. Now I'll go down and make some fresh tea. You stay in bed,' he said slipping on a pair of trousers.

He returned with more tea, drinking it this time while it was still hot.

'Get back into bed Tommy.'

'What! Again? You're insatiable. It's nine o' clock in the morning, you wanton.'

She giggled, 'I didn't mean for that, I just wanted a cuddle.'

Tommy didn't need further persuasion, swiftly removing his trousers he got back into bed. He took her gently into his arms and they lay peacefully for a while, Emma fingering the silver chain with his mother's amethyst ring that he wore around his neck.

'Can I try the ring on?'

'Mmm,' he murmured sleepily.

She slipped it on her finger, and holding out her hand at an angle such as the chain would allow, she admired it.

'See it fits me. I'd 'love to wear it. Can I Tommy, please, can I?' she wheedled.

'Shh.' He kissed her to silence her, wondering why women often chose immediately after making love to ask for things almost as if knowing that in a state of after sex euphoria, he'd find it hard to refuse. She wasn't the first woman to ask to wear the ring, a memory of Catriona asking the same question flashed through his mind.

'You don't love me,' she pouted. 'If you did you'd let me wear it - it's only a ring.'

'Don't be silly Emma. Me loving you has got nothing to do with me not letting you wear it. After all, you've got your engagement ring, and like you say it's only a ring. And now,' he said slapping her buttocks playfully, 'it's time we got out of bed - the day's half gone already.'

The next six months were living hell for Tommy. Emma's moods swung from irascible and scratchy to loving and affectionate. She'd throw tantrums and along with them sometimes more solid objects that came to hand, including a dozen eggs that came hurtling across the kitchen one evening when Tommy suggested she calm down for the baby's sake.

'Don't you bloody well tell me to calm down,' she screamed. 'That's all you think about these days, the baby. What about me? It's not you that has to walk around looking like a freak. Just look at me - my feet are swollen, my belly is swollen, I look like nothing on earth, and all you can say is, "calm down for the bloody baby's sake" she finished bursting into tears.

'Oh Emma don't,' he pleaded, wrapping his arms around her. He rocked her back and forth. 'You don't look a freak, you look beautiful to me,' he comforted.

She sobbed, 'Oh God, Tommy I hate this baby already.'

Taking her firmly by the shoulders he shook her gently, 'Stop it Emma! Don't even think such a thing. I don't ever want to hear you say you hate a child, unborn or otherwise. Do you hear me?'

Another time when discussing names for the baby. Tommy asked, 'Have you any preferences when it comes to boy's names Emma?'

'No, although I quite like Thomas.'

'I don't mind Thomas for a second name, but I'd rather like to call a boy Gareth.'

'Gareth! What sort of name is that?' she asked crossly.

'It's a Welsh name,' he answered wearily, hoping this wasn't going to cause another argument.

'Humph, I don't see why an English name isn't good enough.'

He didn't reply, but continued, 'What's your favourite girl's name?'

'I don't have a particular favourite,' she said, 'If you want to call her after your mother, her name was Martha, wasn't it?'

'Yes, but I didn't want to call her Martha. I would like a girl to be called Amelia, if you're agreeable.'

'Amelia!' she shrieked. 'Oh I might have known it, you and your precious bloody Amelia. Oh that would please her wouldn't it? To have my daughter named after her!'

'She'll be my daughter too Emma, in case you've forgotten,' he said mildly.

'Oh call it what you want. I don't care anyway. Why should what I want count?' she sulked.

No matter how bad her moods, the one constant thing was her need for Tommy physically. One lunchtime, after a particularly frantic lovemaking session, instigated by Emma she'd ended up bathing his back where her fingernails had raked, drawing blood. His bottom lip was starting to swell where she'd nipped him.

'God! Emma look at me, I'm seeing Mrs. Stewart-Shenley after lunch, she'll wonder what the hell I got tangled up with. I look like I've been dragged through a hedge backwards.'

'Just tell her you got attacked by a wildcat,' she giggled.

He grinned ruefully, 'And to cap it all Emma, I've got to go back to work and I haven't had anything to eat.'

'Are you complaining?' she asked archly.

'No, but I suggest if you want more of the same tonight, you spend the afternoon making me a substantial meal. You know what they say - man can't live on love alone,' and with that parting shot, he ducked out of the door.

As the weather got warmer, so Emma grew bigger - her back ached. Tommy would rub her back and feet with lavender oil.

Dr. Fleming had suggested Emma go to the cottage hospital in Bishops Waltham where he himself would be on hand for the birth. Mrs. Stewart-Shenley had given Tommy the keys for the old Ford in case of a night time emergency.

Tommy came home late one evening at six thirty. Emma was resting on the settee. She opened her eyes as he came in.

'How are you darlin'? Don't get up, stay there.'

He came over and knelt besides her smoothing back her hair from her forehead.

She wound her arms round Tommy's neck, 'I'm tired Tommy. The baby feels so low down and heavy.'

He kissed her, 'I know, it won't be long now Emma.'

She buried her face in his neck, 'I haven't even started supper yet.'

'That's okay, I'm not hungry. I'll grab some bread and cheese later. Can I get you something - scrambled eggs or something?'

She shook her head, still against his neck. 'No thanks, I'm not hungry either - it's so hot. I love it when you smell all sweaty and horsey,' she whispered nuzzling into his neck. 'I wish we could make love Tommy. I miss you so.'

'Mmm, me too, soon Emma.'

He did miss their frequent, often wild lovemaking. Over the last few weeks Emma had become enormous, making it an impossible feat.

They'd been in bed about an hour. Tommy not yet sleeping. He'd rubbed Emma's back and belly tenderly with lavender oil, and as he lay waiting for sleep to come, the smell of lavender pervading the room bringing back memories of his mother and the sachets she'd make to put in the linen drawers.

He was starting to drift into sleep when the sound of Emma groaning brought him back to awareness.

'Are you all right Emma?' he whispered.

'No, I think the baby's coming. The pains are coming fast.'

They reached the hospital at eleven o' clock. Tommy being shooed outside to wait. He went into the small garden and lit a cigarette. They called him back in at midnight.

Amelia Katherine Lawrence had come into the world at a quarter to twelve on the twentieth of July nineteen thirty eight.

He was ushered into a small room where Emma lay with the baby in her arms. She had been born a healthy seven pounds, a crumpled red-faced mite, with a thick thatch of jet black hair, as dark as his own, and with Emma's startling blue eyes. Emma was tired but happy.

'Isn't she just too beautiful Tommy?'

‘Yes she’s gorgeous, but I would expect nothing less with a mother like she has. She couldn’t have been anything else.’

He sat on the bed and putting his arms around Emma and the baby he whispered, ‘Thank you Emma, you’ve made me so happy.’

‘I love you Tommy.’

Just then a nurse came bustling in, ‘Come along Mr. Lawrence, time for mother and baby to get some rest. You’ll be able to see them both tomorrow.’

Tommy brought Emma and the baby home after five days. Two days later Emma’s auntie Annie arrived from Reading, to help Emma with the baby.

Tommy was glad to see her as it meant Emma had company during the day while he was working. He hoped having Annie there would give Emma the confidence she lacked while handling baby Amelia.

From the time they got home from the hospital, till Annie’s arrival. Tommy had had to bathe his daughter, change her nappies and dress her. Emma loved to hold her and give her a bottle, but was nervous of performing all the other tasks. Tommy showed her how to hold the baby, to bring up her wind after her feed.

‘You seem to know just what to do Tommy. It’s just that she looks so fragile, and I’m scared she’ll break, or I’ll drop her. You do it again this time and perhaps I’ll try next time. How do you know how to do all these things?’

He laughed, ‘I’ve got twin brothers, and I was four when they were born. I used to love to help my Mum when my father wasn’t around. ‘

She’d watch Tommy deftly dress her after her bath.

‘I’ll never be able to do that,’ she said.

‘Of course you will, you just need a bit of practice, Annie will help you, you’ll see.’

He was proved right Annie helped, and by the time of her departure Emma was coping admirably.

The baby was two weeks old when Tommy brought up the subject of the christening.

‘We’ll have to get organised by early September, because Amelia starts the new school term, and I’d like her to come and stay for a few days beforehand if that’s okay with you Emma.’

‘No, it’s not all right. I’ve got enough to do without having a guest in the house to look after,’ she snapped.

‘Annie was here two days after you came out of hospital, for a week,’ he pointed out. ‘I’m sure we can manage to have Amelia for two or three days - after all she is going to be one of the godmothers along with Annie.’

‘Over my dead body,’ her voice rose an octave. ‘My aunt Annie is one and I thought I’d ask my friend Joan to be the other one.’

‘Well think again Emma, don’t be awkward for God’s sake. I’m quite happy for Annie to be one and Amelia will be the other.’

‘Oh I’m bloody sure you’ll be happy for Annie to be one if it means you can choose dear Amelia as the other,’ she said her voice dripping sarcasm. ‘I often wonder what kind of a relationship you have with that woman,’ she sneered.

Tommy’s face whitened under his tan, the muscles at the corner of his mouth tightened.

‘Emma I don’t want to fall out with you over this. I know you’re tired and pregnancy is a tough time for a woman, but, Amelia will be the baby’s other godmother, and she will come and stay in my home, and you will be pleasant to her. As for your comments on the relationship between Amelia and myself, I'll ignore them, making allowances for the state you're in.'

'Oh that's very noble of you. Why do you always have to be such a bloody saint? I can't stand that woman and you know it, she's such a mealy-mouthed pious old bitch...'

The sound of the slap rang out as Tommy's hand connected with her cheek. She gasped, putting her hand to her face. Tommy grabbed her shoulders with a grip of steel, his eyes a hard flinty grey, boring into hers. He said between clenched teeth, 'That's enough. She's coming and that's the end of it.' And turning on his heel he slammed the back door behind him.

He trembled with rage as he leaned against the back door. How in the name of hell had he ever let Emma wind him up into such a state that he'd resorted to physical violence? He'd spent a lifetime despising his father for that very same trait. For a moment he'd wanted to kill her for uncharitable thoughts about himself and Amelia. A woman he'd come to regard as a surrogate mother, a woman who'd befriended him as a six year old abused child, a woman who had opened her heart and her home to him.

He saw again Emma's face the moment he'd slapped her - the colour had drained from her cheeks and the tears had overflowed, spilling freely down her face. He felt a mixture of emotions apart from anger, there was pity for Emma, remorse and an overpowering self-loathing for his actions.

What was he going to do? Eleven months into a marriage, with a child, and him resorting to violence, where was this heading? Had he been too hasty in marrying Emma? Had he married on the rebound from Catriona? Had he loved Catriona, or had he just been obsessed with her? He didn't know any more. Whether he had or not it was too late now.

He sat on the bench seat just outside the back door. Did he even know how to love? So many questions, with no obvious answers.

He put his head in his hands, a gesture of total despair.

Chapter 9

They returned to El Carranchas in early May. The work had wound down. There were fences to be ridden, sheep to be moved, but generally the work had slackened off during the winter - also due to the short hours of daylight - the busy months starting again in October. Many of the men went on leave for three months.

Life at El Carranchas didn't vary much, it was work and an occasional trip to Rio Gallegos or Punta Arenas, just over the border in Chile, to pick up stores, the dipping of the sheep for scab, the lamb marking, the lambing itself and the shearing.

The leisure hours also varied little, the Saturday night socials, the horse races, the gambling, a good sing-song, and the endless games of chess or checkers. Tommy learnt to play Bidou, a game of dice and a variation of poker. It was one of the men's favourite games. He learnt early on that bluffing well was a necessity and, much to his surprise, he soon became adept at it. It was actually the only gambling game he took part in and enjoyed.

It was during a game of Bidou that the trouble started again with Jack Crooks. Several of the men had been playing at a table in the mess hall when Jack Crooks came in. He'd been drinking when he came to the table to watch, the game.

After a while pulling up a chair as he spoke he said, 'I think I'll join you.'

Tommy's heart sank. He'd had no further trouble with Crooks, but he'd always given him a wide berth at any social affairs, especially if he knew he'd been drinking. When Jack drunk too much, it made him mean.

Tommy considered whether to quit playing, but saw Gareth give an imperceptible shake of his head. He knew what he meant. If he quit now as Jack joined the game, it might very well trigger off an outburst, so he remained at his place.

Tommy had been winning steadily and decided, after another half an hour or so had passed, it would be prudent to stop now. This was enough to provoke Jack Crooks.

'What's the matter then? Competition too much for you?' He looked round the table at the men. 'You've taken all their money and now you're going to quit without giving them the chance to win it back. Typical of you,' he sneered.

'They can always win it back another time,' Tommy said coolly.

'You're a smart-mouthed bastard,' Jack snarled. 'You've always got a bloody answer.'

'Hey, steady on Jack,' Toby Martin interjected. 'Tommy plays with us regular - some you win, some you lose, that's the way it goes.'

Gareth jerked his head at Tommy, 'Go on Boyo, if you've had enough.'

Tommy rose from his chair. Jack was enraged that the men hadn't backed him up, but had sided with Tommy. He rose unsteadily to his feet.

'Not so fast. If they don't object to you taking their money, I do,' he said morosely.

'Well that's too damn bad Jack, because I'm quitting whether it suits you or not.'

Jack lowered his head and before anyone, including Tommy, realised his intention, he lunged at Tommy who staggered back barely retaining his balance.

'That's it you miserable bastard you.' Tommy gritted his teeth and, before anyone could stop him, he swung back at Jack. He felt his fist connect with Jack's face. It was like hitting an over ripe orange. Jack retaliated.

Toby Martin took a step forward, 'C'mon now...' Gareth laid a restraining hand on his arm, 'Leave 'em Toby. It's been a long time coming.'

It didn't last long, but proved to be both bloody and vicious with neither man coming out unscathed, but Tommy's final blow laying Jack out cold. Tommy stepped forward and kicked him in the ribs before Gareth could stop him.

'That's enough dammit,' Gareth said harshly. 'You've beaten him fair and square, but don't kick a man when he's down.'

Tommy shook his head as if to clear it, spraying droplets of sweat and blood around from a small cut above his right eye.

'Christ! His face looks like strawberry jam,' Toby said looking at the prone body of Crooks.

'Tommy, get out of here,' Gareth ordered. 'Go to the bunkhouse and get cleaned up. There'll be hell to pay over this,' he said darkly.

'You know something? I don't bloody well care. I'm sick of tiptoeing round that pig. He's on about the same level as my father,' Tommy muttered and turning on his heel, he walked out to murmurs of "well done Tommy" and "he deserved it" and "good on you boy".

Yes he thought, as the wind hit him as he crossed to the bunkhouse, he deserved it, but what kind of repercussions would this fight have for Tommy? You didn't beat a foreman to a pulp and get off scot free. He'd be lucky to keep his job.

He knew he'd been wrong to kick Jack when he was down. He guessed he'd probably broken a couple of ribs. He remembered his father doing the same thing to him when he was fifteen years old.

The next morning he woke feeling as if he'd been run over by a steam roller. His ribs were sore where Jack had landed a couple of good punches, and his right eye was closed, the beginnings of a real shiner already starting to show. The knuckles of his right hand were skinned and stinging. Jack Crooks wasn't seen all that Sunday.

Tommy knew by Monday Mr. Manners would have found out about the fight, that's if he didn't already know.

Eighteen months of Tommy's contract had passed with another eighteen months still to go. He didn't know where he stood. If he was fired for misconduct, did that mean he would have to pay his own boat fare home? He couldn't remember the fine print of his contract. What would he do in England? He knew from Amelia's letters that work was hard to find.

Monday morning after breakfast Jack Crooks appeared. Tommy was shocked at his appearance. Had he really done that? He only recalled lashing out in an uncontrollable rage and punching continuously until his man went down. The next thing he remembered was Gareth telling him to get to the bunkhouse. Jack's face was varying shades of black and purple, his features distorted and swollen, and missing two front teeth.

Jack gave the men their orders. He battled to make himself understood through lips that were twice their normal size. Not once did he look in Tommy's direction.

When he'd finished and the men had dispersed, then he looked at Tommy and mumbled, 'Lawrence, Mr. Manners wants to see you - now.'

Tommy nodded curtly and headed for the office to face Mr. Manner's wrath.

William Manners looked up from the ledger he was studying as Tommy knocked on the open door.

'Come in.'

Tommy entered and stood in front of the heavy old oak desk.

William looked at him for a long moment before saying with a sigh, 'Sit down Lawrence.'

Tommy fidgeted uncomfortably. 'I'd prefer to stand sir.'

'As you will Lawrence.' He took a deep breath, 'Now tell me what in the hell happened?'

'There's nothing to tell sir,' Tommy answered. 'I had a fight with the foreman, that's it.'

'That's not it at all young man. I only wish it were.' He rested his elbows on the desk, and putting his fingertips together, he went on, 'Tell me how it started and why you couldn't have avoided it. I know for a fact that Crooks had been drinking, but you were sober. So what's your excuse, I understand you hit him first?'

'Yes sir, I hit him first and yes I was sober. I don't need an excuse. That man disliked me from the day I came here four and a half years ago. He's tried to needle me on many an occasion and I've walked away, but there comes a time when you don't walk away.'

This was a long speech for Tommy and as much of an explanation as William Manners was likely to get.

There was a moments silence when Tommy thought, here it comes, *I'm fired.*

'You know Lawrence, this puts me in a hell of a position. One of you has to go. You've proved yourself to be a good worker, and you're popular with the men. You're both competent and sober. Jack drinks too much, and is not well liked, but by the same token he is a first rate foreman, although given a few years, you could probably make a better one. He's also been with us for eleven years.'

He paused giving Tommy a penetrating look before continuing.

'What I am about to do is highly unethical and should it become known to the Board, could put my own position in jeopardy. I spoke to Señor Ramirez on the party line yesterday as soon as I heard about your little fracas on Saturday night. He is desperately looking for a manager, and I have taken it upon myself to not only recommend you, but give him a positively glowing testimonial. I've told him that despite your years, you are both responsible and capable. Under normal circumstances you would have been fired, but,' he added with a tight little smile, 'this isn't really normal circumstances, is it? I know you told the truth about being provoked, and I must say I feel somewhat responsible for the situation. I knew there was friction, and I grossly misjudged my man. I had thought that after my warning to Crooks this would have been avoided.'

'Why thank you, thank you very much sir,' he stammered, hardly able to believe his luck.

'That's all right Lawrence. Everything else can be arranged as long as you're agreeable to going to work for Señor Ramirez. I have taken the liberty of having your resignation typed up. You only have to sign it,' he pushed the letter forward, 'and work one month's notice. Crooks will not bother you for your remaining time here. I shall explain to the Board that I personally took the decision to release you, as you'd had a very attractive offer from elsewhere. The only reason I decided to let you go instead of Crooks, is that you are a young man and can go on to better things. In fact, this is probably a good opportunity for you right now. Had I fired Crooks, who is fifty years old, he would have difficulty in finding another job due to his age, and once it became known he has a drinking problem, then he would have had even more difficulty in keeping one. Only one thing remains - here are the keys to the small Ford. Take it and go to the Ramirez *estancia*, stay overnight. You can discuss the terms of your employment with your prospective employer, and come back for work here on Wednesday. Señor Ramirez is expecting you. Good luck Lawrence. I'm sorry this has happened, but I hope it turns out well for you, and wish you everything of the best.'

December saw a new chapter in Tommy's life begin. Estancia Montalban was considerably smaller than El Carranchas with far less staff. Three of the men employed were married with families, each with a small house. Five single men were housed in the bunkhouse. Tommy himself, as manager was allocated a small house in close proximity to the main house.

One of the married couples was English, Kenneth and Jenny Ball, a pleasant, cheerful couple. Kenneth was a shepherd from the Lake District, and Jenny had been a teacher. She now taught the six children on the *estancia*. There were servants at the big house, but they did not fall under Tommy's jurisdiction. There was Maria the cook and her husband Jose, who carried out maintenance work on the house and farm buildings. There was Thomasina, their eldest daughter, who ostensibly was employed as a housemaid, but spent more of her working hours acting as a ladies maid to the Senora and Catriona. Lastly Jorge, Thomasina's younger brother, who tended the gardens, which included a well-stocked kitchen garden growing all their fresh produce.

Tommy settled into his new life quickly which had the advantage of being more friendly and relaxed atmosphere, but had considerable financial advantages for him too.

Tommy had been at Estancia Montalban for a little under a year, and had gone to Punta Arenas where he was overseeing a shipment of wool and picking up stores, when by a stroke of luck he ran into Gareth, who was also collecting stores for El Carranchas.

They spent the evening together catching up, before making their way back to their respective *estancia*'s the following day.

Gareth told Tommy that Jack Crooks was very subdued these days, and that rumour had it, after the fight with Tommy, he'd had his final warning. He was eager to know how Tommy liked working on a smaller place.

'Sounds great,' he said wistfully as he listened to a detailed description of the men and their families. 'A pity there aren't any vacancies. I could do with a change. El Carranches isn't the same without you Boyo.' He grinned his old infectious grin.

'Young Juarez is talking about moving on soon. He's got a girl up in Buenos Aires,' Tommy said. 'I think Señor Ramirez will let me replace him if he leaves. D'you fancy coming to work with me? '

'Would I? But it's hardly likely to fall into place to suit us is it?'

As it happened it did. Pedro Juarez moved on, and Tommy lost no time in approaching Señor Ramirez. So it was that Gareth came to work on Estancia Montalban. The two friends were pleased to be together again. Evenings they kept one another company, the two of them often being invited to the Ball's for supper where they would pass a pleasant hour or two.

Christmas came and the men ate a special Christmas lunch, after which Tommy took a stroll down to the stables to feed Diablo a carrot he'd scrounged from the cookhouse. He snickered from his stall as he heard Tommy's footsteps. Tommy stroked his neck, talking to him softly, while feeding him the carrot.

‘Ah, so you would rather spend Christmas with your horse than with people then?’ a teasing voice said.

Tommy looked up startled to find himself not alone. Catriona was standing in the doorway of the stable yard.

‘No, I wouldn’t say that,’ Tommy smiled at her. ‘Diablo was a bit lame yesterday and I thought I’d just check him out.’

‘Do you like working here for my father Tomas?’ she asked pronouncing his name the Spanish way.

‘Yes I do, very much,’ he nodded, ‘And now if you’ll excuse me Miss Catriona, I think I’ll go back and join the company.’

‘What’s your hurry? Aren’t I company?’ she pouted.

‘Yes you are, and very charming company too, but I think you should be with your family.’

‘My parents have gone for a siesta and Thomasina has gone to join her family. I’m lonely.’

She sounded so plaintive that Tommy felt sorry for her, but this was awkward. She was still a child in Tommy’s eyes, and he was determined to treat her as such, despite the fact that she was obviously attempting to flirt with him.

‘If you think I’m such charming company, perhaps you’d like to walk down to the river with me,’ she suggested.

‘No, I wouldn’t,’ Tommy replied, sensing that no matter how much of a child he thought she was, that was not how she regarded herself.

‘Listen young lady,’ he said trying to inject a lighter note into his tone, ‘I don’t really think your father would approve of you keeping company with his farm manager.’

‘Oh my father likes you very much and, besides I think you’re very attractive, Tomas. Are all Englishmen as attractive as you?’

Tommy knew she'd deliberately misunderstood, but this had gone far enough. He sighed, 'You're much too young to be passing comments on the attractiveness or otherwise of men. How old are you, fifteen? You should still be playing with dolls at your age,' he said harshly.

Just then a familiar voice came on the wind, 'Hey Boyo, you're not still fussing over that horse are you?'

'Yes, I'm in here,' Tommy called out breathing a sigh of relief.

Gareth appeared, but not before Catriona hissed, 'I'm sixteen. I'm not a child and you know it.' Opening the yard door, she said in a voice loud enough for Gareth to hear, 'I'm so glad your horse is all right now.' She smiled hello at Gareth as she swept regally past him.

'What the hell was she doing here?' Gareth raised his eyebrows.

'You may well ask.' Tommy wiped the sweat from his upper lip with the back of his hand, although the day was cool.

'That, Boyo, is trouble if you're not careful. Did I save the day coming along when I did?' he laughed.

Tommy snorted, 'Yes you did, and it's not funny. She's a child for God's sake. She sixteen years old.'

Gareth looked sceptical. 'Don't kid yourself. That one's sixteen going on twenty six. Years mean nothing. She's a woman before her time, and she's got her eye on you. You realise what kind of trouble that could be?' he asked seriously.

'Yeah, I realise, but I'm not stupid. I've got a good job and I don't intend losing it.'

Gareth gave him a long hard stare.

Tommy did his best to avoid contact with Catriona whenever possible. Unfortunately Señor Ramirez ran his office from his house.

On one occasion when Tommy had been to the office discussing the wool prices being offered that season, he was leaving the office and had almost reached the front door when he heard a soft footfall behind him.

'Hello Tomas. How are you?'

He turned. 'I'm well thank you Miss Catriona,' he replied. He quickened his stride and was almost at the door, but Catriona was quicker. She brushed past him swiftly and put her hand on the door handle.

'Why are you in such a hurry?' she asked in a soft voice.

'I have work to do,' he replied curtly.

'If I didn't know better,' Catriona said, her eyes sparkling with mischief, 'I'd think you were trying to avoid me. Why only the other day when I came over to the stables, you rode off in such a hurry I thought the devil himself was after you.'

Tommy found himself blushing. He didn't think she'd realised he'd seen her coming. 'I'm sorry, I didn't see you Miss Catriona,' he lied.

'Oh I think you did Tomas, but no matter - there will be other times.' She smiled sweetly.

He cursed her silently. 'Well if you'll excuse me Miss, like I said I have work to do.'

She opened the door, holding it for him to pass through. There were inches between them as he brushed past her, smelling her heady perfume.

'As you're so busy, maybe I shall have to visit you in your quarters on a Sunday,' was her parting shot.

Tommy was shaking as he walked across to the cook-house. God forbid that she should do such a thing. Although these encounters were rare, they were an ordeal for Tommy.

Gareth commented one day. They had ridden in one evening and were turning into the stable yard when Catriona appeared suddenly through the small side gate leading from the big house gardens. She looked surprised at seeing Gareth, and had beat a hasty retreat.

Was she hoping to catch you on your own Boyo?' he laughed.

Tommy gnawed at his bottom lip. 'I think so.'

Gareth studied him. 'Is it becoming a problem Tommy?'

'Yes I'm afraid it is. Gareth she scares me - no, I mean it,' he said seeing the half-smile on his friend's face.

'I'm afraid to go across to the office in case she waylays me. She even threatened a few weeks ago to visit me in my quarters on a Sunday. D'you think I should mention it to her father, or just keep trying to avoid her?'

'Keep quiet. Her father's not going to appreciate being told his daughter is a randy little piece that's trying to get his farm manager to take her to bed. Don't worry, she won't visit your place on a Sunday. I'm here Boyo to come to your rescue.'

As it turned out, Gareth was not there when he needed rescuing.

Chapter 10

Amelia came to stay for four days. She delighted in her namesake and was given the honour of holding the baby in church, at Emma's insistence. Tommy noticed that Emma was sociable and pleasant during Amelia's visit, but he himself had withdrawn from Emma. He tried not to let his feelings show as he didn't want Amelia to feel uncomfortable. The evening before Amelia was due to return to Swallowfield, Tommy suggested, while Emma was putting the baby to bed, that Amelia walk down to the stables with him, as he wanted to check on Satan, who he thought might be going lame.

On their way Amelia said, 'Thank you so much Thomas for asking me to be my namesake's godmother, and for inviting me to stay, it's been lovely. I hope my inviting you for Christmas won't cause any problems. Please don't worry I shall understand if you can't make it, or if you'd rather spend your first Christmas in your own home with your new addition to your family.'

'No, Amelia it won't cause a problem. The problem is already there, but don't worry, it will be sorted out long before then,' he replied grimly.

She reached out and touched his arm sighing, 'Things are all right between you and Emma aren't they Thomas? I don't mean to pry or be an interfering old woman, but you look so tired, and not entirely happy.'

He smiled fondly at her. 'It's okay Amelia, you're not an interfering old woman, but no, things aren't all right, although I had hoped you wouldn't notice. I tried not to let it show. I hope it didn't spoil your stay. Don't look so stricken,' he went on, seeing the expression on her face, 'It's nothing serious -we're still adjusting to married life. I've been a bachelor for so long and have still got a lot to learn, and it's not easy for Emma either. In a little over a year she'd met me, married me, moved away from her family for the first time, and had her first child. She's used to living in town, and she's not used to the country, and as if that wasn't enough, she's still very young,' he finished

'No, of course it didn't spoil my stay. Emma made me most welcome. It's just that I know you so well and I suppose I just sensed that all wasn't as it should be. I feel better now you've assured me it's nothing serious my dear.'

Tommy burst out laughing, 'Oh Amelia you're the world's worst liar. You really are worried about me. Well don't be. You think I'm making excuses for Emma and you might be right, I am, and I suppose in a way it has been our first major upset, but we can't just run away, we'll work our way through it. And I'm looking forward to Christmas, I shall be able to see Georgie, Sylvia and the girls, and even Maude and the old man, as well as Emma being able to see Frank and Annie.'

They'd reached the stables and Tommy led out Satan, the magnificent seventeen hands, bad tempered black stallion. He walked him round the yard a couple of times on a lunge rein and made him trot so he could study his gait. After about five minutes he vaulted up onto his back. Satan snorted, laying his ears back flat, and rolling his eyes.

Eventually after satisfying himself there was nothing wrong he dismounted and led Satan back to his stable. They set off to stroll the ten minute walk back to the house.

The following morning, goodbyes said. Tommy took Amelia to the station. He gave her a big hug saying, 'Stop fretting Amelia, things will come right you'll see.'

He didn't feel so optimistic himself, but he'd wanted to reassure Amelia. Despite Emma's efforts he'd not forgiven her, and he hoped there would be no more scenes and tantrums now they were to be alone again.

A few weeks after Amelia's visit the autumn evenings were beginning to draw in. Tommy came home with the beginnings of a black eye, a dark purple smudge appearing across his cheekbone. Emma rushed to him full of concern.

'What happened Tommy? Are you okay?'

'Nothing much,' he muttered. 'That blasted Satan is aptly named. He played up something rotten the whole afternoon - skittish and bad tempered - like a temperamental woman eventually coming through the copse on the way home a rabbit ran across the path and spooked him and he tried to throw me. I had a hell of a job to stay on him, and a low branch caught me across the face. 'Where's Amy?' he asked.

'Outside the back door in her pram. Never mind the baby, let's have a look at your eye.'

She crossed to the chair where Tommy sat struggling to remove his riding boots. He looked up at her to say it was nothing when she reached out a hand and gently stroked his cheek.

'It's getting chilly out now I'll go and bring her in,' he said rising abruptly brushing her hand aside.

Her eyes filled with tears. 'She's well wrapped up Tommy. She's all right for a few minutes. What about me? You haven't said hello to me properly yet.' She looked up at him longingly.

He bent his head allowing his lips to graze her cheek briefly. Carefully avoiding her eyes, he headed for the door to bring his daughter in. He delighted in Amy - so like Emma in her features, despite her dark mop of hair.

Later that night in bed Tommy lay in the darkness staring up at the ceiling unable to sleep in spite of being bone weary. The ache in his leg was plaguing him, his struggle with Satan after a long day in the saddle was telling.

Emma reached out for him, 'Tommy, I'm sorry, I love you. Please don't be so cold with me. I'm truly sorry for what I said about you and Amelia.'

Tommy didn't reply, but took her hand that was resting lightly on his chest.

'And I really did try and be nice to her while she was here. Are you still cross with me for what I said?' she whispered.

'I know Emma, I know,' he squeezed her hand, 'And no, I'm not cross. I'm surprised that you could query my relationship with a woman of Amelia's age, who's been like a mother to me. Amelia would be a good friend to you, if you'd let her. What is it about her that you don't like?' he asked gently.

'She means so much to you and she so obviously adores you. She came into your life such a long time ago, and she knows you so much better than I do, I feel excluded. I suppose I'm jealous of her Tommy,' she confessed.

'Be reasonable Emma. Amelia will always mean a lot to me. She was my teacher, an example of everything that was good and right when I was a kid, she's been my friend for twenty six years. You're my wife, I married you, we have a beautiful baby, don't spoil what we have by being jealous of someone that isn't even in competition with you. Don't waste your energies. Ours is a totally different kind of relationship - not comparable at all,' he sighed.

It was true when he told Emma he wasn't annoyed with her any longer. He was troubled by a feeling of shame for the stinging slap he'd given Emma. He couldn't bring himself to say sorry. Why? Sorry was only a word after all.

He couldn't tell her of the terrible doubts he'd had after he'd slapped her. He knew they needed to work at making a go of their marriage. Emma could be warm, generous, with a sunny disposition when things were going her way, but he was only too aware of her faults. She could be volatile, impulsive, possessive, and on occasion very selfish.

Emma let out a barely audible sob - a sound that tore at Tommy's heart. Rolling over he kissed her mouth. She ran her fingers through his hair. Pressing his head to hers she opened her mouth feeling his tongue, arching her body up to meet his as he slipped his hands under her buttocks, and then he was inside her, moving slowly - waves of passion sweeping over him brushing all doubts from his mind. Even the physical ache in his leg which had plagued him earlier was forgotten as he lost himself in Emma.

The following day brought a letter from Gareth. He would be returning to England in the New Year. His father had died and there were things to be attended to. Megan, his sister, had already expressed a wish to move. He would see her resettled and, on his return to Argentina, he planned to marry Thomasina.

Tommy bought a second-hand car in November which they travelled up to Swallowfield in, for the promised Christmas visit to Amelia. Their stay went off well with Emma trying really hard to be nice to Amelia, which she found wasn't nearly as difficult as she'd expected, she later admitted to Tommy.

Amelia looked after the baby one evening so that Tommy and Emma could go dancing in Reading. They visited Annie and Frank on Christmas Eve, and Georgie, Sylvia and the girls on Boxing Day afternoon for tea, which

Amelia was also invited. Tommy was soon on the floor in front of the fire playing horsey with his nieces, which consisted of Tommy on his hands and knees the two little girls riding on his back, this caused shrieks of delight while Amy who was now six months old sat gurgling contentedly on her mother's lap. Georgie watched his elder brother indulgently.

The only thing that marred their holiday was their visit to Maude and George. This was the day before they were to return home. They drove up the lane to East Lodge to be welcomed by a smiling Maude. They exchanged gifts – a new tobacco pouch for George and some fancy soap for Maude. In return. Tommy received a bright yellow knitted scarf, and for Emma two embroidered handkerchiefs, with a soft woolly lamb Maude had made for Amy. After a while Maude went to the kitchen to prepare tea, Emma following a moment later to offer her help, leaving Tommy holding Amy.

There was a silence until George said, 'The car belongs to the people you work for then. They let you borrow it, did they?'

'No, it belongs to me. I bought it last month. I thought it would be nice to take Emma and Amy out sometimes on a Sunday,' he answered quietly.

'Humph! You and your fancy ideas, always aping your betters,' George grunted disparagingly.

'Why in the name of hell should buying a car be aping my betters? Who exactly, in your opinion, are my betters? I've got a decent job as farm manager, why shouldn't I spend a bit of money to give my family some pleasure?'

His eyes had turned colder than the icy wind that had started to blow that morning.

'Farm manager! Sounds like a fancy sounding title for a glorified farm hand.'

'What would you know anyway? You have no conception whatsoever of what I do for a living - you never have had. From the day I left this house you've no bloody idea what I've done to earn my living, and not only have you no idea, you've never cared one way or the other.' Tommy said. He could taste the bitterness in his words.

The two men glared at each other. The door opened and Maude and Emma came in bearing laden tea trays. The atmosphere could have been cut with a knife. Maude looked from one to the other.

'What's been going on?' she demanded.

'Nothing Maude,' Tommy muttered.

'Don't you tell me nothing, young man. I'm neither blind nor stupid, and as for you,' she turned to George, 'I suppose you're being cantankerous as usual. Why is it you can't leave him alone, and just be pleased he still visits after all that's gone on in the past? I'm not sure as I would in his shoes,' she added. 'Sit down Tommy. Emma pour him a nice cup of tea, and here let me hold Amy while you drink it in peace. Come to Nana then, my little love.' She held out her arms to take Amy from Tommy.

He let her take Amy, furious with himself for rising to the bait and reacting the way he did to the old man's sarcasm, at the same time feeling a grudging admiration for Maude who seemed to know exactly how to handle his father.

George sat looking sheepish for a few moments and then made a half-hearted attempt to be sociable by speaking to Emma.

'So how do you like living near Winchester then, girl?' he asked gruffly.

'Oh it's very nice. The cottage is lovely and we're very happy, and Tommy loves having the horses to ride around the estate, and now we've got the car we'll be able to come up and visit more often, and visit everybody,' she finished innocently.

Tommy felt an uncontrollable urge to laugh at the irony, but stifled it on hearing Maude say, ‘Well that will be nice, Emma. We’re always pleased to see you and Tommy, aren’t we my pet?’ she said tickling Amy under the chin.

Tommy flashed her a grateful look. She was all right was Maude.

Later that evening when Emma was putting Amy to bed Tommy sat drinking coffee with Amelia, Tommy related the afternoon’s incident.

‘He can still rattle me Amelia. Why does he always try and belittle me? Is he sick or something? Does he get some kind of perverse pleasure out of it?’

‘Yes to both of those questions Thomas. He is sick and, yes, he does get pleasure out of riling you, I’m afraid. You see, he’s still jealous of you, and has been from the day you were born.’

‘Jealous of me? What have I got for him to be jealous of?’ he asked in genuine amazement. ‘I just don’t see it, Amelia. It’s beyond my understanding.’

‘Thomas your mother absolutely adored you that was where it all started, and now you’re an adult with a lovely family, and you’ve done so much more with your life than he has ever done. But please Thomas, don’t let him get under your skin. Don’t give him the satisfaction. Rise above it, and ignore his cruel comments my dear.’

They sat for a few moments saying nothing, drinking their coffee in companionable silence, until Tommy spoke.

‘Do you think there’s going to be a war Amelia? This bloke Hitler seems to be strutting about making a lot of noise. First there was Austria and then this business with Czechoslovakia. You know Chamberlain’s being weak, after that meeting when he went to Germany in September, the result of that was for us and France to back down over Czechoslovakia. Hitler seems pretty shrewd. He sensed that neither us nor France would actually fight. Everyone seems to give in to him.'

'It doesn't look good Thomas. I must admit. He's like a farmyard cockerel, but they mustn't treat him as a joke. I agree with you. I think he's a very serious threat... Ah, Emma come and sit down and let me pour you a cup of coffee.'

'Is she asleep now?' Tommy smiled, 'Come and sit down Emma.' He patted the settee invitingly, all thoughts of war temporarily forgotten.

Thank you very much for having us to stay,' Emma said. 'It's been lovely. You've really spoiled us all.'

'That's all right Emma. It's nice to have someone to spoil. I can't get over how much Amy's grown since September.' Amelia was pleased to see that things appeared to be back to normal between Tommy and Emma.

They retired to bed early that night as Tommy wanted to get an early start in the morning, as the weather forecast had predicted snow.

They arrived home just as it started, huge fluffy flakes drifting lazily down. Tommy lit the kitchen range, glad that he'd chopped plenty of wood before going off on holiday, and now stored in the outhouse beside the old copper that Emma boiled the washing in.

They had stopped in Beauworth village on their way home and Emma had bought meat from Coles, the butcher to last for a few days, calling in at the grocer next door for a few odds and ends as she put it.

Later that afternoon Tommy lay stretched full length on the colourful rag rug in front of the fire, his head propped up on a cushion. Amy lay in the crook of his arm. Emma sat in the armchair watching them fondly. A beef stew bubbled merrily on the range. A warm glow enveloped them.

'I'd better light the lamp Tommy. It's a bit like the black hole of Calcutta in here,' she said peering at her brand new wristwatch - Tommy's Christmas present to her. She rose and crossed to the table in front of the window.

'Oh there's a car coming up the lane. I wonder who it is. Just someone going up to the big house I s'pose,' she said.

She lit the lamp and was about to draw the curtains when the car swung in front of their gate, its headlamps lighting up their pathway.

'It's stopped. Tommy. It's a taxi and there's a man getting out and he's coming up the path. I think he must be looking for someone else 'cause the taxi's not pulling away.'

'I'll go Emma.' Tommy made a move to rise as the knock came at the front door.

'It's all right, you hang on to Amy. I'll go.'

She went to the door and Tommy heard the murmur of voices. After a few moments he heard the taxi pulling away and the front door being closed.

'Who was it Emma?' he called out.

'A visitor for you.' She smiled as she came back in and there, filling the doorway behind her, was Gareth, a familiar lopsided grin on his face.

'Well I can see you lead a life of absolute luxury. Married life agrees with you,' he laughed. 'Well don't look so surprised Tommy. I wrote you a letter saying I was coming. Didn't you get it?'

'God, Gareth!' Tommy said rising to his feet. 'Yes, of course I got it, but it said you'd be here in mid-January, and it's only the twenty eighth of December. I can't believe you're actually here.' His whole face was alight with pleasure. He held out his hand.

Their greeting included a lot of hand shaking, back slapping and an occasional light punch on the arm, each one repeating over and over exclaiming how good it was to see one another.

Eventually Emma spoke up, 'Well, I gather you're delighted to see one another, and I know it's Gareth from Argentina, but don't you think you should introduce him properly to your wife and daughter Tommy?'

'Of course,' he put in quickly, and putting his arm around her shoulders, he said, 'Gareth, this is Emma, and this gorgeous creature,' bending down to pick up a wide eyed Amy, 'is my daughter, Amelia, better known as Amy.'

Gareth held out his hand to Emma, 'Hello Emma. I've heard all about you from Tommy's letters, but he didn't tell me that you were so beautiful.' His eyes twinkled, his Welsh lilt becoming more pronounced.

'You'll have to watch him, Emma. He's a real ladies' man,' Tommy grinned.

'Take no notice of him Emma. I just appreciate a beautiful woman and envy him his two,' he turned to smile at Amy in Tommy's arms. 'And as for me being a ladies man, well I'm afraid they go for the tall, dark and handsome type, like your Boyo here. I got used to playing second fiddle to Tommy as far as woman are concerned. I'm sure Thomasina only agreed to marry me when she realised Tommy wasn't coming back,' he teased.

'Get away with you. Thomasina always had an eye for you. What took you so long? So how come you're back so early anyway, what happened?'

'Well Señor Ramirez knows the situation with Megan, with me wanting to get her settled. I haven't even let her know I'd be home early. He knows that Thomasina and I will be getting married when I get back, so he suggested the sooner I go, the sooner I'd be back. He reckoned with help from Catriona's husband they'd cope till I got back.'

Momentarily a shadow crossed Tommy's face.

‘Well now you’re here, and with the snow, wouldn’t you like to stay overnight, while you see how the weather develops, and perhaps tomorrow get in touch with your sister? It’s okay for Gareth to stay for a bit isn’t it Emma?’

‘Of course,’ Emma nodded.

Chapter 11

Gareth had received a letter from his sister telling of his father's heart attack. He had expressed a wish to see Gareth, and soon. Señor Ramirez gave permission for Gareth to take long leave. Tommy worked doubly hard, taking on many of the jobs he would have given to Gareth. Señor Ramirez expressed his gratitude and suggested Tommy might also like leave when Gareth returned. Tommy agreed.

Two weeks after Christmas, Tommy rode out to inspect a wind pump. As was his habit, he'd told Señor Ramirez and the cook-house where he was headed. When he hadn't returned when expected, Señor Ramirez set off taking Kenneth Ball with him.

They spotted Tommy's horse after about an hour and a half, with Tommy's body a few yards away.

He was lying with his right leg doubled up under him. The left side of his face was caked with blood from a deep gash in his head.

Kenneth Ball threw himself from the saddle. 'Tommy, Tommy! He's unconscious Señor,' he said turning as Señor Ramirez dismounted, 'and his leg's at a funny angle.'

Tommy had heard the voices, and the sound of someone groaning which he vaguely knew was himself. His leg hurt. God, what was happening? He felt himself being handled. He recognised Señor Ramirez's voice.

‘Put him across the saddle Kenneth - a little more this way. We must get him back to the homestead, doing as little damage as possible.’

‘I can ride,’ he mumbled through parched, cracked lips.

‘He’s conscious Señor, he’s trying to say something, but I’m not sure what.’

‘It doesn’t matter much Kenneth. Our immediate problem is to get him back home and before dark.’

Tommy woke up in a strange room. He knew he’d been drifting in and out of consciousness, but now he was fully awake. He knew he’d been held down by firm hands in his delirious ramblings. He’d felt those same hands bathe him, feed him a few sips of water and wipe his burning forehead with cool, scented cloths.

He lay still taking in his surroundings - a large room painted white, with high ceilings, polished golden wood floors. The curtains and bedspread were of loose weave cloth, a pattern in dark reds, blacks and browns on an ecru background. On the floor were scatter rugs carrying the same colours.

His leg was stiff, and felt strange like it wasn’t part of him. As his mind cleared, so he panicked - the sweat stood out on his upper lip. For one ghastly moment he thought they’d amputated his leg. He threw back the covers. His leg had a splint on, that’s why it felt stiff. He wanted to cry with relief. He looked down at himself. He was wearing a white cotton nightshirt that came half way down his thighs. Who had undressed him? Whose hands had tended him? Just then the door opened and the welcome friendly face of Maria appeared.

‘Ah Tomas, you are awake, and how are you feeling?’ She bustled across the room and, pulling the crisp white sheet back over him, she asked, ‘Would you like me to help you sit up?’

He knew then whose hands had tended him. Maria was a motherly, buxom woman with a brood of children, one produced at roughly eighteen month intervals, the eldest being Thomasina at twenty two, down to seven year old Martin.

'Who put this splint on Maria, and how long have I been here?' he croaked.

'I put the splint on, and you have been here for two days.' She brushed his hair back from his forehead with a gentle hand, 'And now I shall go and tell the Señor that you are awake. Everyone has been very worried about you.'

Señor Ramirez came to see him, assuring him everything was fine - yes, that included Diablo. He mustn't worry, but rest and recover.

Later that night he lay in the darkness trying to remember exactly what had happened. The accident was still a little hazy. He heard the door open, and turned his head slightly. 'It's all right Maria, I'm not asleep.'

The door closed softly, and the sound of light footsteps crossed the room. He knew immediately who it was, although the room was only lit by dim moonlight.

'Catriona?'

'Yes Tomas,' she answered sitting on the edge of the bed. 'I have been so worried for you.' She put out a hand and softly stroked his cheek.

He took her hand in his to stop her. 'You shouldn't be here, please,' he begged weakly.

She leaned forward until her face was inches from his own.

'Please kiss me Tomas,' she whispered.

'No,' he exhaled, 'No Catriona, you don't know what you're doing, please...'

It was too late. Her lips were covering his. They were soft and tempting, tasting of rose petals. He could feel her young breasts through the thin material of the nightshirt. He was drowning. Her perfume wrapped round him like a mist. He felt himself responding as the tip of her tongue touched his lips. Suddenly it was all over. He mustered all his strength to push her gently away.

'Please don't do this,' he whispered. 'You've no idea of what you're doing. You're still a child.'

'No Tomas, I know exactly what I'm doing,' she paused, 'I'm not a child, I'm seventeen and I want you as a woman wants a man. I want you to make love to me. I know you want to,' she sighed, 'and you will.' Leaning forward once more she kissed him swiftly on the lips and slipped quietly from the room.

He lay there in his weak state. He hadn't cried since the death of his mother, but unable to control it a tear rolled down his cheek. He was tormented. Damn her, she was right! He did want her. Gareth, he silently lamented, where the hell are you? You said you'd be here to rescue me.

Tommy was weak and dehydrated. He was scared his leg might not mend. What if he couldn't ride again, or even walk properly. The gash on his head, just above his ear had been deep. His head was still heavily bandaged. He had a ringing sensation in his left ear.

He felt utterly miserable. He was well attended to. Maria fussed over him and mothered him. Señor Ramirez visited him every morning and talked about the daily happenings on the *estancia*.

He had books that Señora Ramirez brought him from their library - but he was still miserable.

He had regular visits from Catriona, which scared the life out of him. He wanted to leave his bed and run when she entered the room. Sometimes she would come in the afternoon while her parents and the servants were having their siestas, or it would be late at night when her parents were in bed.

She'd sit beside him on the bed and talk of Europe – she'd been there twice. She'd talk of books she'd read, the *estancia*, a subject she was quite knowledgeable on, in spite of her youth, but always it would end the same, with Catriona leaving the room vowing never to visit the invalid again, as somehow Tommy would discourage her advances, he tried never to let his guard slip.

These visits were agony for Tommy with a young woman in such close proximity. She'd sit on the bed lightly touching his hand.

Tommy rarely thought about women. Firstly, it didn't do you any good, as there were none available, and normally, by the time he'd finished a hard day's work, he usually fell asleep thinking of very little, other than the work to be done tomorrow.

His few sexual encounters since leaving England had been in Buenos Aires or once on a rare visit to Punta Arenas, and then it had been brief casual affairs with no emotional involvement.

Catriona was a different kettle of fish. She was the boss's daughter, spoiled and adored by her parents, an only child that stood to inherit the *estancia*, and Tommy guessed he'd be out of a job if Señor Ramirez thought he harboured any ideas regarding his precious child. He knew that Catriona, however, harboured many thoughts regarding him.

Tommy dreaded her visits and yet, in some perverse way, he looked forward to them. He loved the way she threw back her head revealing her small, perfect white teeth when she laughed.

On one such occasion Tommy had been sitting up in bed when she'd put her hand over his. As she talked, she'd laced her fingers with his.

She looked at him appealingly as she'd asked, 'Don't you like me Tomas? Do you find me unattractive?'

'Catriona, don't be silly. Of course I like you, but you know what I've told you. I'm twenty seven, and no matter how grown up you think you are, I'm much too old for you. I still think of you as a child. And as far as what you look like, yes, you're very pretty,' he answered disengaging his fingers from hers.

He'd deliberately understated referring to her as pretty, where in fact she was already a ravishing beauty.

Her body was that of a young woman, all the angles smoothed away, the gawkiness gone and, in its place, a curvaceous figure, a tiny waist a man could span with his hands. Her face framed with tumbling black curls, and sparkling dark eyes, that could set a man's blood racing.

But this time she was not so easily put off.

'Do you think I couldn't please a man of your age, am I too...' she searched for the word, 'inexperienced?'

He couldn't look at her, but closed his eyes wearily. 'Yes, you're too inexperienced,' he replied taking what he thought was the easy way out.

'Then teach me,' she demanded.

His eyes flew open. 'Stop it, for God's sake,' he grated, and grabbing her by the shoulders, holding her at arm's length,

'Why are you doing this to me, to yourself? What for? If I've told you a dozen times, no. Damn you, I don't bloody well want you. Can't you understand that?'

She gulped, and then the dam broke. The tears rained down her face unchecked. Before Tommy knew what was happening she'd collapsed against his chest sobbing wildly. For a moment his arms remained at his sides, but as the sobbing intensified, he reluctantly brought up his arms and wrapped them round a near hysterical Catriona.

'Shh, don't, please darlin' shh.' He held her, murmuring words of comfort into her cloud of hair.

Gradually her sobs subsided and she raised her tear stained face to his. 'Kiss me, Tomas,' she begged. Her chin quivered and she immediately whispered, 'Sorry.'

From that moment Tommy was lost. He lifted his head and kissed her wet cheeks, then the corner of her mouth, then her eyelids, before moving to her lips once more. Her lips parted beneath his and this time it was Tommy whose tongue invaded her mouth. She moaned and was on the bed beside him, her busy fingers unbuttoning his nightshirt. She was whispering over and over, 'Love me Tomas, please love me.'

His hands were on her back pulling her to him. She pressed herself against him moaning softly with desire. Tommy by now was fully aroused.

'You're driving me crazy, Catriona,' he murmured. 'I want you so much, but I can't,' he indicated the heavy wooden splint.

She pulled up her skirts and pulled down her pants, wriggling herself out of them. She knelt astride him. 'Touch me Tomas.'

He needed no further urging. He was kissing her, caressing her, exciting her to such a peak that, suddenly she started to shudder with ecstasy. She sensed his need for satisfaction and instinctively she knew what to. 'Keep still. Let me do the work,' she whispered as she lowered herself onto him. She ground her hips into him writhing with pleasure, till she brought him to a point too strong for him to control. He gasped as he felt her convulsion starting again, as he came inside her. She flopped against him, both of them spent.

That night he swore to himself that it would never happen again. He was torn apart by guilt. He knew that she'd been tempting him for a year, and begging him daily for three weeks, but that didn't salve his conscience. Lord, don't let her be pregnant!

Tommy lay awake. What had he done? He couldn't believe he'd succumbed. He'd let himself be seduced, he'd been a willing participant. He heard the hall clock strike every hour. He relived the scene minute by minute. As she lay on his chest afterwards, she'd said, 'I never dreamed it would be so good Tomas. Tell me, was I too inexperienced to please you?'

'No, you're very beautiful, and you pleased me very much.'

She laughed showing those white teeth.

'I must go now,' as she kissed him full on the mouth. 'I shall see you tomorrow.'

He watched the pearly dawn push the night aside before the solution finally came to him.

Señor Ramirez paid his daily visit at eight o' clock the following morning as was his custom. Noticing Tommy's pallor and the deep shadows under his eyes, he once again assured him that there was no need for him to worry about the work. It was all being done. Was there anything Tommy needed to make him more comfortable?

He wanted to die of misery and shame, Señor Ramirez's generosity made his betrayal a thousand times worse. He was wracked by guilt. He was left with no option but to leave as soon as he was recovered enough to travel.

'I was wondering Señor, you have been so good to me and I don't wish to be ungrateful, but now that I am much better, do you not think it would be better if I moved back to my own quarters. Maria says Jose has made me some crutches,' he went on, 'and I could perhaps practice walking soon.'

Señor Ramirez frowned. 'Are you sure you are ready? You don't think you might be rushing things? After all it has only been just a little over three weeks since your accident.'

Tommy felt even more wretched as he answered, 'No really, I feel the sooner I don't have Maria to wait on me hand over foot, the sooner I shall learn to manage for myself.'

He wasn't really sure at all that he'd be able to cope, but he saw it as a solution to his problems. His quarters were some five hundred yards from the main house. It would make it much more difficult for Catriona to visit him. She couldn't possibly be seen visiting his quarters during the day and, leaving the house at night to come to him, would also run the risk of getting caught.

Señor Ramirez smiled at him and nodded, 'Well if you're sure. Maria can still cook for you, and will arrange to have your food sent across. I can see you are determined to get better quickly.'

Yes, Tommy thought, the quicker I recover, the sooner I shall be able to leave. But he hadn't counted on Catriona.

He was moved that very morning. Kenneth Ball and Tom Stokes came to the house. They were to carry him to his quarters. They were in his room with Maria fussing over the best way to lift him, and to take care not to knock his leg, when Catriona came down the passage.

'What's happening?' she asked, surprised to see the men in the house.

'We're losing our invalid. He wants his independence. He's moving back to his quarters,' Maria answered, 'although I don't know how he thinks he'll manage without me to make him comfortable and look after him. Jose has made him some crutches and he's eager to try them out.'

Catriona stared at Tommy, the blood draining from her face. Tommy was first to drop his eyes as the memory of the previous night flooded his brain.

Tommy was happy to be back in his quarters. Jenny Ball was there to welcome him, duster in hand.

‘My goodness Tommy you gave us such a fright,’ she said. ‘Kenneth was so worried about the night him and Señor Ramirez found you. We’ve had daily bulletins from Maria on your progress, but it’s nice to see for ourselves. I’ll come across in the mornings and again in the afternoons to see if there’s anything I can do. You look tired Tommy. Are you sleeping okay?’ she finished.

‘No, not last night,’ Tommy mumbled.

‘Well get some rest then. We’ll see you later.’ Kenneth said.

Tommy slept solidly. The next thing he knew Kenneth was peering round the door.

‘Ah you’re awake then?’ he asked

‘Yes.’ Tommy pulled himself up in bed. ‘What time is it?’

‘It’s lunchtime,’ he grinned, ‘and I can see Thomasina heading in this direction carrying a tray. Old Martinez was grumbling why wasn’t his cooking good enough for you? You always enjoyed it in the cook-house. They’re falling over themselves to look after you. Anyway are you up to a visitor?’

Tommy looked wary, ‘Depends on who it is?’

Kenneth opened the door wider and a black and white collie slid round the door. In one huge bound she was on the bed, whining, licking his face joyously, happy to be reunited with her beloved master.

‘Bella,’ he laughed, hugging her to him. ‘There’s my girl.’

‘Would you like to keep her with you for company?’ Kenneth asked, ‘We’ve had her at home with us, much to the kids’ delight. ‘

‘You wanna stay with me Bella?’ he asked. She thumped her tail regarding him with her intelligent brown eyes. ‘Yes,’ he nodded, ‘I think she does.’

Thomasina appeared in the doorway bearing a huge tray. Kenneth relieved her of it, and put it on the table beside Tommy's bed.

'Thank you Thomasina,' Tommy smiled at her.

'You are welcome. My mother says you must eat it all,' she giggled.

'I will, I promise.' Tommy suddenly grinned feeling much more cheerful than he had been of late. He realised for the first time since his accident he was actually hungry.

He had received a long letter from Amelia a week before Christmas, which he suddenly felt the urge to reply to. Kenneth put writing materials to hand so that, after lunch, he could write his letter.

'Kenneth, do you think you could come over tonight after work this evening?' he asked. 'I really would like to try getting out of bed and seeing if I could manage a few steps on those crutches.' He eyed them dubiously.

'Sure,' Kenneth nodded. 'I suppose someone must be here to catch you when you fall.'

That evening Tommy managed to get out of bed unaided, while Kenneth watched. He walked round the bed several times, and made it to the bathroom. After half an hour he felt a little giddy and tired.

'Don't overdo it Tommy, this is your first time up and about and you've done very well. Get back into bed now.'

'Yes I feel that's progress. Maria seems to have done a good job with her splint. Thanks Kenneth, go on home now, I'll be okay. '

For two days he rested, read books and practiced walking on his crutches. He no longer felt giddy when he stood up. His appetite had returned, and he had Bella for company.

His third morning he managed his longest trip to date. He'd made it to the cookhouse where he was welcomed by old Martinez. He sat for a while chatting to the old man before making his way back to his quarters, Bella trotting happily beside him. Tomorrow he thought, I'll see if I can make it to the stable yard.

He still tired easily and it was a warm day. Getting back to his house, he removed his light woollen shirt and lay on the bed. He fell asleep, and woke to the rattle of dishes.

He opened his eyes to find Catriona standing beside his bed.

'What are you doing here? What if anyone sees you?' he demanded, 'And where is Thomasina?'

'Aren't you pleased to see me? I have missed you very much.'

Her warm eyes caressed him. 'Thomasina was happy to let me bring your lunch tray, as I have given her much to do, to keep her occupied.'

He was suddenly aware of his nakedness. 'Please pass me my shirt,' he nodded towards the shirt which he'd flung carelessly across the back of a chair.

She didn't move, but stood looking down at him. Slowly without a word, she sat on the bed.

'You haven't answered my question,' she said at last, 'Aren't you pleased to see me?'

Tommy drew his breath. Her nearness made him nervous.

'Catriona, please don't make a scene. What happened between us should never have been. I blame myself. Do you realise you could have a child because of what we did?' His heart froze at the thought. 'It mustn't ever happen again,' he finished.

The look she gave him was unfathomable, but she said meekly enough 'I know Tomas. I'm sorry, but it wasn't your fault.'

He visibly relaxed, he felt as if a weight had been lifted from his shoulders. She'd accepted his decision. She stood and reached for his shirt, passing it to him, she raised her hand and touched his cheek with her fingertips, and giving him a wistful smile, she left.

Late that night Tommy woke to the sound of Bella growling low in her throat. He listened. Was that something or someone outside his door? He reached for his crutches beside the bed. In three steps he was at the door, his hand reaching for the handle. It turned before he touched it. Bella stopped growling recognising Catriona's smell as she stepped into the room.

'What in the hell are you doing here?' he asked despairingly, knowing full well exactly what she was doing there.

For an answer she stepped close to him, her body just touching his. He couldn't push her away. Both arms were needed to balance on his crutches. She wound her arms slowly round his neck, as she stood on tiptoe to kiss him hungrily.

'Come let me help you back to bed,' she whispered, her lips barely touching his.

He groaned. He was defeated, and he knew it. He couldn't fight her any longer. He didn't even want to.

Chapter 12

Throughout the night the snow continued to fall silently, swirling, drifting cloaking everything in a thick white blanket by morning.

Tommy wasn't due to return to work till the first of January. He and Gareth cleared a path where the snow had drifted with shovels and, at Tommy's suggestion, walked the three miles into Beauworth laying in some extra provisions, and allowing Gareth to send a telegram to Megan informing her he was staying with Tommy and, weather permitting, would travel on to Castleton some time during the next couple of days.

Walking through the village, Gareth remarked on the quaintness of English villages, going on to say that after the wide open spaces of Argentina he could never imagine himself living back here again.

'I must admit, I never expected to come back here again at one stage, but you never know what's round the corner. I love my work, and my family, so it suits me fine,' Tommy said.

'Meggie wants to move to England, tho' God knows what for. She doesn't know a soul, but she says for the last fifteen years she's looked after our father, she's entitled to her freedom, a new life of her own, whatever that might mean.'

'How old is she Gareth?' Tommy asked. 'And what does she do?'

'Twenty nine. It's a shame I suppose she hasn't had much of a life, apart from being a free housekeeper to my father as well as being his receptionist at his practice, until he retired a couple of years back. We were always very close as kids, and although we've kept in touch and written on a regular basis, I haven't actually seen Meggie since I came home that time seven years ago, remember?'

Tommy nodded remembering only too well. It was during Gareth's absence that the accident had happened - that the affair with Catriona had started. If Gareth had been there, who knows, maybe the thing with Catriona might never have happened.

'It's strange to see you married with a kid Tommy. Do you ever wonder what might have happened if things had worked out differently with Catriona?' Gareth asked.

'No,' Tommy answered shortly. 'Not a lot of good in wondering what might have been is there. Emma's a good wife and we're okay.'

'She's certainly a looker, and I can see she's only got eyes for you, despite me turning on all the charm I could muster,' he teased.

Tommy grinned, 'You can turn on all the charm you want - it's good for her. I'll tell you when to draw the line. It's a bit of a quiet life we lead here in the country, and Emma's a city girl really. She doesn't complain, but I often wonder if she misses it.'

'She looks content enough to me. You always did have a way with women, you lucky dog you.'

"I'd rather you didn't harp on about my winning ways with women in front of Emma. She tends to be a bit on the possessive side - a bit jealous,' he shrugged. 'Goodness knows why, I've never given her cause to be.'

That evening Tommy noticed Gareth made extra effort to include Emma in the conversation, making no joking references to Tommy's prowess with the ladies. Instead he asked Emma to tell him about how her and Tommy had met, going on to ask about the comparison between Reading and Winchester, and which did she prefer for shopping, explaining to her that his sister Meggie wanted to move to England. He didn't know if she had anywhere specific in mind, but would like to see her settled before returning to the Argentine for his forthcoming marriage to Thomasina. The following morning the snow had already begun to melt, the sparkling white crispness giving way rapidly to a mucky brown-slush. Tommy took Gareth to Winchester to catch his train. For most of the journey Gareth remained silent, seemingly deep in thought.

'Come on then, what's on your mind? I can see you're preoccupied.' Tommy asked.

'Yes I am Tommy. I was wondering whether it would be too much of an imposition if I were to suggest that if Meggie doesn't have any preference as to where she lives in England, if she might like to look round your area.'

'No, why should it be an imposition? You can show her round some of the villages, there's Kilmeston, Cheriton, Bishops Waltham, plenty of places, even Beauworth itself. She's bound to like one of them.' he suggested

'It's just that I'm not very happy about her moving Tommy. You know she's lived in that house all her life and, as the local doctor's daughter, everyone knows her. I know the house is a bit big for her,' he went on, but if she moves to England, she knows nobody, and you know I don't expect to be coming home again in a hurry. I've got a bit of money saved up and Thomasina and I hope one day to buy some land of our own, move up country a bit. I do worry about Meggie, I'm afraid I'm still old fashioned enough to think that a woman needs a man to look after her. '

Tommy laughed uproariously, 'Oh God! Gareth where have you been living, on the moon? Women are very independent creatures these days and, as far as needing a man, wake up,' he prodded Gareth's ribs. 'A prime example of a woman alone coping admirably is Amelia Nelson. With her independent spirit she'd be horrified at the suggestion that she needs a man in her life,' he chuckled.

Gareth grinned, 'Okay, Okay, perhaps you're right. Maybe I'm being overprotective, but I'd still like to know that Meggie has someone looking out for her, and I'd certainly feel better if I knew that someone was you.'

Tommy returned to work and Emma got back into her routine. She baked, she cleaned, she sewed and she cared for Amy, but Tommy knew that the centre of her world was himself, everything she did was with him in mind. Sometimes it weighed heavily on him. He wished she had other interests outside, a friend of her own age.

January the twenty second came. Tommy's thirty fourth birthday. As a surprise, Emma had arranged for Blanche Watkins, the cowman's wife to babysit Amy for the evening while she and Tommy went to Winchester for a rare meal out, just the two of them. Emma wore a soft green dress that clung to her curvaceous figure, knowing that it was Tommy's favourite colour. She looked soft and radiant, and they made a handsome couple as they entered the dining room of the Royal Hotel.

'I thought you might enjoy a nice romantic dinner, just the two of us, for your birthday,' Emma said once they were seated.

'But of course, who wouldn't enjoy a candlelit dinner with a woman as beautiful as you look tonight?' he replied gallantly.

He privately would have been just as happy to stay at home, but they went out so rarely, and he knew how much Emma enjoyed dressing up and going somewhere special.

'Oh Tommy, I do love you so. You say such lovely things sometimes, but I wonder after your friend Gareth's comments, whether you don't just have a way with the ladies.'

He covered her hand with his own, his long sensitive fingers curling round hers. He shook his head, 'Gareth was only joking Emma,' he assured her with a smile. 'When have you seen me look at another woman?'

'Well I must admit, I haven't - yet, but if I ever do I think I'd kill her, whoever she was,' she replied giggling. 'Seriously Tommy, you won't ever look elsewhere like some married men do, will you?'

'Not unless you give me cause to,' he teased.

'Oh no Tommy, I'd never look at anyone else and I think I know how to please you,' she said coyly, her eyes sparkling.

Later that night she proved she knew how to please him when their lovemaking reached new heights.

February saw the return of Gareth who brought his sister Megan, to look round the area. They stayed at the Fox and Hounds pub.

Megan turned out to be a surprise to Tommy. He had visualised a down trodden, dowdy spinster, and was prepared to feel sorry for her. He'd imagined a feminine version of Gareth. Not so, where Gareth was fair-haired and stocky, Megan was tall and willowy, with a cloud of light brown curly hair, and the most unusual shade of green eyes. She was soft spoken and intelligent, with barely a trace of a Welsh accent, and unlike her brother there was a trace of shyness. There was something about her, an air which reminded Tommy of Amelia Nelson, a quiet elegance giving her a touch of class.

For the next week Gareth and Megan drove around the surrounding villages looking at properties for sale. Much to Emma's envy Megan drove her father's car with great panache, never crashing the gears like her brother did.

'Give me a pony and trap any day,' Gareth grinned.

'That's progress Gareth,' Megan said fondly.

On Sunday, at Tommy's suggestion, they packed a picnic and drove up to Swallowfield to see Amelia, with the idea in mind that Gareth and Megan could look around that area the following week.

It turned out to be a huge success, all of them enjoying the day. Amelia was thrilled to see Tommy and his family again so soon, and delighted to meet his friend, who she'd heard so much about over the years, and the gentle Megan who she had had an immediate affinity with. The outcome of the visit was for Amelia to invite brother and sister to stay with her while they looked around the area.

A week later they returned to the Fox and Hounds.

Over supper at Tommy and Emma's Gareth announced, 'Well that's it then. Now all Megan has to do is make up her mind whether it's to be the house in Swallowfield or the cottage next to the church in Kilmeston. Which is it to be Megan? I've confirmed my passage back, sailing on the tenth of March.'

'Which do you like best Megan?' Tommy asked.

'I'm not sure - I like them both. I just can't make up my mind. If I were to choose Kilmeston I would only be a couple of miles from you and Emma,' she said shyly. 'I'd like that, and if I choose Swallowfield I would know Amelia and, of course your brother Georgie and his family who we met last week, when Amelia invited them to tea.'

In the end Megan didn't have to decide. Two days later the house in Swallowfield was taken off the market. The thatched cottage next to the church in Kilmeston was signed up that week.

Arrangements made, the move planned for the first week in April, Gareth to sail in March, content in the knowledge that Tommy and Emma would help Meggie settle in.

Megan returned to Wales, and the following day Tommy took Gareth to the station to catch the train to Southampton.

In the car Gareth was unusually quiet. Tommy put it down to the fact that he was leaving his sister and England once more. Suddenly he turned to Tommy, 'You know that Catriona married Eduardo Sanchez six weeks after you left, don't you?'

'No,' Tommy slammed on the brakes. 'How should I know?' he asked with barely a tremor in his voice.

'Didn't she write?' Gareth asked, 'Not at all, not ever?'

'No. Now what in the hell are you trying to say Gareth?'

Gareth shook his head not meeting Tommy's eyes, he mumbled, 'Nothing Tommy.'

'What d'you mean - nothing? What's all this about?' he went on, not waiting for an answer, 'What's it to me if she married? I'd finished with her,' he said savagely. He barely suppressed his anger.

'I know Tommy,' he nodded. 'I'm sorry I brought the subject up. It's not important. Listen pal, changing the subject, you'll keep an eye out for my Meggie won't you? I don't want to lay too much on you, but she's only got me and I'm a long way away.'

Tommy sighed, 'Of course I will Gareth. Rest assured, she's got Emma and I now, and I think Amelia took quite a shine to her too.' With these words of assurance, he put the car into gear and moved off.

A few weeks later Megan's move to Kilmeston went off smoothly. Tommy and Emma were waiting for the removal van to arrive. Emma had swept the cottage through, cleaned the windows, and had bought a few essentials. She'd made a casserole for lunch which they ate in Megan's cheery kitchen. By four o'clock in the afternoon, everything was in place. Tommy and Emma with Amy starting to get tired and fretful left for home, with arrangements made for Megan to pick Emma and Amy up on Monday morning in her new Baby Austin, having got rid of her father's Morris, to make the trip to Winchester to look for curtain material for the cottage.

Sunday morning they went to church - the first time in a while they'd attended a service. One of his earliest memories had been of his father making him, as a three year old, walk two miles to church, in new boots, and two miles home, his heels blistered and bleeding, his mother distressed and in tears. Amy sat quietly on Tommy's lap.

She was nine months old and was starting to pull herself up. Holding onto the furniture, she'd stagger a couple of steps, falling occasionally on her well-padded bottom, but she'd get up and try again as long as Tommy's arms were held out ready to catch her. Her first word had been 'Da' as she'd held up her arms to Tommy one evening on his return home from work.

Over tea that afternoon Tommy asked, 'What time are you going to Winchester tomorrow Emma?'

'Megan said she'd call for me at about nine o' clock,' she answered. 'Why?'

'Well here's something extra for you to spend.' Delving into his wallet he handed her three pounds.

She jumped up and threw her arms round his neck, 'Ooh thanks Tommy, but that's such a lot of money, can we afford it?' she said kissing him enthusiastically.

He smiled, 'Well it's nice for you to have someone near your own age to be friends with. You do like her don't you?' he asked.

'Yes she's all right. She's very quiet though. Not a bit like I thought she'd be like after I'd met Gareth. She's very attractive, isn't she? Don't you think so?'

Tommy shrugged, realising his answer might be the deciding factor as to whether or not Emma and Megan became friends, he said carefully, 'I don't know, I suppose so, can't say as I've taken much notice. I prefer blondes myself.'

In fact he really hadn't taken much notice, she was his friend's sister and for Gareth's sake, he wanted to do as he'd promised and befriend her, without arousing any feelings of jealousy from Emma.

The next few months passed swiftly with threatening rumblings throughout Europe of war. The first of September nineteen thirty nine saw Hitler sending his troops into Poland and the third of September Chamberlain announced that Britain had declared war on Germany.

Even Tommy, who thought Emma was being optimistic, when she'd said it probably wouldn't last long, never thought the war would drag on for nearly six years. Those six years were to bring so many changes to Tommy's life.

Chapter 13

By the end of February Maria removed the splint from his leg, and he took his first unsteady steps without crutches. Maria assured him all he needed was practice. He must walk to strengthen the leg and work the muscles. He would be left with an imperceptible limp. The ringing in his left ear gradually subsided, but unfortunately his hearing in that ear deteriorated.

By the middle of March he was ready to ride again. It was a slow and painful process, but Tommy was determined. His perseverance paid off. By mid-March he was able to ride again.

Kenneth and Jenny Ball were amazed.

'If I hadn't seen it with my own eyes, I wouldn't have believed it possible that anyone could recover that quickly.' Kenneth said, watching Tommy riding Diablo for his half hour daily practice.

Señor Ramirez was also surprised, 'Don't overdo it Tomas,' he cautioned.

'I won't Señor. I'm building up slowly, two fifteen minute sessions a day in the saddle, with as much walking as I can in between. '

'You're a very determined young man Tomas, and it's nice to see you getting better by the day.'

Catriona had convinced him not to leave Estancia Montalban. She could see no useful purpose by him giving up his job. 'Who knows how things might turn out,' she'd said. Possibly had he known, he would have packed his bags and gone a thousand miles away, but for now he was very much under her spell. The affair was developing into a wild and passionate relationship, with Tommy finding the deception and guilt difficult to live with. Catriona, it appeared to Tommy, had no such qualms.

Tommy felt they were courting disaster to continue. It was like a runaway train and they, the passengers, were unable to get off. He was powerless to stop it. He despised himself for his weakness. Why couldn't he end it?

Catriona was beautiful, fascinating, used to getting everything she wanted, and she wanted Tommy. He was totally besotted, obsessed - he would have done anything for her.

She had imposed herself like a sickness. Every waking moment she was there invading his mind. Images of her in the throes of lovemaking set his pulse racing. No matter how he tried, he couldn't blot out those images.

Gareth was due back any day now. Tommy wasn't sure if he should take him into his confidence or not. He knew he could rely upon his discretion, but the less people that knew, the better. As far as they were aware, there was no one who knew at this stage. At night Catriona would sneak out of the house as often as she could to join Tommy in his quarters.

Gareth returned looking relaxed and rested. He'd enjoyed his visit, but still had no desire to return to Wales. His sister, Megan was well, still tending his father, with no young man in her life.

'Not that she's got much time for a life of her own,' he commented. 'She's kept pretty busy with my father. She's a smashing girl who'd make some lucky bloke a great wife one day.'

'Do you think you'll ever marry, Gareth?' Tommy asked idly one evening.

Gareth replied, 'What brought that on Boyo? Not wanting to take a wife are you?'

Tommy grinned sheepishly, 'Well sometimes I think it might be nice. You know, a woman to warm your bed at night, and raise a family with.'

Gareth raised his eyebrows. 'Go on Tommy, you're going soft on me. Who's been getting at you while I've been gone? It must be the blow to your head during your accident,' he laughed.

Tommy blushed. 'No, no one,' he said hastily, 'but sometimes I feel a bit envious when I've been to Kenneth and Jenny's for supper, and then I go back to my empty quarters.'

Gareth laughed uproariously, 'Ah Tommy, don't be confused. It's time you went on leave and got yourself a woman. That's what you need not marriage.'

Tommy remained silent. He had a woman, but Gareth didn't know that.

Time marched on and despite Señor Ramirez's urging. Tommy decided not to take long leave. On the one hand he had his employer trying to persuade him, because he thought Tommy needed a break, as he looked tired since the accident and, on the other hand he had Catriona begging him not to go.

'Please Tomas, don't go away for three months,' she pleaded. 'You might meet an English girl. You will forget me.'

He laughed at her. 'Don't be silly Catriona. How could I forget you?'

'You will, and I couldn't bear it. I can't lose you.'

He took her hands in his and kissed her palms, first one and then the other.

'You're not going to lose me,' he said between kisses. 'I promise.'

Tommy compromised. He went to Buenos Aires for a month. He needed breathing space, time to think. He knew the secret trysts with Catriona were wrong. Sooner or later it would come to light. Someone would find out, with disastrous consequences for both of them. He had to make a decision.

He revisited all the places he and Gareth had frequented, but it wasn't the same without him. He had no interest in women. Catriona had captivated him, other women paled by comparison.

Less than month later, he'd had enough of his own company. Enough time to decide where his life was going and he was no further forward than when he'd set out.

He returned to Montalban and the rest of the year sped by. The situation with Catriona remained unchanged, apart from the quarrels being more frequent.

Each year on Christmas Eve the Ramirez custom was to have an *asado*, the cooking of meats over the coals. Tommy had never seen anything like it in England. All the people on the *estancia* gathered, there were gifts distributed to the children. The coals would be lit during the early afternoon, in readiness for early evening. The carcasses of three lambs would be splayed open and wired to their metal crosses, resembling miniature crucifixes, and put round the coals to be turned frequently.

Tommy had felt uneasy all day. He'd been troubled lately with the way things were going between him and Catriona. She would be eighteen next month and he'd suggested that possibly he should talk to her father.

She'd shrieked like a banshee at him, 'Talk to him, talk to him about what? What are you going to say to him? I've been sleeping with your daughter for a year. Do you think I should marry her? He'd kill you, and probably me too,' she added grimly.

'Catriona, we cannot go on like this - sneaking round corners.' He rubbed his hand over his eyes, a weary gesture. 'Don't you know the chance we're taking? You could become pregnant at any time. What the hell would we do then?'

'I'd get rid of it of course,' she snapped.

'What!' he exploded.

'You heard me - I'd get rid of it. There are lots of ways to get rid of unwanted children. The servants know about these things,' she pouted.

'Christ! I don't believe you.' He shook his head in disgust. 'You're eighteen years old, a Catholic, and you stand there as blasé as you like and tell me there are ways to get rid of unwanted children. You cold bitch you.'

How in the name of hell did he ever let himself get into this situation? At that moment he looked at her with loathing.

'This has all come about because I was fool enough to let you seduce me.'

'Don't be such a hypocrite,' she spat at him. 'For all your guilt and talk of conscience, you welcome me into your bed at nights. Please Tomas,' she cajoled, 'we get so little time together - let's not waste it quarrelling.'

She moved swiftly into his arms, rubbing her body against him like a cat. He grasped a handful of her hair and kissed her roughly, till he tasted blood. They made love, but not lovingly. There was no tenderness, no joy, no thoughts of pleasuring on Tommy's part - just a violence in the act, perpetrated by Tommy, yet shocking him. It was over in minutes, leaving both of them gasping for breath. Shocked to the core.

Christmas Eve came and the company assembled. The gifts given. The serious business of eating and drinking had begun. Tommy stood to one side deep in conversation with

Señor Ramirez. A few feet away Gareth, Kenneth and Jenny Ball, Maria and Jose chatted comfortably.

From the corner of his eye Tommy saw Catriona approaching. She slid her arm through her father's. He paused to smile at her briefly, then continued his conversation with Tommy who could feel her eyes burning into him. He'd nodded to acknowledge her presence. As soon as there was a break in the conversation, she smiled at both the men, her eyes were glittering wildly.

'Do you know Papa, I don't believe your manager and I have exchanged two words since the day he came here,' she began in a loud voice, 'and how many years ago would that be? Tomas isn't it? '

Tommy stared at her intensely, his eyes not leaving her face. What bloody game was she playing now? Her father too, looked at her, a look of puzzlement in his eyes.

'Two years Miss,' Tommy replied.

'As long as that, and which lady is your wife?' she asked brightly.

'I'm not married,' he replied through clenched teeth. He wanted to take hold of her and smack her like a naughty child.

She rolled her eyes saying, 'Why, I can hardly believe it – a handsome man such as yourself, still single.'

Catriona's voice had become shrill and had caused a lull in the conversation from the people around them as they watched, aware that there was a drama being played out before them. The trouble was that neither the players, nor their audience seemed to know what it was about.

'Excuse me Señor, Miss Catriona, I need to have a word with Kenneth before I forget.'

Señor Ramirez nodded, 'Of course Thomas, enjoy the rest of the evening.'

Later that same evening Tommy and Gareth were having a cigarette on the steps that led to Tommy's quarters. Bella had flopped down beside them, she was never far away.

'Tommy, what's going on?'

'What d'you mean? Nothing's going on.'

'Yes there bloody well is, and don't tell me to mind my own business.' he finished emphatically.

'I suppose you mean with Catriona,' Tommy sighed.

'C'mon Tommy, stop prevaricating. I've known for months something was going on, and that little scene earlier just confirmed it. Spit it out.'

Tommy told him everything, starting with the accident. Gareth listened in silence.

'And that's it - it's been over a year. I keep saying I'll finish with her, but that's easier said than done.'

Gareth slowly blew out a plume of smoke before speaking, 'Boyo, you have gone crazy. Just tell me how did you ever let this happen? And even worse, why is it still going on Tommy? You are in deep trouble,' he said seriously.

'I know,' Tommy answered. 'What must I do?'

'For crying out loud, why are you even asking? You know damn well what you must do, and you'd better do it now.'

Tommy never knew where he plucked up the courage, but that same night he told Catriona it was over. The quarrel that ensued was long and bitter, and went deep into the night. It started with recriminations and threats, followed by tears and pleading, but Tommy wasn't to be moved.

'It's over I'm telling you. I should never have let it happen at all. I'm sorry,' he said gently. 'Please Catriona don't cry. You know nothing will ever come of it, and you're young you have your whole life ahead of you.'

In the inky blackness of the night they walked back through the stable yard where the only sound was the occasional stamp of hooves. They stood beneath a silver birch tree, by the garden gate.

'I love you Tomas, and it's not over,' she said with a sob.

He didn't answer, and eventually she turned and ran swiftly up the path to the kitchen door. He watched her until the night swallowed her up.

He knew he'd had to end it. There had been no choice, but that didn't make it any easier. He'd been choked when she told him she loved him.

He missed her, he was miserable, his every waking moment was filled with thoughts and memories of her. The feel of her skin against his, her lips under his own. He worked harder than ever, often riding in at dusk, hoping to tire himself out, so that he could be free of thoughts of her at night, but no matter how exhausted he was, even in his sleep she invaded his dreams.

By the end of March nineteen thirty three Tommy could have counted on one hand how many times he'd seen Catriona, and then always at a distance. When he'd told her it was all over, he hadn't believed that she'd accept it.

One afternoon in April Tommy rode in accompanied by Kenneth Ball. The wind had been blowing hard all day. His leg ached, and he was weary and dispirited. They were unsaddling when Gareth came out of the barn.

'Tommy there's a message for you. Señor Ramirez said to tell you he was going to Rio Gallegos and they'd be back sometime tomorrow, but please to carry on bringing the sheep down.'

'Okay I wonder what he went to town for anyway,' Tommy mused, 'I'm going in next week for stores.'

'Dunno, but the Señora and Catriona were with him,' shrugged Gareth. 'They probably wanted a shopping trip.'

The following afternoon Tommy saw a plume of dust made by an approaching vehicle. As the vehicle drew level it slowed down and came to a halt. Tommy swung Diablo's head and trotted over.

'*Buenas tardes* Señor, Señora.' Tommy noticed that Catriona was not with them.

Señor Ramirez raised his hand in salute. 'Did you get my message Thomas?'

Tommy nodded, 'Yes Señor, we brought the last of the sheep down this morning.'

'Come over to the office in the morning Thomas and we'll go through a list of stores we'll need for winter.'

He smiled and pulled away, but not before Tommy had seen his wife's face. She was pale and drawn, her eyes were swollen and red rimmed. She had obviously been crying.

The following morning Señor Ramirez apologised for not stopping longer the previous afternoon, but, he explained, his wife had been very distressed as they'd been saying goodbye to Catriona, who was going to stay with her grandmother in Spain for a while.

Tommy wanted to ask why? For how long? Instead he said, 'That's nice for her, Señor. I'm sure you'll both miss her.'

'Yes, we already do, but she's been very unhappy of late. Her mother tried to talk to her, but she wouldn't tell her what was troubling her. Things have been difficult this past year, tears and tantrums - all part of growing up I suppose. You know what the ladies can be like,' he finished.

Gareth tried to distract him by talking about their next leave, but in vain. Tommy couldn't work up any enthusiasm. His whole being was concentrating on holding himself together, trying to get through one day at a time, hoping it would get easier as time passed.

It was probably the ideal solution anyway he told himself. He didn't have to see her, temptation had been removed. He'd loved her with an intensity that had surprised him. With the prospect of her absence from his life, he felt as if a part of him was missing.

Chapter 14

Tommy wondered how long Catriona would be gone. Over a year passed, nineteen thirty four slipped into nineteen thirty five and it was during that winter that Señor Ramirez and his wife went to Spain for three months leaving Tommy in charge. They returned in early October. Tommy was to meet them when they docked in Rio Gallegos.

Nothing had prepared him for the shock of seeing Catriona again. There had been no mention of her returning with them.

Tommy found himself staring like some callow youth. If he thought she was beautiful at seventeen, she was positively stunning at nearly twenty.

'Hello Thomas. Everything all right at home?' her father asked, shaking Tommy's hand.

'Yes,' Tommy stammered. He could hardly take his eyes off her.

'You remember Catriona, don't you?' he smiled.

'Yes, of course. Yes Señor, all's running smoothly, we've had no problems.'

He felt a total fool and was aware of those dark eyes regarding him with amusement.

'Hello Tomas. Nice to see you,' she said coolly as she stepped past him to get into the car, the door of which he had already opened. He stood there taking in the heady, spicy smell of her perfume as she brushed against him. He remembered her naked in his bed and wondered what he'd given up. Did she ever think of those days, of him, and what they'd once shared?

Apparently she did, because the next day she sought Tommy out.

He was in the barn sorting through some pipes and fittings to fix one of the wind pumps just beyond the shearing shed when he heard a sound behind him.

He straightened up saying, 'It's okay, Gareth. We've got enough pipe and a joint. I was just going to bring it across...'

'I'm sure Gareth will be very pleased to hear that Tomas,' she said.

He swung round. She was dressed in black boots and a long black divided skirt, a bright yellow shirt made of some silky material, which showed off her masses of dark hair tied back with a ribbon of the same colour.

'Hello, Catriona,' he said awkwardly.

'Is that all you have to say to me?' she asked, a faint smile playing at the corner of her mouth. 'I rather hoped it would be more after - what's it been - nearly two years?'

'I don't really know what to say. When you left you didn't even say goodbye.'

'I didn't think you'd care Tomas. You'd made it perfectly clear that you didn't want me. I was young and hurting too much. I didn't want to see you again.'

'I'm sorry Catriona. I never meant to hurt you,' he said in a low voice. 'I've thought about you often,' he added.

'Have you now? Well that's something I suppose. Oh, Tomas,' she suddenly threw back her head and laughed, a gesture he'd always loved, 'Don't look so guilty. You were probably right to end it all. Even broken hearts mend.'

He grinned ruefully. 'You look good Catriona. I must have been crazy not to want you.' He could have bitten his tongue out. What had made him say such a thing?

She walked towards him slowly with insolent grace. She flaunted her full luscious body with every movement, knowing his eyes were upon her. She finally stood in front of him, putting her hands on his shoulders. Their bodies were inches apart.

'And do you want me now Tomas?' she breathed, her eyes never leaving his face.

He could feel her warm breath on his cheek, his nostrils filled with the familiar scent of her.

'Well, do you?' she asked again.

'God, yes,' he groaned.

They were in each other's arms kissing, her lips soft and sweet as honey under his own. She wrapped her arms around his neck. He put his hands on her hips and pulled her roughly to him. It was as if the last two years had been wiped out in a few moments.

Catriona broke off their kiss long enough to sob, 'Oh Tomas I've missed you so.'

They couldn't keep their hands off each other, stroking, caressing. Tommy's breath was coming in ragged gasps, when Catriona pulled away from him slowly.

'Not here - not now. Later. I'll come to you,' she whispered.

She slipped silently from the barn. He stood there for a moment trying to gather his thoughts. He had thought he was over her. She'd only been back twenty four hours, and they were back where they'd started from, the attraction between them stronger ever. She was even more desirable than before.

A voice broke into his thoughts, 'Boy, she has become the most gorgeous creature I have ever seen, but go careful Tommy. Remember the old saying that fools rush in where angels fear to tread. You've been there before Boyo.'

'Mmm,' Tommy bent down gathering up the length of pipe to hide his embarrassment. 'I found the pipe and fittings we need and was just going to bring it across.'

'Well, are you going to tell me what she had to say for herself?'

'No, I'm bloody well not,' Tommy snapped.

Gareth hesitated for a moment, 'Tommy we've been friends for eleven years, and I can see trouble ahead. I looked out for you when you first arrived as a raw twenty year old, you're old enough and capable enough to make your own decisions, and live with the consequences, but I can see one of you getting hurt. I don't want it to be you. Back off Tommy, that's my advice for what it's worth. Okay subject closed, no more to be said.'

'I know, sorry pal. Ever heard the old saying, "good advice is seldom taken". C'mon Gareth we'd better get that wind pump fixed, we haven't got all day.'

She came to him that night. It was as if she'd never been gone. Their lovemaking was better than ever. They lay sated and exhausted, her head resting on his shoulder, her arm flung across his chest, her fingers stroking him lightly.

'I don't remember seeing this before.' She fingered his mother's amethyst ring which he now wore on a silver chain around his neck. 'Where did it come from?'

'It belonged to my mother, and I put it on a chain so I don't lose it.'

'It's pretty.' She slipped it on. 'Oh look it fits perfectly.'

'Mmm,' he murmured, gently removing it from her finger.

When his mother had given it to him she had said she hoped he'd find a girl he loved enough to give it to one day. He looked at Catriona through half-closed eyes. He was reluctant to part with it. He did love her, but something held him back.

The following day Tommy and Gareth were bringing in the last of the sheep for shearing. They had been a little later this year. They were riding down the long home paddock towards the *galpon*. The south easterly wind was bitterly cold although the sun shone brightly. Earlier they had come across a dead ewe, the *carranchas*, carrion hawks, had already gathered round the carcass. They waited till the riders were almost upon them before they hopped off to one side uttering their harsh rasping squawks as they moved a couple of feet away until the riders had passed.

The thorny calafate bushes were in bloom, their bright yellow flowers reminding Tommy of the colour of the shirt worn by Catriona yesterday. Legend has it that if you brace its thorns to eat its delicious blueberries, which were ripe in December, either you or your bones will return to Patagonia. Tommy had always laughed at the legend, but he'd never eaten a calafate berry.

Tommy went to see how Kenneth was getting on in the *galpon*, with the shearing crew hard at work. He never failed to be fascinated as the small slightly built Chileans worked. Within two or three minutes of starting, the clipped sheep would be shoved unceremoniously backwards through a little doorway behind the shearer. Their movements were both economic and efficient.

Tommy had tried his hand at shearing, but being tall, found it both difficult and back breaking. A fast man might shear two hundred sheep a day.

The thick, hot greasy smell of lanolin filled the air, mixed with the pungent smell of sheep droppings. After checking with Kenneth that all was well. Tommy couldn't wait to get outside in the fresh air.

Shearing finally over, there were only a few weeks to go to Christmas. The situation with Catriona remained the same. The stolen nights, the arguments, always ending unresolved. Tommy was becoming more disillusioned, increasingly discontented. So many times after their nightly encounters he would feel empty. Something was missing. He wanted more from the relationship. He wanted to sit across a table from her, to eat together, to sit with her in the long evenings and talk. He wondered what it would be like to walk down by the river holding hands, in daylight for the rest of the world to see.

Christmas nineteen thirty six came, bringing the customary Christmas Eve *asado*, the lambs cooked whole on their crucifixes, the succulent meat served with salads, and spicy rice, the gifts for the children, sherry for the ladies and beer for the men. There were guests this year, among them the Sanchez family from an adjoining *estancia*. Señor Sanchez and his wife, with their son. The twenty six year old Eduardo seemed besotted with Catriona, dancing attendance upon her. She, it seemed to Tommy, hung on his every word. She threw back her head and laughed at his jokes, smiling up at him constantly.

That night Tommy waited for her, but she didn't come. Neither did she come the following three nights. On the fourth night, just after midnight, she slipped quietly into his room, and into his arms.

'Where have you been? I've missed you,' he said softly, his lips almost touching hers.

'I have been busy Tomas. I have had guests to entertain, my cousins and Eduardo.'

Tommy knew that recently their relationship was reverting back to what it had been previously. He could see no future for them, unless he talked to her father. He loved her, and so many times in the last year she had declared her love for him.

'Catriona, we need to talk,' Tommy started.

'Ssh, I didn't come to talk,' she said huskily between kisses.

He pulled his head back laughing down at her.

'We've got plenty of time for that,' he promised. 'I want to talk about us.'

'Us?' He felt her body tense in his arms. 'What about us Tomas? '

'Do you love me?' he asked.

For an answer she pressed herself against him, 'You know I do.'

'Catriona will you marry me?' He held her face between his hands.

'How can we Tomas? My family - what would my father say?'

'I think it's time we found out?' he suggested.

'What's the hurry Tomas? We have plenty of time. I'm still very young.'

'I'm tired of waiting Catriona, I love you, and I want to marry you.'

Her answer to that was, 'Take me to bed.'

This was her solution to everything. As if by the physical act all other problems would be swept away.

Afterwards they lay quietly. A strip of moonlight lit the room. Tommy kissed her gently, his hand resting on her hip as she lay facing him.

'I'll speak to your father this week,' he said.

'No.' Her voice was like the crack of a whip. His eyes flew open. 'No, please Tomas let me speak to him,' she continued in a softer tone. 'Let me speak to him first, to prepare him.'

'That's not the right way to do it Catriona. I must speak to him,' he insisted.

'Please Tomas, I know my father. Let me speak to him first, and then you can approach him,' she pleaded.

'Okay, when?'

'When the time is right. Soon...' she added seeing the expression on Tommy's face.

And so for the time being he had to be content with that.

The following week Tommy and Gareth were out checking boundary fences, a two man job. They camped out overnight. Bitterly cold crisp white frost covered them by morning. Gareth rekindled last night's fire and got the coffee on, while Tommy attended to the horses.

Gareth never mentioned Catriona after his words of advice, and he looked surprised when Tommy brought the subject up.

'You know it's still going on with me and Catriona don't you? I'm going to have to do something about it, make some kind of decision.' Gareth remained silent. 'I think I'm going to have to speak to her father.'

'Bloody hell Tommy! Rather you than me. He'll either welcome you with open arms, challenge you to a duel to avenge his daughter's honour,' he grinned half-heartedly, 'or possibly he'll just fire you.'

'Yeah well, I'm prepared for whatever the outcome might be, like you said I'm old enough to make my decisions and accept the consequences. And guess what, right after I've had some of that coffee and chow, I'm finally going to pick some of those calafate berries and try them.'

He did just that, but not before the needle-like thorns had inflicted their injuries, drawing blood from his hand in several places. He tasted the sweet berries.

'Mmm okay, but not exactly worth the battle scars,' he said ruefully trying to stem the flow of blood.

'That's it then Boyo,' Gareth laughed, 'I guess Patagonia is your destiny one way or another.'

By mid-January Tommy raised the subject again with Catriona.

‘Have you spoken to your father yet?’ he asked as she was now promising to do on a daily basis.

‘No, he’s still very upset about my grandmother’s death.’

‘Catriona you’ve been coming up with one excuse after another. That was well before Christmas, and you said yourself she was very old and her death was not unexpected. I’m not prepared to wait forever.’

‘Please be patient,’ she entreated.

‘No, I’ve no patience left. You speak to him now - tomorrow,’ he threatened, ‘or...’

‘Or what?’ she interrupted. ‘What will you do Tomas?’

He sighed, ‘I shall leave and go back to England.’

Until he uttered those words the thought of returning to England had never occurred to him.

She laughed softly, ‘I don’t think you would ever do that Tomas. You wouldn’t give me up again would you? Remember how you missed me last time?’ she taunted.

She came up to him and raised her face to him. He pushed her roughly away.

‘Yes damn you, I remember how I missed you, but don’t be so sure of yourself.’

‘It’s not me I’m sure of Tomas. It’s you, but I’ll leave you to think about that.’

He cursed her silently. She was just playing him along – was this her revenge? If he hadn’t been so weak, it would never have begun again. He slumped wearily on his bed, his head in his hands. He should just carry out his threat to leave. Bella had died last year, there was nothing to keep him here. Maybe he should wait a while longer, perhaps till April.

The following day something happened to make him change his mind. Señor Ramirez and Tommy were in the office.

‘Thomas if I were to go away next year for practically the whole year, do you think you could manage for that long?’

‘I don’t know Señor, a year’s a long time with no one at the helm. We’d manage I’m sure, but we’d miss you, and I’d have to be able to get in touch with you.’

‘Of course Thomas that could be arranged. It was just that I was hoping to take my wife on an extended visit to her family in Spain.’

‘What about Catriona?’ The words were out of his mouth before he could stop them. Señor Ramirez looked at him for a long moment before answering.

‘Well just between you and me, her mother and I have plans concerning her, which we have discussed with her. We’ll see how things develop.’

Tommy’s heart turned to stone - what plans? There must be some mistake. Catriona hadn’t mentioned any plans.

That same afternoon Señora Ramirez and Catriona left the *estancia*, no one seemed sure of their whereabouts.

Tommy was furious. He was in a foul black mood for ten days, after which he started to calm down, and by the time they returned after two weeks, he was in a slightly more rational frame of mind.

That first night back she came to him. He was hungry for her, and they fell upon each other.

They lay sleepily spent, Catriona snuggled up to his side, her hand resting lightly on his stomach.

‘I love you Tomas. That was so good for me. Was it good for you? ‘

‘It’s always good with you.’ he answered. ‘Catriona, I meant to ask you,’ he began, as he remembered his conversation with Señor Ramirez the day Catriona had left the *estancia*. ‘Your father said something about him and your mother going to Spain for a year, and when I asked about you, he said they had plans for you. What did he mean, what plans?'

She sat up and quickly swinging her legs over the edge of the bed, she started to throw her clothes on.

'Catriona, what's wrong? Answer me. What plans?'

He was very much aware that something was drastically wrong. He too started to dress hastily.

'I wanted to tell you, honestly I did Tomas, but I couldn't. I didn't know how.'

'Tell me what? Tell me now,' he demanded.

'They want me to marry Eduardo Sanchez,' her voice dropped to whisper.

A dangerous light glittered in Tommy's eyes as he said quietly, 'That's nice, and what did you say?'

He was standing facing her across the bed.

'I agreed today.' She didn't look at him as she made a dash for the door, but Tommy was too quick for her. He grabbed her wrist in a vice like grip before she'd taken three strides.

'Look at me dammit,' he grated. 'When were you going to tell me? Were you perhaps going to slip down to my quarters on your wedding night, just to let me know it would be the last time, or would you have written me a note while you were on your honeymoon?' He shook his head in disbelief. He was shocked and dazed.

She looked at him her dark eyes full of tears, 'Oh please, it doesn't have to make any difference. It doesn't change what's between us. I love you Tomas, not him. I can't lose you.'

'What d'you mean it doesn't make any difference, of course it does. It makes the world of difference to me. It changes everything. You think I'm going to stay here, watching you with your new husband, and be your lover on the side. I don't take other men's wives to my bed. I thought you loved me.'

The anguish was there in his voice as he uttered those last words. He let her wrist drop, as he turned away in disgust.

'I do love you Tomas, but I can't give up everything. I had to make a choice. I think my father would disown me if I told him I wanted to marry you. It was a chance I couldn't take. Should I give up my inheritance, and have you, or give you up and keep my inheritance.'

She looked at him pitifully, her lower lip trembling, the tears starting to spill.

'You bitch, you never even bothered to speak to him, did you? You want it all, a husband, the *estancia* and your lover on the side. His voice was barely steady. 'Go now Catriona, please.' He almost choked on those words. He turned away, not moving as he heard the door close behind her.

The next morning he gave one month's notice. His explanation to Señor Ramirez being that he felt in need of a change after nearly seven years. He suggested he look no further than Gareth Rees for his replacement.

'I'm so very sorry to lose you Thomas, thank you. I wish everything of the best for you.' He gripped Tommy's hand firmly.

He told Gareth of his decision, and of the recommendation he'd made to Señor Ramirez.

'Thanks Tommy, I shall miss you. Are you sure you're doing the right thing? I'm not asking you to tell me your reasons, just be sure Boyo.'

'Yes Gareth, I'm sure.'

Tommy felt a kind of relief, a lessening of pressure since he'd made his decision to leave.

As Gareth shook his hand he grinned, that familiar cheeky grin, 'Well Boyo you've eaten the calafate berries, you'll be back.'

Tommy laughed with him, 'Yeah I did, didn't I? But don't worry I don't believe in legends, so neither me nor my bones will come back to Patagonia. I'll write pal. Good luck!'

Chapter 15

May nineteen forty. The German War Machine was on the move. Breaking through the French lines at Sedan, they caught the British forces unprepared and they retreated to the coast, converging on Dunkirk. A flotilla made up of every conceivable kind of boat approached the beaches, rescuing two hundred thousand men, transporting them back to Britain. Thousands were mowed down, dying on the beaches, leaving them littered with abandoned military equipment and bodies.

Winston Churchill made a stirring speech, which would go down in history, as he broadcast to the nation.

By Amy's second birthday in July, the Nazi flag flew over France, Belgium. Holland, Denmark and Norway. The rest of Europe were either Hitler's allies or neutral. Britain stood alone. London was literally in flames. By the end of nineteen forty Tommy went to sign on. He failed his medical, due to his leg and his deafness in one ear.

That night he raged to Emma, 'Bloody ridiculous. They need people. I'm as fit as the next bloke, so my hearing not so good in one ear, and I've got a limp. No good telling me I'm doing important work feeding the nation. Women could farm and grow food. '

He was frustrated, feeling utterly helpless.

'Hush Tommy, I know how you feel, but Amy and I need you too,' she consoled, looking relieved that he'd been turned down.

'God! Even Megan's doing more than I am for the war effort, with her ambulance duty in Winchester three nights a week. It's driving me crazy Emma.'

Driving him crazy or not, he had to live with it and eventually, as more able bodied men signed on. Tommy took on more of the farm duties.

Maurice Watkins, Blanche's husband, left for the front, followed closely by Sam Smith. That left no one in the dairy. Tommy rose earlier than ever to start the milking with the help of Bob Stocker, the tractor driver.

Mrs. Stewart-Shenley was grateful to Tommy for taking on so much more than any one man could be expected to, as she put it.

Tommy volunteered for ambulance duty two nights a week in Winchester, as Megan had said they could never have enough people. He did Saturday and Sunday evenings, from six to ten. Emma complained.

'But Tommy, with all this extra work on the farm, I never see you anymore. Why must you volunteer for even more?'

'There's a war on Emma,' he replied.

Still he managed to visit Amelia, along with Sylvia and the girls. Georgie too had joined up.

'It's only the sick, the lame and the useless left behind to look after the women and children. I wonder which category I fall into Amelia?' he asked wryly.

'Don't torment yourself Thomas. There are so many people dependent on you to see us through these terrible times.'

He snorted, 'Whatever I do here won't make any difference to the outcome of this bloody war.'

'I know, but as I've said, so many people are reliant upon you. Mrs. Stewart-Shenley for one couldn't manage without you. Emma and Amy need you, Sylvia and the girls lean on you and, on top of all that, Megan and myself both draw from your strength and look to you for support. How is Megan by the way?'

'I don't know, Amelia. I haven't seen much of her lately. The estate takes up a lot of my time, and Megan does three nights a week on ambulance duty. I try and call round on a lunchtime when I can, but I don't make it very often. She looked tired last time I saw her,' he sighed.

'So do you Thomas,' she replied.

Christmas and the New Year passed with very little to celebrate. Tommy, Emma and Amy were joined by Amelia, who came to stay for a few days, with Megan coming for Christmas lunch.

June nineteen forty one brought more bad news. Hitler had invaded Russia, but there was one piece of good news, Emma announced she was pregnant.

'I went to see Dr. Fraser today. He's come out of retirement now Dr. Fleming has gone off to the front. He says the baby's due in December. No wonder I've been feeling so awful lately - that miserable pukey feeling. What a time to bring a baby into the world.'

'There's nothing wrong with now Emma. Perhaps it's what we need, with all the loss of life, a new baby,' he said holding her tight, and kissing the top of her head. Amy'll be so excited, and I'm pleased, aren't you?'

'No, not particularly,' she muttered. 'And neither would you be if you had to go through the next six months in my shoes. Don't you remember what a bloody awful time I had when I carried Amy?'

'Yes, but it will be easier this time Emma. The first time a ewe lambs it can be difficult, but the second time it's usually easier,' he consoled her.

She burst out laughing. 'Are you comparing me to a bloody sheep Tommy Lawrence?'

He laughed with her. 'It'll be all right Emma, you'll see.'

Amy was delighted and when Megan called in for a few minutes on Saturday morning, she couldn't wait to tell her that for Christmas she was going to have a baby brother or sister.

'Congratulations Emma, you must be thrilled, and you too Tommy.'

'Oh yes, he's like a dog with two tails, but as for me being thrilled I'm not so sure,' she said doubtfully. 'I had a miserable time last time with Amy, and I'm afraid I gave Tommy a bit of a hard time too, didn't I? 'She looked at Tommy.

He grinned, 'Just a bit, but I've got broad shoulders. How have you been anyway? We haven't seen much of you lately Megan?'

'No, I know, I'm sorry. Now you're pregnant Emma I'll try and pop in more often just to see how you are. Tuesday morning I'm rolling bandages for the Red Cross, three nights a week is ambulance duty, and for the last month I've been acting as Dr. Crossland's receptionist three mornings a week, as his lady has gone off to join the W.R.E.N.S. or some such. I was telling Tommy the other day,' she went on, 'I heard from Gareth and Thomasina last week. They're expecting their second child already.'

'That's nice,' said Emma flatly.

'I can't stop. Emma, you look after yourself now and if there's anything I can do, let me know,' she concluded.

'Yes, I'd better be off too I'm running late,' Tommy said, giving both Emma and Amy a swift kiss. 'I'll be back about fourish Emma for supper, and it's my ambulance stint tonight.'

At the gate he turned to Megan, 'Thanks Megan, that's kind of you to say you'll try and pop in more often. I know she's worried about the prospect of another baby. Bye now, see you soon.'

He watched Megan drive away, and headed for the stables.

Tommy came home at four thirty. 'I'm starving Emma,' he called out as he came through the door. 'Hello my darling,' he said picking up Amy as she came running to meet him, 'Give Daddy a kiss then.'

'Food's ready. I'll dish up,' Emma said moving swiftly away as Tommy went to kiss her.

He glanced at her and seeing she wasn't in the best of humours, he said, 'What's up Emma. You don't look very happy. Do you feel all right?'

'I'm perfectly all right thank you,' she replied with exaggerated politeness, and putting his food in front of him, she sat down.

Taking Amy on his knee saying, 'Do you want to share Daddy's supper?' He looked up. 'Where's yours Emma? Aren't you eating?'

'I'm not hungry just now. You never mentioned that Gareth and Thomasina were expecting their second child,' she said, her lips a tight line.

'Mmm, I forgot,' he mumbled through a mouthful of cottage pie.

'Really, just like you forgot to mention that you'd even seen Megan. When did you see her by the way?'

'I called in one lunchtime last week - Wednesday it must've been, on my way back from the market. Why what's this all about?' He looked up, his fork halfway to his mouth, his eyes meeting hers. He shook his head. 'Don't start Emma. Megan's supposed to be a friend of ours remember. I haven't had time to call in for at least three weeks, so last week I made the time.'

He pushed his half eaten plate from him.

‘And just forgot to mention it to your wife. I thought you said you were hungry,’ she said motioning to the plate.

‘Yes Emma, I forgot to mention it. I didn’t think my calling in to see a mutual friend was of such earth shattering importance and,’ putting Amy down on her feet he rose from the table, ‘with regards to my appetite, I just lost it.’

He left the room, and at five thirty he left the house.

Don’t let the moods and tantrums start. Why should she suddenly out of the blue, for no apparent reason, be jealous of Megan? He knew they’d never formed a close friendship, but they’d always got along well enough. Why this sudden burst of antagonism towards Megan?

The following Saturday, driving back from Amelia’s, having been up to share the news, with the families, about the baby, Emma put her hand on Tommy’s knee.

He smiled and patted her hand absent-mindedly, his thoughts on how long it would be before he had enough petrol coupons to make the trip up again.

I’m sorry Tommy,’

‘Sorry! What about?’ he asked.

‘When I knew I was pregnant, I vowed to myself that this time I wouldn’t give you such a hard time, and I’ve already started, haven’t I? The other day about Megan - I mean. I know I was being silly,’ she went on, ‘and that you’ve never looked at her. I suppose it’s because I know how much she’s in love with you.’

‘What!’ he was incredulous. ‘Whatever gives you that idea?’

‘Oh, a woman knows. I can tell by the way she looks at you when she thinks no one is watching. It’s all right, I don’t blame her. You’re a very good looking man and so sexy,’ she giggled. ‘So sexy in fact, that I can’t wait to get home, get your daughter to bed, and have you all to myself. She moved closer resting her head on his shoulder. 'I do love you so Tommy. You're so good to me.'

'It's okay Emma,' he squeezed her hand. 'It's a combination of everything I expect. This bloody war's getting us all down. It's been nearly two years and no end in sight. Now what's all this about having me all to yourself? Sounds good to me,' he grinned.

She groaned, 'Oh bloody hell Tommy. You're on ambulance duty this evening, it's Saturday.'

He laughed, 'Well you'll just have to wait till I come home, won't you? The longer you wait the better it is.'

In July Amelia came to stay for a week, for Amy's birthday. She announced her plans for her retirement that coming Christmas. Megan joined them for the birthday tea. Emma had been saving sugar from their rations for months, and she made a Victoria sponge, using her last jar of home-made jam as filling. Egg and cress sandwiches completed the feast.

By mid-November Emma was enormous, but looking forward to the baby coming. She was hoping for a boy, but Tommy said he'd be happy with either. Georgie had been wounded and had been hospitalised. Sylvia was hoping he'd be home for Christmas.

The baby came on the fourth of December - another girl. Three days later, on Sunday the seventh of December nineteen forty one, the Japanese bombed Pearl Harbour. America entered the war.

The new baby was to be called Laura Anne. She was a tiny replica of Tommy. That olive skin, right down to the mop of jet black hair. Emma was tired and Amelia arrived just before Christmas to find Emma pale and wan.

'Emma needs to rest Tommy,' she said. 'Yes you do Emma,' as Emma started to protest. 'Get your strength back.'

Earlier in the year Tommy had spoken to Mrs. Stewart-Shenley about a larger house and was told immediately that he could move into the Lodge at the main gates, which had been vacated by the gamekeeper some weeks earlier. So for Amelia's visit they were no longer as cramped as they had been on previous occasions.

Amelia took over the running of the house, leaving Emma free to tend to the children.

Megan joined them for Christmas day and, lunch over, she and Amelia went to the kitchen to wash the dishes, leaving Tommy sitting at the table with Amy, helping her with a jigsaw puzzle, Emma was sitting in the armchair in front of the fire, nursing Laura Anne.

In the kitchen Megan asked Amelia, 'What's wrong with Emma? She looks terrible - so tired and drawn. Has she been to the doctor?'

'Yes,' Amelia nodded. 'Tommy said he took her the day before I arrived - the baby too. Dr. Fraser says they're both fine, although I believe he said Emma is a little run down. He's given her a tonic I believe.'

'Tommy looks tired too,' remarked Megan.

'I think he's more worried than tired,' Amelia said scouring the last pot vigorously, 'although he does work awfully hard.'

January the fourth saw Georgie discharged from hospital and sent home. Tommy took Amelia back to Swallowfield, Emma insisting on going with them to see Sylvia and Georgie, and her aunt and uncle, and paying a very brief visit to Tommy's father and Maude. Tommy had swapped ambulance duty with another volunteer to enable them to stay over one night.

Tommy's first priority was to see how Georgie fared. Sylvia opened the door, Maggie and Jenny close on her heels to greet their Uncle Tommy. She looked flushed and nervous as she ushered them in.

'Oh Tommy,' she threw her arms round him, 'He'll be so pleased to see you. He's so thin and down. Oh listen to me. Congratulations! Here let me see her Emma. Hello Amy, my but you've grown,' as she opened the door to the small sitting room.

Georgie sat on the settee, his leg still in a plaster cast, resting on a stool.

'Well then baby brother, how goes it?' Tommy grinned. 'Some people will do anything, even go so far as breaking a leg, to get a few weeks off from the war. Opposite leg to me, we've ended up with one good pair of legs between us,' he joked.

'Hello our Tommy. God! It's good to see you. Emma let's see the new addition then,' Georgie smiled weakly holding out his arms to take the baby.

Emma placed the baby in his outstretched arms. 'There you are, Laura Anne, meet your Uncle Georgie.'

Tommy watched him closely, saw how thin and haggard he looked, saw his eye twitch, and his bottom lip trembled ever so slightly.

'Come on then girls,' he said taking the baby from Georgie, and handing her back to Emma. 'Take all the kids to the kitchen and make us blokes a nice cup of tea.'

As the door closed behind them, Georgie's face crumpled. Tommy moved swiftly across to the arm of the settee, putting his arms around Georgie as he sat down.

'It's that bad, eh?' He held him close saying nothing further, just wishing he could take some of his brother's pain away. Georgie gave a muffled sob.

'Christ Tommy, I don't want to go back. It's nothing like I thought it would be. Every bloody day you're seeing someone you know getting blown to pieces, and every day you wake up wondering if it'll be your turn today. I don't want to die Tommy. What'll happen to Sylvia and the kids if I'm gone?'

Tommy closed his eyes. 'Come on, Georgie, you won't die. It'll take more than the German army to do away with a Lawrence. Have you heard from Matthew since he joined the R.A.F.?'

Georgie nodded, 'Yeah, he was okay last time I heard. He's stationed up in Lincolnshire. Sorry about that Tommy,' he coughed, 'you must think me an awful coward. I'll go back when the time comes. I haven't really got any choice.'

Tommy gave his shoulder a hug, as the door opened and in came the tea.

The visit over, they left Amelia's early on Sunday. Megan had promised to go round and light the fire so the house would be warm on their return. It had turned bitterly cold overnight with freezing cold temperatures. They arrived home to find the house warm, and the smell of roast chicken greeted them. Megan was already halfway into her coat by the time they came in the front door.

'Special treat,' she said, 'Mr. Leyland killed one of his chickens for Dr. Crossland yesterday, but the doctor doesn't eat meat, so he kindly gave it to me and, seeing as I can't eat a whole chicken, I thought of a family that could,' she smiled. 'I've stuffed it and done some veggies ready Emma.'

'Hey, what's your rush?' Tommy said, 'Stay and eat with us Megan, after doing all that.'

'No, some other time Tommy. Emma you look tired. Let this lump of a husband finish cooking the lunch.'

'Mmm, I don't know what's wrong with me. I feel so lethargic all the time. I need my batteries recharging or something. Anyway, thanks Megan, it smells lovely, you're welcome to stay you know.'

'Yes I know Emma, but like I say some other time,' and with a wave she was gone.

The next day Emma woke up with a cold. A week later she could hardly breathe. At Tommy's insistence he took her to see Dr. Fraser.

'It's all on my chest,' she wheezed.

'Yes, I can hear that young lady. It doesn't sound good at all I'm afraid.'

'Well I can't be ill Doctor, I've got my husband and family to look after. Laura Anne's only six weeks old.'

'I'm afraid Mrs. Lawrence, they're all going to have to manage without you.' He looked at Tommy who was holding Laura in his arms, Amy standing solemn eyed at his knee. 'Your wife needs to go to hospital. She's got pneumonia. I'm afraid her lungs are badly inflamed,' he said gravely.

'Oh no Tommy, I can't,' she gasped.

'Oh yes you can Emma. You must. Don't worry - I'll manage. Megan will help me with the children,' he nodded to Dr. Fraser. 'What must we do now?'

'You take your wife to the hospital now, along with this note, and I will see her there later. You can then go home, and visit her this evening, six till seven are visiting hours I believe.'

Tommy drove to Kilmeston arriving at Megan's just after lunch. She looked at him in amazement.

'What on earth are you doing here, and where's Emma? What's wrong Tommy?'

'It's Emma, Megan. For God's sake I need your help,' he got out.

'Of course, but what's happened?' she insisted.

He looked dazed. 'She's in hospital. She's got pneumonia. What am I going to do Megan?'

She'd never seen Tommy at a loss. He'd always been the strong one. She took charge.

‘You’re going to leave the girls with me, better still, I’ll come home with you. I’ll follow you in my car. The baby’s things are all at your house, and Amy will be happier in her own home. I’ll stay all day and come home in the evenings when you get back from the hospital. It’ll only be for a couple of days,’ she assured him. ‘I’ll follow you in a while. I’ll stop at the phone box and cancel my ambulance duty and my mornings for Dr. Crossland. After all if I was ill they’d all have to manage without me.’

And so they managed - Tuesday, Wednesday into Thursday the fifteenth of January.

That evening after an early supper. Tommy set off for the hospital saying, ‘I’ll be back about half seven Megan. I hope Emma’s a bit better tonight. Her colour looked a bit better yesterday even though she couldn’t talk properly.’

Chapter 16

By eight o'clock Tommy still wasn't home. Megan began to worry. On leaving to visit Emma his last words were, 'I'll be back about half seven.'

Megan had put the kettle across to boil as they usually had a cup of coffee on his return from the hospital, while he told her of Emma's progress. He'd said last night her colour had looked better, but her breathing was still very laboured. He had hoped she'd be a little better tonight.

Megan hoped so too. It was such a shame that Emma had got pneumonia, and as a doctor's daughter she was fully aware that it was potentially life threatening. But Emma was young and normally in good health, so she was sure she'd pull through.

She thought about Emma. They'd never really become close friends. Emma seemingly wanting to keep a little distance between them. Megan had respected that and had never tried to force their friendship.

Gareth had told Megan when he'd jokingly commented on Tommy's winning ways with the ladies, that Tommy had afterwards taken him aside and asked him please don't make jokes about his prowess with the ladies, as Emma was possessive and tended to be jealous, although he'd hastily added he'd never given her cause to be. Megan wondered if this could be why Emma kept her at arm's length, or did Emma suspect that Megan had feelings for Tommy. She hoped not. She would be mortified if she thought anyone knew her thoughts and feelings for Tommy. Tommy had been kindness itself when she'd moved from Wales, but she sometimes wondered if it wouldn't have been better if the sale of the cottage in Swallowfield hadn't fallen through. She liked Amelia Nelson and Tommy's brother and his wife Sylvia, and had she moved there instead of Kilmeston, she wouldn't have had to see so much of Tommy. She couldn't decide if that would have been better or not. It would have been agony not to see him at all, and it was torment to see him so often, knowing he belonged to someone else, a married man and therefore out of bounds as far as she was concerned.

Amy and baby Laura were both fast asleep. She glanced at the clock for the hundredth time, eight fifteen. Next week was Tommy's thirty seventh birthday. If Emma was out of hospital she'd offer to look after the children for an evening so that they could go out if Emma was well enough, or even to give them an evening at home on their own.

Thoughts of an accident went through her mind. Tommy did drive fast. Oh please she prayed silently, don't let anything happen to him, she couldn't bear it. Just then she heard his car. She prepared to make the coffee. They usually sat for an hour or so, talking of his days in the Argentine with Gareth, sometimes talking about the war, wondering where and when it would all end.

As soon as he came in she knew something was very wrong. He stood there, his arms hanging at his sides: his eyes lifeless, the colour of dull pewter, she'd never seen a man look so utterly defeated.

'She's dead Megan. Emma's dead.'

Megan's hand went to her mouth - she'd heard his words, but they barely registered. Emma dead! How could she be? She was twenty eight years old, two years younger than herself, she'd just had a baby six weeks ago. She stared at Tommy, unseeing. He hadn't moved. It was as if he was in a trance. Her lips formed the word, 'Tommy,' but no sound came out - the only noise was the ticking of the clock.

After what seemed like an eternity she managed to whisper, 'Tommy, oh Tommy, I'm so sorry, how...'

Her voice brought him out of his trancelike state. He blinked. 'She went so quick Megan. I was sitting there holding her hand, she opened her eyes and smiled at me, and then she sort of gasped, then she just stopped breathing. What am I going to tell Amy? How do you tell a child of her age,' he faltered, 'that she's never going to see her mother again?'

Megan could feel that prickling sensation in her nose, the lump rising in her throat, the tears ready to spill. She mustn't cry. He needed her help now, not her tears or her sympathy. There would be time for sympathy later. Now was the time to be practical.

'Don't worry there's time to think of that tomorrow. You'll have to let Annie and Frank know, your family and of course Amelia.'

He shook his head wordlessly.

'Would you like me to see to it first thing in the morning? I could phone Annie and Frank and send a telegram to Amelia. She can let Georgie and Sylvia know, and your father and Maude. Shall I take the children home with me now?' she turned from making the coffee to see that shock had taken over.

Tommy had started to shake uncontrollably. His teeth rattled in his head and the blood had drained from his face. Megan stepped forward and catching his arm she propelled him towards a chair where he slumped down. She knew Emma kept brandy in the corner cupboard, so she poured him a large one, passing him the glass, 'Drink,' she instructed. He took it dumbly, his hand shaking so that the brandy slopped down his shirt. She took the glass from him and held it to his lips which were bloodless. The glass chattered against his teeth. He gulped as the fiery liquid hit the back of his throat. Gradually the colour returned to his face. Megan poured the strong coffee and heaping sugar in she made him drink that too.

'Are you okay?' she asked, 'What about the children?'

'No, I'm all right Megan. Leave the children. You go home. I'll manage, but what time is Laura's next feed?'

'Around elevenish, when she wakes, everything is ready over there,' she nodded towards the kitchen surface, 'You've only got to heat it. Are you sure you'll manage?'

He nodded, 'Yes I'm fine now, I'll be grateful if you contact Frank and Annie and if you could come round and help me in the morning with the children, that's if you can.'

'Of course I can, I'll pop into the village first, send the telegram to Amelia, ring Frank and Annie and I'll be here as soon as that's done.'

'Thanks Megan. What would I do without you? Now go and get some sleep. I'll see you out.'

At the door he gave her a customary hug as he said, 'Thanks again Megan, I'll see you in the morning.'

That hug was nearly her undoing, she broke away quickly and ran down the path to her car fumbling for her keys.

She got to bed around midnight, she sat down and dashed a quick letter off to Gareth that she'd post it in the morning. Sleep eluded her. She closed her eyes but all she could see was Tommy's face as he'd told her - the anguish mixed with shock and disbelief. She thought of the children. The tears finally came in great gasping sobs, tears of grief for Emma, tears of sorrow for Tommy and the children, mingled with tears of guilt for her feelings for Tommy, which she was helpless to do anything about. She finally slipped into an exhausted sleep the tears still wet on her cheeks.

The following morning, phone call made from the kiosk outside the Post Office, telegram sent and letter posted she went straight to Tommy's house.

He looked terrible. His eyes were red rimmed, his face ashen. If she'd slept little, it was obvious he hadn't slept at all.

'Annie and Frank will be here about midday and they will bring Amelia with them.' The baby had started to cry. 'It's all right, I'll see to her. Have you told Amy yet and where is she?' she asked looking round and seeing no sign of her.

'She's in the other room playing with her dolls. I've lit the fire in there and put the fireguard up. I explained about Emma, but I don't think she understood. I told her that Emma had gone to Jesus in heaven - I know Emma used to tell her Bible stories.' He rubbed his forehead, a gesture of utter weariness. 'I want things to be as normal as possible for her. Christ Megan, I don't know what I'm going to do, or how I'm going to manage, but I'll get by somehow. Can I leave you for a while? I must go and tell Mrs. Stewart-Shenley I'll need some time off work.'

She nodded, lifting the crying Laura from her pram. 'Yes carry on Tommy.'

'I'll fetch Amy,' he said opening the door and crossing the hallway to the sitting room. 'Come Amy, Auntie Megan's here. Come and say hello,' she heard him say.

Amy came through clutching her favourite doll, a disreputable looking creature known as Topsy, dressed in bedraggled green satin.

'Hello Amy, are you going to help me feed your baby sister?' Megan invited.

'I'll be back shortly Megan,' Tommy said.

'Where you go Daddy, me come.' Amy clutched at his leg.

'No Amy, it's too cold out. I won't be long. Stay and help Auntie Megan,' he said picking her up and kissing her fiercely with a *See you soon, be a good girl* he was gone.

With Tommy gone Megan set to making a cottage pie for lunch, sitting Amy down with a set of wooden bricks which, when put together in the right order made various farmyard scenes. Laura was fed, changed and sleeping peacefully in her pram. She quickly dusted the sitting room, and had put on some fresh coffee, knowing Tommy's preference for a good strong cup of coffee above tea. It had just started to bubble, the aroma filling the house when Tommy returned.

'Can I pour you some coffee Tommy?' Megan offered.

'Mmm please, smells good.'

'How did it go with Mrs. Stewart-Shenley?'

'Fine, she was shocked to hear about Emma, but she said I must take all the time I need, but there's lots to do right now and not many hands to do it. The war has taken half our workforce.'

We're experimenting with indoor lambing in the old barns, and we've got about a hundred ewes pregnant, and it's going to snow,' he tailed off. 'God, Emma and I were laughing not two months back about me comparing her to one of my sheep.'

'Tommy I know you've hardly had time to think yet, but can I make a suggestion?'

He nodded, 'Please do.'

'Won't you let me take the children? Just for the time being,' she added hastily. 'I'm only a couple of miles away and you can come round every day after work and see them. It will give you breathing space, time on your own to think, to plan your future and theirs,' she finished gently.

'Thanks Megan, but that's putting a lot on you. I don't know.'

'Please Tommy I want to help. You and Emma were so kind to me when I moved from Wales, and it's the only way I can think of to repay you. You still have to go to work and you can't do that and look after two children, one of them a six week old. I know you need your work to keep you occupied. I understand, but be practical.'

He shook his head. 'I know Megan. I can't think straight yet. Annie, Frank and Amelia will be here soon. We'll discuss it further then. Amelia will probably come up with the most practical solution.'

They arrived at lunchtime. Tommy greeted Annie and Frank before turning to Amelia, who held out her arms. They held one another for a long moment, neither of them speaking, until finally Amelia gently disengaged herself saying, 'It's all right Thomas. I'm so sorry. Don't worry we'll manage.'

The cottage pie was more than adequate, as no one was very hungry. Tommy declined altogether. Taking Amy on his knee, he fed her, while the others picked disinterestedly.

Lunch cleared away, Megan made tea. Annie wanted to know what Tommy's plans were for the children.

'I haven't got that far yet Annie. Have you got any ideas?' he asked.

'Well you can't raise two children, girls at that, on your own. That's for certain. Amelia here has just retired and lives alone. Megan,' she nodded in her direction somewhat condescendingly, 'is a single woman with no experience of children,' as if this automatically disqualified her, 'I think the best thing under the circumstances would be for Frank and I to take them and bring them up as our own, but of course I suppose the final decision must rest with you. After all you are their father. '

For the first time since Emma's death, Megan saw a spark in Tommy's eye.

‘Yes you’re right Annie. I am their father.’ His eyes were cold. ‘And kind as your offer is, I feel I must decline it. I don’t want my children being brought up by someone else, and I don’t want them growing up in a pub.’

‘Well don’t be too quick to refuse Tommy,’ she said huffily. ‘It’s not every day you’re going to get someone offering to take the responsibility of raising your children for you.’

‘I know Annie,’ he answered softly, a determined set to his mouth, ‘and as I’ve said, much as I appreciate it, the answer is no thank you. I’m not looking for someone to take the responsibility from me. It’s mine and I’m very much aware of it. ‘

During this exchange Frank sat silently, eyes downcast, neither agreeing nor disagreeing. Megan had watched Tommy closely, glad he had taken a stand against what she’d considered to be Annie’s highhanded attitude. Amelia had also remained silent.

Tommy turned towards her now, ‘Well Amelia what do you think?’

‘It seems to me Thomas, that all you need is a temporary arrangement until you have time to think everything through. I would suggest you take Megan up on her offer to take the baby and again, purely on a temporary basis, until you arrive at a permanent solution, I could take Amy with me. After all, I have been a schoolteacher all my life and am quite used to children. Amy is my goddaughter and I do love her very much.’

Tommy looked from one to the other. ‘Thank you Amelia, but are you sure you can manage? Amy’s becoming a bit of a handful lately.’ Turning to Megan, ‘What about your work Megan, with Dr. Crossland and ambulance duties? Are you sure?’

‘Yes Tommy, I can keep up the ambulance duties. They don’t coincide with yours, so you could stay with Laura the evenings I have duty, and as for Dr. Crossland, that was only temporary. I was just helping him out. He has a new lady starting the beginning of February. He'll manage.'

'That's settled then Thomas, I shall manage admirably. I'll stay with you until after the funeral. I've taken the liberty of packing a few things, then I'll return home with Amy.'

'Well there really doesn't seem to be any need for us to stay Tommy, you've obviously made your choice. I just hope you don't regret your decision, but we are here if you need us,' Annie sniffed. 'And I do hope that this doesn't mean that we won't see anything of Emma's children, after all she was our niece.'

'Thank you Annie. Please don't be offended. The funeral arrangements will be made in a few days, and we'll let you know, and no, of course it doesn't mean you won't see the children. I'm sure I speak for Amelia when I say you're welcome to call and see Amy whenever you want, and I will personally make sure you see Laura whenever possible,' he said wearily.

Annie departed, placated, saying that they would be down for the funeral. After their departure Tommy announced that he was going to saddle up Satan and take a quick look round the farm before darkness set in.

Again Amy clung to him. 'I'll bring Satan round on my way back and you can ride down to the stables with Daddy okay. Wrap her up warm Megan, I'll be back for her in about an hour.'

'What happened Megan?' Amelia asked as soon as they were alone.

Megan related the events that led up to Emma's death, and Tommy's shock. Amelia listened saying nothing until Megan had finished.

'My poor Thomas, and poor Emma too - to be taken so young. He looks devastated. I can't believe it. I'm so glad you're here to help. He'll need all the help he can get.'

‘I’ll help him in any way I can Amelia, but I’m not sure how he’ll cope with it all, Emma’s death, the prospect of having to bring up two children alone. I’d do anything for him,’ she paused noticing Amelia’s penetrating look, ‘after how kind he was to me when I moved here, and with him being Gareth’s oldest friend,’ she added hastily.

‘He’s a lovely man, and he has great strength of character. He’s very resilient. He’ll come through it all right. I don’t think he’ll be alone for too long. He’s a good looking man, and despite being a widower with two children he’s quite a catch. He has a good job, and when the war is over there’ll be a shortage of eligible young men.’

‘Of course I forget you know him so well. You’ve known him from five years old haven’t you? What was he like as a child? Tell me. Help me to understand him better. I feel there’s so much I don’t know about him.’

‘Oh dear, I’m not sure he’d approve of me telling you, but he had a very abusive childhood. His mother adored him but I’m afraid she seemed to be helpless against his bullying father. As a small boy he used to visit me but I soon realised he’d tell me only what he wanted to and he close up like a clam if I asked too many questions. But I do think that helped to make him into the strong person he is today.’

There was no more time for Megan to ask Amelia any further questions as Tommy returned to pick Amy up. She was ready and waiting, looking out of the window. Megan took her down the path, her red woollen pixie hood like a bright beacon. Megan could see he’d ridden Satan hard. The horse was in a sweat as he leant down from the saddle to put Amy up in front of him. He gave Megan a half-smile, ‘It’s all right Megan. Don’t look so worried. We’ll manage, and again how can I ever thank you.’

‘I know. Listen Tommy I’m going to take Laura and go home now. I’ll bathe her at about half past six in the evenings, so you come, if and when you can.’

‘I’ll be there.’

True to his word he was there that very night and every night, a ritual that Megan grew to cherish.

Chapter 17

Tommy woke on Tuesday morning, the day of Emma's funeral, a day of weak watery sunshine. The mourners were few. Much to Tommy's surprise his father and Maude came with Georgie still on crutches, and Sylvia, who had left the children with a neighbour. Annie and Frank were there, and from the estate, Blanche Watkins, Bob Stocker, Mrs. Stewart-Shenley, and himself and Amelia.

Megan had stayed at the house with the children, laying out cups and saucers, and attending to refreshment for the immediate family, before they set off back to Reading by train. Frank and Annie had driven down.

They returned to the house a solemn little group. Maude held the baby while Megan and Amelia tended to the food. Tommy talked quietly to Annie and Frank, while Amy chattered happily to Georgie and Sylvia.

After an hour or so Annie and Frank said their farewells and Tommy followed Megan to the kitchen.

'I know everyone means well but I shall be glad when it's over and the taxi arrives to take them to the station. I've had enough now.' He was shattered. 'You must think me very selfish and ungrateful Megan.

She took his hand in hers, and he gripped hers firmly returning the pressure.

'No Tommy, you are neither of those things. We all know that. They'll be gone soon,' she assured him.

It was with relief Tommy saw the taxi pulling up outside. Megan prepared to leave too.

'I'll see you later,' he told her as he saw her out.

At last it was just himself and Amelia. Amy sat quietly almost asleep, on his lap, her thumb in her mouth, a recently acquired habit.

'When do you want to leave Amelia?' he ventured.

'Saturday, if it's all right with you Thomas.'

'Yes,' he nodded. 'That's going to be another wrench having to part with this one,' he said, kissing the top of Amy's head. 'I'll see Laura every day at bathtime, so she'll get to know me. I'm all she's got.'

He caught at his lower lip with his teeth as the realisation of what he'd just said dawned on him, that he was all that both of his children had, and just at that moment it felt like a very heavy burden to bear.

'Listen Amelia, as long as I can manage petrol coupons I shall come and see Amy every Saturday, and if I can't, then I'll have to think of trains, or even buy a bicycle. If it suits you I'll stay overnight coming back on Sunday. Another thing Amelia, what about money for Amy's keep...'

'Oh no Thomas,' she interrupted. 'Save the money. How much do you think a little girl of three eats anyway? Please let me do this - such a small thing,' she pleaded.

He was about to argue, but capitulated, realising how ungracious it would be, and seeing how much it meant to Amelia.

'Thank you Amelia, I'm very grateful. I shall be forever in your debt.'

Amelia rose and crossing to where he sat with Amy, she put her arms around him, 'Hush now Thomas, no talk of debts between us.'

He felt his shoulders tense and a muscle in his cheek twitch. He covered her hand with his, saying a simple, 'Thank you. '

That evening he went to Megan's where he bathed baby Laura and gave her a bottle.

Megan sat watching, 'You're very confident holding such a tiny baby. You're a natural father Tommy.'

He smiled, 'When the twins were born I used to help my Mum, as long as my father wasn't about. I love the smell of newborn babies, and when Amy was born Emma was nervous so for the first few days before Annie arrived I did everything, more or less, just to show Emma that babies weren't that fragile. Emma used to say she was afraid she'd break.'

The next few months were hard for Tommy. Constantly on his mind were the children. They needed him, and he needed them. They gave his life a purpose, a reason to go on. He thought of Emma and felt guilt. He knew in his heart he'd never loved her the way she'd loved him, with an all-consuming passion, but he had loved her and he missed her.

Winter moved on, heralding spring. The war dragged on. It was all doom and gloom. The Japanese seemed invincible in the Pacific. Britain was forced to give up Hong Kong, Malaya, Singapore and Burma. The Dutch could no longer hold out in Indonesia.

By April the ears had formed inside the wheat, all that was needed was the right amounts of warmth, sunshine and rain.

By the beginning of May the Americans were beaten in the Philippines, by which time Laura Anne was six months old. Tommy divided himself between his work and his daughters.

True to his word he visited Amy every Saturday. She would be kneeling in the window seat of Rose Cottage from eleven' clock onwards, and nothing would budge her as she waited for Tommy's car to appear.

She was often to be found in the afternoons at her Aunt Sylvia's playing with her cousins, Maggie and Jenny, when she wasn't shadowing her beloved 'Mielie' as she called Amelia. They made biscuits with Amelia's meagre sugar ration, they did puzzles and Amy loved Amelia to read her stories. Tommy had worried that Amy might be too much for Amelia to cope with, but quite the contrary, Amelia told him Amy made her feel young again.

Every evening with the exception of Saturdays, Tommy was at Megan's to bath and feed Laura. Recently she'd taken to laughing delightedly when she heard his voice.

It had become customary for Tommy to stay on a Friday after Laura was put to bed, and have supper with Megan. He knew she would have been willing to cook for him every evening, but he wanted to fend for himself. That didn't stop him looking forward to his Friday evenings with Megan, a home cooked meal and some female company.

He felt totally at ease with Megan. She had the knack of being, and putting others, at ease. Like her brother she was well read. Sometimes they'd talk of books, of Argentina and himself and Gareth's time together. He confessed to Megan that if it weren't for the children, he would have returned there after Emma's death. He talked about his days at Melchet Court, where he'd learnt from the butler, Mr. Grimes about fine wines. Of Mrs. Baker the cook and her sumptuous banquets when the family were entertaining. He confided his first love had been the gypsy girl Miriam, who he had sneaked out every night, from the library window, to meet for the whole of that long hot summer, until the gypsies moved on.

One Friday evening in July after supper Tommy said, 'Come Megan let's put Laura in her pram and walk to the Fox and Hounds. It's a lovely evening. We can sit in Mrs. Porter's garden for a while and have a beer or something.'

This was the first time Tommy had felt any inclination to go anywhere, other than his weekly visits to Amy. That was the first of several Fridays throughout the summer they could be found in the pub garden.

They sat at the rustic wooden table, the pram beside them. Megan asked for a shandy, while Tommy although not normally a beer drinker, ordered himself a pint of bitter.

Sitting comfortably in one another's company Tommy began, 'You know Megan, you've been looking after Laura for six months now, and I've never thanked you properly. It was only supposed to be a temporary arrangement.'

'Well I hope I'm proving to be a satisfactory Nanny and you're not planning on firing me,' she said lightly.

He smiled, something he didn't do very often.

'No Megan but,' he went on seriously, 'I do think that looking after Laura restricts your life. You're only thirty two and you never get to go out. You have no life of your own.'

'And what might I ask do you think I'd be doing without the restrictions Laura puts on me? Cavorting round night clubs perhaps, a constant round of social activities with the local gentry?' she teased.

'No, but what I did notice was that the new vicar seems to have an eye for you, and maybe without the encumbrance of my daughter like a millstone round your neck, he might show more than just a passing interest.' He raised his eyebrows, 'Don't say you haven't noticed?'

'Yes, as a matter of fact I have but, seeing as you pride yourself as being so observant Mr. Lawrence, I'm surprised you hadn't noticed that the attraction isn't reciprocated from my side. Seriously Tommy, Laura is not a millstone round my neck, she's the joy of my life, I love her to bits, she's become like my own, but I know she isn't,' she put in hastily, 'and I know the day will come when I shall have to part with her. Maybe you'll marry again, but please don't take her away before you have to.'

He heard the distress in her voice, and put out a hand and rested it lightly on hers, he felt her tremble at his touch.

'It's okay Megan, please don't be upset. I was just trying to think of your needs first for a change, instead of mine and Laura's. And as regards to marrying again, I doubt it, I'm not exactly catch of the year, a thirty seven year old widower, with two small children,' he ended ruefully.

Strolling home he suggested she come with him to Amelia's tomorrow. 'I can sleep on the settee and Amelia loves to see both you and Laura.'

She hesitated. She'd gone with him a couple of times since Emma's death.

'Come on Megan,' he urged, 'I want Amy to see Laura more often, now she's getting bigger.'

And so he persuaded her. On his departure he normally put his arm around her shoulders giving her a brotherly hug, a kiss on the cheek saying, 'Thanks for supper. See you Sunday.'

That night he took both her hands in his, and looking deep into her eyes, he said, 'Thanks for supper as always Megan, and don't worry I'm not about to take Laura away from you, at least not in the foreseeable future. I'll pick you up about tennish in the morning,' and leaning forward he kissed her cheek, letting his lips linger a moment too long.

He shouldn't have done it, but he couldn't help himself. She was so different from both Catriona and Emma. She was very lovely, and such a gentle character he was drawn to her almost against his will, but he knew he mustn't give Megan the wrong impression since he wasn't ready for any kind of relationship.

Amy was kneeling in her usual place, watching for Tommy when his car turned the corner.

'Mielie, Mielie,' she yelled excitedly, 'Daddy's here and Megan and my baby sister.'

Before they were barely out of the car she was flying down the path to meet them. Tommy laughed, as he scooped her up in his arms smothering her face with kisses.

'How's my big girl then? Have you been good this week?'

She nodded vigorously, 'Mielie's made you an apple pie Daddy, an' I helped didn't I Mielie? And Uncle Georgie took us last night after tea to fly the kite.'

Amelia smiled at this outburst. 'Yes you did help darling, and don't strangle your father,' she admonished seeing Amy's arms wound tightly round Tommy's neck.

Tommy put Amy down and greeted Amelia with a hug, 'Hope you don't mind me bringing Megan and Laura, Amelia without any warning. '

'Don't be silly Thomas. I'm delighted,' she held out her arms to Megan, 'How are you Megan? You look radiant my dear. What have you been doing to her Thomas?'

Tommy saw Megan's blush as he cast her an amused glance.

'It's good to see you too Amelia. I do hope you don't mind me coming. Tommy insisted you wouldn't.'

'Of course not. I haven't seen you in ages, and you know you're always welcome, with or without Thomas.'

'Yes well I'm looking forward to a weekend being spoiled by my womenfolk.' he grinned, 'So Georgie's home this weekend, I'm glad he didn't have to go back to the front, it's good that he was posted to Aldershot to an admin job. I think I'll take a stroll down to see him,' he said, removing Laura's cumbersome pram from the boot, where it had to be laid on its side in order to fit in. 'I'll take the girls with me, that's if I've got time before lunch?'

Amelia nodded, 'That's nice Thomas, Megan and I can go sit in the garden and chat. We'll have lunch at two.'

Sunday morning Tommy took the children to see his father and Maude. Tommy originally had been very anti-Maude, but on getting to know her he'd actually grown quite fond of this no nonsense woman, who had taken all of George's grandchildren to heart, having none of her own.

Maude took Amy to the garden to pick gooseberries for Amelia, Tommy was waiting for them to come back when his father said, 'I s'pose you've brought other 'un with you,' he muttered.

Tommy drew in his breath sharply, 'What other one is that?' he asked fully aware of who his father meant.

'That hoity-toity madam that looks after your nipper and,' he said with a leer, 'probably looking after you too if the truth were known, not that I blame you for that, a man must get it where he can...'

'That's enough,' Tommy thundered leaping to his feet. 'You crude bastard you. That woman looks after my child damn you. She's not a whore, and I'm not you. Just because you couldn't wait till my mother was in her grave, before you were in another woman's bed, we're not all the same.'

He knew he was shouting. He knew he was losing it, but he couldn't stop. That this crass, vulgar man should make assumptions about himself and Megan, and then presume to pass judgement incensed Tommy.

'Where in the name of hell d'you think I'd be without her and Amelia? They're caring for my children, until I'm in a position to care for them myself. Those children are mine, and no one is going to take them away from me, just because you never cared for me...' he tailed off as the door opened and Maude and Amy stood there, Amy clutching a bowl of gooseberries.

‘Well back to normal are we? I must say it’s a fine way to carry on. Just as well we don’t have neighbours because if we had, they’d have heard every word,’ she nodded. ‘Just as I did Tommy. Oh it’s all right,’ she said raising her hand. ‘I’m sure your father said something to provoke your outburst, but nevertheless it doesn’t make it easier for me.’

‘I’m truly sorry Maude, you can ask him when I’ve gone what he said. Perhaps it would be better if I didn’t come again. I must admit I get heartily sick of being forever on the defensive. It’s like sitting on a bloody time bomb.’

He turned to his father saying, ‘The only reason I come is for the children. I want them to grow up with a sense of belonging, a sense of family, but maybe it’s not worth it. You’re never going to change.’

Nodding curtly to Maude he grasped Amy’s hand causing her to drop the bowl of gooseberries.

‘Daddy,’ she wailed, ‘Mielie’s goosegogs.’

‘Never mind the gooseberries baby. I’ve got a sour enough taste in my mouth.’

He swept her up onto the end of the pram, where Laura had been sleeping peacefully, and strode up the lane.

Amelia took one look at his face, ‘What’s wrong Thomas? Not your father again.’ It was more of a statement than a question.

‘Yes Amelia, but not open for discussion,’ he said abruptly.

Throughout lunch Tommy was inwardly fuming, and didn’t contribute anything to the conversation. Saying goodbye after lunch he gave Amelia a swift kiss on the cheek saying, ‘Thank you Amelia, look after yourself, and my little angel. Hey Amy that’s you.’ He picked her up showering her with kisses. ‘I’ll see you next Saturday.’

The journey home was silent until just before they reached Kilmeston.

‘I’ll be round later for Laura’s hour Megan. Meanwhile there are some things I must attend to on the farm.’

‘All right Tommy.’ she said quietly.

Chapter 18

The remainder of the afternoon passed slowly. She played with Laura and took her for her customary walk, but her heart wasn't in it. Her thoughts were elsewhere. She reflected on the last few weeks. Tommy had shown an interest in things outside of his work. It had been at his suggestion for the odd Friday evening visits to the pub garden, and now this last weekend when Tommy had asked her to go with him to Amelia's. He'd taken both her hands in his and kissed her cheek with assurances he wasn't planning to take Laura away from her. Had she imagined that kiss was anything more than brotherly, that he had perhaps lingered a moment longer than usual. Later, alone she'd put her hand to her face where his lips had been. She shook her head, as he'd pointed out, she was thirty two years old, it was time she started acting like it she told herself, not like some silly lovesick teenager.

She'd thought that evening had been a breakthrough. Since Emma's death there had been an invisible barrier, she couldn't get past the shadows in his eyes. She used to wonder where he'd gone, but when he'd looked into her eyes, she felt the barriers had dropped briefly. That evening he'd smiled, he'd relaxed and she caught a glimpse of the old Tommy.

He'd joked about his 'womenfolk' and Megan found herself blushing wondering if she was included, but quickly told herself not to be foolish. She was there as his friend, to look after his child.

When Tommy had gone to visit Georgie, Megan looked forward to an hour or so of female company, in the shape of Amelia. She hadn't made many friends since she'd moved from Wales, she knew this was partly due to her shyness, added to the fact that most young women of her age were married with families, leaving her very little in common with them. She did however get along very well, despite their age difference, with Amelia who had been very kind to her and Gareth when she had been house hunting. Both were unmarried, well-educated forward thinking women.

Amelia had offered tea or a pre-lunchtime sherry. They'd plumped for sherry taking it into the garden.

Amelia's small back garden was a riot of colour, hollyhocks in pinks, whites and reds, larkspur, and an abundance of roses and honeysuckle climbing all over the walls stretching up their tendrils round the bedroom windows, with their diamond shaped panes. The perfume was rich and heavy.

'The garden looks lovely Amelia,' Megan said sitting down. 'Your roses are especially beautiful. Just look at that white climbing one.'

'Yes Tommy bought and planted that for me when he came back from the Argentine. He's such a lovely man, don't you think so?' she asked none too subtly.

'Yes Amelia he is,' Megan smiled.

'You love him very much don't you Megan?'

Megan didn't reply immediately. She could feel the delicate pink stain spreading up her neck.

'Yes Amelia, I do. But is it so obvious? You don't think he knows do you? Oh Amelia I'd die of embarrassment if I thought he knew.'

'No dear, he doesn't know. The idea has never crossed his mind.'

I've loved him from the very first moment I met him,' she confessed. 'I knew it was hopeless. I knew I shouldn't, because he was a married man, and I knew how much Emma adored him. I always tried so hard not to let my feelings show. Up until now I thought I'd been successful.'

'There, there Megan,' she reached out and patted her hand. 'Don't worry, no one knows. I've grown very fond of you, and because of that I'm probably more observant as far as you're concerned. I could wish for nothing better than for you and Thomas to get together. He deserves to be happy, and I'm sure he could be with you. I have to say he seems more at peace with himself lately, and I think your influence has contributed to that.'

Megan had a lovely weekend up to the point where Tommy had returned from his father's. She had been taken aback by the manner in which he'd cut Amelia short saying "not open for discussion". It was a side to Tommy she had never seen.

The silent journey home. Tommy stony faced, his mouth a grim line. His whole demeanour stern and forbidding.

Later that evening, his sleeves rolled up bathing Laura, his expression relaxed once more, as Laura splashed and chortled contentedly.

Megan thought now might be a good time to bring up the subject of the way he'd spoken to Amelia.

'Tommy I think Amelia was upset about the way you spoke to her at lunchtime. I know you were very angry, but you really were quite rude.'

He looked up, 'Was I? I didn't mean to be, but you're right, I was very angry.'

'That's really no excuse for talking to her like that. I think you owe her an apology,' she said.

Tommy looked amused, 'Consider it done Megan, and I apologise to you too, for losing my temper.'

'You don't owe me an apology. I wouldn't have let you talk to me like that in the first place,' she said tartly.

Tommy actually laughed at that, 'Why Megan, I had no idea you could be so feisty.'

'There's quite a lot you don't know about me Tommy Lawrence,' she replied.

Autumn swept in with its vivid yellows, reds and bronze shades. The end of November saw Megan's birthday which fell on a Friday, ten days before Laura's first birthday.

The night before Tommy was there for his ritual hour with Laura, who was now growing at an alarming rate and into everything. Megan couldn't believe how much the little girl looked like Tommy. There was nothing of Emma. She shared Tommy's olive skin, dark grey eyes and thatch of jet black hair. The resemblance to her father was uncanny in so small a child

On leaving, he put his arm around Megan's shoulder giving her a peck on the cheek saying, 'Miss Rees it's your birthday tomorrow, and I'd like to take you out. I'll be round for Laura's time tomorrow as usual, but I've organised for Blanche to come with me to babysit. I shall expect you to be dressed to kill as I'm taking you out to dinner. And,' he went on, 'we now have two things to celebrate, your birthday and Monty holding out at Al Alamein, and forcing Rommel back. Maybe it's the turning point in this bloody war. Mind you, what we'll get for dinner with rationing being what it is I can't imagine, but I'm willing to risk it if you are.'

'Oh Tommy it sounds lovely, thank you, but you don't have to take me anywhere. I'm quite happy to cook supper as usual.'

'I know I don't have to, but I want to,' he flashed her a grin. 'C'mon Megan you deserve it, a night out, we both do.'

The following evening Tommy was there as promised with Blanche Watkins to babysit.

'Hello Megan,' she said. 'My you do look nice dear. Happy birthday and I hope you have a lovely evening.'

She'd washed her hair, and her soft brown curls shone. She wore a soft woollen two piece in a delicate shade of lavender and a white silk blouse. The outfit clung to her slender figure. Normally she wore no make-up, but tonight she did. With her high heeled shoes she was only a few inches shorter than Tommy. Her eyes sparkled with anticipation. She couldn't remember when she'd last gone out socially.

'Thank you Blanche. I was told to be dressed to kill,' she smiled, 'so I hope I've succeeded.'

'You certainly have,' Tommy's look showed his approval.

'Thank you, both of you,' she said feeling a surge of pleasure at the compliments.

The Eagle Hotel in Winchester was their destination. The menu was limited. They plumped for tomato soup, followed by chops, finishing off with cheese. The wine cellar was sadly depleted, but they opted for a good Chablis, the waiter informing them that it was the last one of that particular vintage, and goodness knows when they'd ever get more.

Immediately after the main course there was a power cut. Candles were hurriedly lit. Tommy sat back with a cigarette, after asking Megan first if she minded.

'No, go ahead Tommy. In fact would you mind if I had one too?' she laughed seeing the look of surprise on his face.

'Not at all.' He held out the packet. 'I didn't know you smoked.'

‘I only have one occasionally. A bad habit my brother got me started on. I started having one every evening with him after supper.’

‘Mmm sounds like Gareth’s got a lot to answer for. He started me smoking when I was a naive twenty year old, unaware and innocent of the dangers of wine, women and song, not to mention tobacco.’

‘I’m so glad he’s married and settled down with a family of his own. What’s Thomasina like Tommy?’

‘She’s a lovely kindly soul with all of her mother Maria’s attributes. She can cook, keep house, and if she turns out just like Maria, it’ll be a new addition to the family at roughly eighteen month intervals,’ he laughed. ‘That’ll keep your brother on his toes. It was Maria that tended to me after my accident, Thomasina’s father Jose fashioned me a pair of crutches. They’re a lovely family. What about you Megan? Do you ever think about marrying and having a family of your own?’

‘I think it’s a bit late for me. I’ve missed the boat. I’m thirty three today and most women of my age are already married. I spent much of my life looking after my father, so I have a little money put by, and the trust from my mother was invested wisely. Dad saw to that. Then when he died he left me the house, and a small legacy, so it’s really just a case of wondering what to do next. Maybe I’ll be like Amelia, alone but happy with my own company,’ she finished.

‘Well don’t let looking after Laura hold you back Megan. I’m serious, don’t leave it too late before deciding what you’re going to do next. Oh heck, I almost forgot,’ he said, his hand going to his pocket. He withdrew a small box. ‘Happy birthday and a special thanks for all your help this year.’

She opened it to reveal a small gold butterfly on a delicate chain.

'Why Tommy!' she gasped. 'Thank you, it's beautiful. I'm not used to such extravagant presents.'

The three piece band in the corner started to play Glen Miller's "String of Pearls".

'Would you like to dance?' he invited holding out his hand.

She rose gracefully. He put his arms around her, she shivered at his touch. She hadn't danced for so many years, that she'd forgotten how much she'd once loved it.

He held her close saying, 'You know the last time I danced was my birthday, three years ago. It seems a lifetime ago.'

She smiled, 'I had similar thoughts Tommy. You're a very good dancer.'

He looked even more amused, 'Once again I've got your brother to thank for that. He taught me to dance, so he didn't just teach me bad habits. Gareth taught me to ride a horse, play chess, Bidou, and if it wasn't for him, we wouldn't be here together right now.'

Megan eyes were almost on a level with Tommy's which she found slightly disconcerting. Could he see into her soul? She felt exposed, and did he know? She was grateful for the candlelight.

They were home by eleven thirty. Tommy switched off the engine and going round he opened her door. As she moved towards the path, he put out his hand staying her.

'Megan,' he said softly.

She turned to face him, 'Thank you again Tommy for a lovely evening.'

He looked into her eyes and, taking her face between his hands he kissed her very gently on the mouth. She took a sharp intake of breath as he released her.

'We should do it again sometime, Megan. I'll come in for Blanche, and I'll see you on Sunday. You haven't forgotten next weekend you're coming with me to Amelia's as it's Laura's first birthday. '

Alone in her bed she re-lived the evening, every moment of it. God! She mustn't read too much into it. When he'd taken her in his arms, she'd wanted it to go on forever. As they danced, she'd been so afraid that he might be able to read her thoughts. Like she'd told Amelia she would be mortified if Tommy knew how she felt about him. She wanted to continue to be his friend.

When his lips touched hers it had taken all her willpower not to put her arms around him returning his kiss. She knew he was still vulnerable, and it wouldn't be fair. And if she had encouraged him at that point where might it have led? Would it have taken them somewhere that they might later regret? But for all these thoughts it didn't stop her from wanting him. She finally fell into a troubled, restless sleep.

Chapter 19

Megan knew that Christmas was a bad time for Tommy. For the children's sake, and with her and Amelia to help they'd make it as festive as they could.

Amelia and Amy returned home in early January, leaving the house silent and as cold as the grave. Megan hated going round there, and Tommy had told her he hated going home.

As the anniversary of Emma's death approached, Tommy became more withdrawn. Megan wished they could all just go to bed one night and wake up to find the week had passed.

That year the fifteenth fell on a Friday. Megan had cooked supper. It had become customary for Tommy to have supper with Megan every Friday after Laura's bath and bedtime. She'd made up the fire and was waiting for Tommy to arrive. She glanced at her watch, he was already a little late. She wished he'd hurry up as Laura had a cold and had been crotchety all day.

The sooner she was in bed the better. By six thirty it was obvious Tommy had been held up, so she quickly bathed Laura and put her to bed.

As the evening wore on she began to worry, remembering that fateful night a year ago. Not once had Tommy missed Laura's bath time. Was he sick? Had he had an accident? The roads were icy. Could that wretched Satan have thrown him out in the woods somewhere? Was he lying out there freezing, unconscious maybe? By nine o' clock she was frantic. She couldn't go looking for him - she couldn't leave Laura. She was at her wits end when she heard the car door slam.

She rushed to the front door, and as she opened it, he stumbled in.

'Tommy are you okay? I've been so worried,' and then it hit her - the overpowering smell of brandy.

'That's nice Megan. Almost like being married and having the little woman sat at home worrying about my safety.' He blinked owlishly in the light.

'Oh Tommy,' she half laughed with sheer relief, 'you're drunk.'

'Yes I think I am,' he slurred.

'You need food, and plenty of black coffee to sober you up.'

'It's not food I need Megan,' he said grasping her firmly round the waist, and pulling her roughly towards him.

'Don't be silly Tommy,' she said, putting up her hands to fend him off. 'You're drunk,' she repeated.

'I know, and you're beautiful. You're a very desirable woman, Megan Rees.'

She could feel his breath on her face, smell the brandy fumes. Before she realised his intention, he was kissing her, his mouth on hers, crushing her against him. Oh God! This wasn't how it was supposed to be. She struggled to free herself, wrenching her mouth from his, she managed to gasp, 'Tommy, stop it, please don't.'

Now she was scared. He was a strong man. She had to stop him. He was kissing her again, begging her between kisses, 'Let me love you Meggie, please.'

Her resistance only seemed to fuel his desire. Suddenly she relaxed against him. He drew back to look at her and, in that moment, she slapped him with all the strength she could muster, a stinging open handed blow across his cheek. His head jerked to one side with the force of the blow, but it had the desired effect - it brought him to his senses. He let go of her abruptly, causing her to stagger back.

'Now sit down Tommy, I'll make some coffee, and as soon as you've sobered up a bit, you can go home.'

He slumped into a chair putting his head in his hands, 'Christ Megan! I'm sorry,' he muttered. 'I don't know what came over me.'

'Well I do, you're drunk, that's what came over you,' she said firmly, 'and that's all it is.'

She went to the kitchen, and looking into the mirror she straightened her hair, tucked her blouse in, it had come out of her skirt in the struggle, and she closed her eyes, waiting for the kettle to boil. The tears coursed down her face. Coffee made, she wiped her eyes, blew her nose and, picking up the tray she returned to the other room. He was sitting where she'd left him. The rattle of cups made him look up.

'Megan I'm sorry. I don't know what to say.' He didn't quite meet her eye. She saw the imprint of her hand across his cheek.

'Forget it Tommy, it doesn't matter. Nothing happened,' she said pushing a cup of coffee towards him. 'Please talk to me Tommy. You must talk.'

He looked up, and his eyes finally met hers, they were deeply troubled, full of anguish.

He sighed, and to Megan's relief he started to talk.

'From the moment I woke up this morning I thought of Emma, I honestly believed when I set off for hospital that last day, that she'd be home in the next couple of days. I miss her Megan. Then I started to think about Amy and Laura. It's been a year and I'm no nearer a permanent solution than I was the day Emma died. What am I going to do? They need the love of two parents, a home and to be together. I can't give them up.'

'I know Tommy, nobody's asking you to give them up, but it's only been a year. Give it time, these things have a way of working out. I know it's not an ideal situation but, so far you've managed to go to Swallowfield every single Saturday to see Amy. Amelia says she gets so excited every week when she knows you're coming. She hasn't forgotten you, and she's very happy with Amelia. I can tell that on the few occasions Laura and I have come with you. And as for Laura,' she went on, she's still a baby, but she already knows who you are, her first words were "Da-da", and you see her every day.'

'I know Laura thinks you're her mother Megan, you're the only woman's love she's ever known. I know I should be grateful, and I am, but tonight just before I was going to come round, I poured myself a stiff brandy to see me through, and then another and another until practically the whole bottle was gone. I don't know how much longer I can go on.'

He rose and crossed to the dying fire, as if to gather some warmth. Megan didn't know if it was the brandy or her imploring him to talk that had loosened his tongue, but she did know that this was the first time he'd spoken of Emma's death. He stood with his back to her, but she saw his shoulders move, and heard his stifled sob.

She came and stood behind him and put her hand on his shoulder. He turned slowly. She could see he felt shame for what had happened earlier, but she knew that the shame was also that she should witness his weakness.

He averted his face as she put her arms around him, burying his face in her hair, she felt his hot tears scalding her neck.

'I'm so very sorry Tommy,' she said, holding him tight.

He put his arms around her and clung to her, great sobs wracking his body. She comforted him the way she would a child. They stood for several minutes, until his sobs subsided.

'I must go Megan,' he mumbled as he disengaged himself from her arms, and swiftly left.

At lunchtime the following day, Browne's, the greengrocer's van pulled up outside Megan's house and Mr. Browne himself got out carrying a bunch of flowers - red carnations and winter greenery.

Megan went to the door, 'What's all this about then Mr. Browne,' she smiled.

'Well I don't know Miss Rees. Mr. Lawrence came down this morning and asked me if I'd got anything in my greenhouse. Well of course I don't grow much in the way of flowers any more, what with the war on and all that, more important to grow food now.' He paused to draw breath. 'Anyhow I still grow a few flowers in the corner of my greenhouse, for the missus like, and she made 'em look quite pretty with a few bits of green. Oh and I nearly forgot, there's this note.' He took a crumpled envelope from the pocket of his khaki dustcoat.

Megan took the flowers indoors and laying them on the kitchen table, she tore open the note.

Dear Megan,

I am so sorry about last night. I am ashamed of the way I behaved - you don't deserve it. Please forgive me.

Yours Tommy.

The day went by so slowly. Megan growing more nervous with every passing hour. How was she going to face him? She'd lain awake last night reliving his lips on hers, hearing his voice whispering, begging her to let him love her. She wanted him so badly, but not like that, full of drink, his mind full of Emma. Later when she'd held him close, she'd wanted him to make love to her, then she wouldn't have fought him off. Her face burned at the memory.

At six o'clock she heard the familiar tap at the door and Tommy came in looking subdued, 'Am I welcome, or am I banned?' he asked putting his head round the door.

Laura shrieked at the sound of his voice and staggered towards him holding up her chubby arms. He picked her up, kissing her saying, 'Hello my baby.'

'Well Laura's pleased to see you,' Megan answered not quite being able to bring herself to look at him.

'And you Megan, are you pleased to see me? Did you get my note? '

'I'm embarrassed Tommy, for both of us,' she said walking to the window and staring out into the darkness

Putting Laura down, he came and stood behind her putting both his hands on her upper arms he said, 'Don't be Megan. You have nothing to reproach yourself for. Listen to me, I am truly sorry. I'd do anything for it not to have happened, but it did. Please don't let it spoil our friendship. You, your brother and Amelia are all I've got. I can't afford to lose you. I promise nothing like that will ever happen again. And another thing, if only you knew what my head felt like this morning, you'd have mercy on me.'

She laughed, 'Oh Tommy, it serves you right.'

'Then am I forgiven?' he asked.

'I haven't got a lot of choice, I see you every day, and now you'd better get started with Laura's bath time.'

Early May Tommy told Megan about a new Army land girl that had started on the farm, Liz Shelton. 'God we could do with extra help. She's a good worker, and I'm already wondering how we managed before she came.'

'That's good Tommy,' Megan said, who privately thought Tommy worked much too hard.

Over the next few weeks Megan was to hear Liz's name crop up time and again in conversations with Tommy. She found herself more than a little curious about the new land girl. Now the summer evenings were here Tommy had suggested to Megan that they resumed something they had started last summer, and that was very occasionally on a Friday evening they'd stroll down to the Fox and Hounds, Megan pushing Laura in the pram. Now Laura was getting bigger Tommy had bought a pushchair, a little less cumbersome than the pram.

So it was that on one Friday evening Megan was to have her curiosity satisfied regarding Liz Shelton.

Megan sat on a wooden bench at an old rustic table in the pub garden. Tommy lay stretched out on the grass playing with Laura, who was now eighteen months old, and a mirror image of Tommy. She loved to see him with his children, who both adored him.

'Megan would you like to come to Swallowfield next Saturday? I'm going to bring Amelia and Amy back with me, and I know Amelia loves to see you. We can stay over and come home Sunday. What do you say?'

Megan didn't hesitate, their easy friendship had reverted back to what it had been before what Megan thought of as that hiccup back in January.

'That would be nice Tommy, if you're sure. It means you have to sleep on Amelia's settee, not the most comfortable night for you. '

While she was answering Tommy she watched a young woman coming up the path wearing jodhpurs and a bright yellow shirt that was straining across an ample bosom. She had flaming red hair and wore bright scarlet lipstick. She was as curvaceous as any Hollywood starlet.

'Hello Mr. Lawrence,' she called out as she bounced up the path.

He looked surprised, 'Oh hello Liz. Can I get you a drink?' he offered getting to his feet.

'Thanks, a small shandy would be fine. I really only came down for some ciggies.'

'Here, come and sit with us and meet Megan,' he indicated the bench. She came over but did not sit.

'Hello,' she nodded in Megan's direction.

'Megan this is Liz Shelton, our landgirl. What cigarettes do you want Liz?' he asked.

'Twenty Woodbines please,' she fumbled in her pocket for money.

'It's all right I'll get them,' he offered and went into the pub.

'Is this his little girl?' Liz nodded towards Laura.

'Yes this is Laura his youngest one,' Megan replied.

'She's gorgeous isn't she,' she said sitting down on the grass beside Laura, 'But then so's he, isn't he? Very sad about him losing his wife, wasn't it? Have you known him long?'

Megan's heart sank. This brash young woman with her bright red lips obviously fancied Tommy. They worked in close proximity every day. Stop it she told herself you've no right to feel jealous. Before she had chance to answer any of Liz's questions, Tommy returned.

He sat back down on the grass holding out his arms to Laura.

'She's a beautiful little girl, Mr. Lawrence, such lovely eyes, she looks just like you. I love kids, I've got three young brothers. I'd like to have lots of babies one day.'

Megan saw the sidelong glance she gave Tommy.

'Yes, well lots of babies cost lots of money Liz. You'll have to find a rich husband,' he teased.

She shrugged, 'Oh I quite like the idea of love in a cottage. Money doesn't mean much does it?'

'Only when you've got plenty,' he grinned. Megan sat quietly watching this exchange until Tommy said, 'Shall we go then Megan? It's past Laura's bedtime.'

'Yes I'm off too. Ta for the drink and the ciggies. See you tomorrow Mr. Lawrence.' She flashed Tommy a dazzling smile, and giving Megan a cursory nod, with a wave of her hand she strode off.

'Goodbye Liz, nice to have met you,' Megan smiled.

Over the next few weeks Tommy mentioned Liz Shelton several times. Megan felt a small stab of jealousy. She told herself that she was being foolish, that it was only natural he should mention the people he worked with.

Another time he was slightly late coming to bath Laura, his explanation being that Liz had said that she loved to ride, and Tommy had promised that if their work was finished on time that afternoon he'd let her ride the steadier grey, and he would take Satan as he needed to go up through Cokers Wood to check on the new gates that were being put in. He said he didn't know how competent she might be, but he said how much he'd actually enjoyed riding just for pure pleasure.

'And,' Megan had asked trying to keep it casual, 'How competent is she?'

'Yes she's not a bad rider, and she works hard, so I thought it would be a bit of a treat for her.'

One Friday lunchtime Megan was surprised to see Tommy striding up her front path.

'Is something wrong Tommy?' she asked as she opened the door.

'No, I've just been into Winchester to the cattle market. We were selling some calves, and I called in to tell you, please be ready to go out this evening. I'm bringing Blanche with me to babysit Laura. After I've put Laura to bed, we can go. I need to talk to you Megan. Where is Laura by the way?'

'That sounds very mysterious Tommy. Where are we going? And Laura's just been put down for her nap. Would you like a cup of coffee?'

'No thanks Megan, I'll see you tonight.'

A shiver of apprehension ran through her. It sounded ominous. Was Tommy going to tell her he was thinking of remarrying, just to prepare her perhaps? Had he fallen for Liz Shelton's flirtatious charms? The whole afternoon similar thoughts whirled round her mind. How could she part from Laura? But she'd always known it could happen. Tommy was far too attractive to remain unattached. She took Laura for a walk after her nap. They went to the pond to feed the ducks. Megan loved to see her laughing and squealing with delight as the ducks came right out of the water for the bread.

She took special care with her appearance, wearing a floral dress in muted shades of greens and pinks. Her long tanned legs were bare. By the time Tommy arrived with Blanche she was a nervous wreck.

Laura bathed, talcum powdered and put to bed. Tommy said, 'Right, are you ready Megan? We'll be off Blanche. We won't be too late.'

As soon as they were outside Megan asked, 'Where are we going. Tommy?'

'Just for a short drive. Then I thought we could go into Winchester for a bite to eat. But first I have to talk to you.'

He drove to Bracken Hill, a local beauty spot overlooking the surrounding villages. Parking the car, he suggested they walk. Megan had remained silent throughout the short drive. She felt physically sick. They walked along the footpath for a few yards, where there was a weatherworn wooden bench. Tommy said, 'Let's sit Megan. I've something I want to ask you.'

Megan was filled with trepidation. 'Oh please Tommy,' she burst out, 'what's this all about?'

'God Megan, don't look so scared. I'm not very good at this, but what I'm trying to say is - will you marry me?'

She stared at him, hardly daring to believe what she'd heard.

'Don't look so taken aback, Megan. You must have known it was coming.'

'No, Tommy. No, I didn't know it was coming,' she stammered, blushing to the roots of her hair. 'I had absolutely no idea.'

Her mind was in turmoil. He'd never given her any indication of what his feelings towards her were. If it came to that, what were his feelings? What had prompted his proposal? Probably nothing more than the fact that his children needed a mother, and he could do with someone to run his home.

'Megan,' he said quietly, 'aren't you going to put me out of my misery?'

I'd like to marry you very much Tommy, but I'm not sure.'

'Would you like more time to think about it?'

'No, time has nothing to do with it,' she hesitated not sure of how to go on.

'Then what is it Megan?'

She couldn't look at him as she whispered, 'You don't love me Tommy, do you?'

There was a hushed silence broken only by the sighing of the breeze through the trees. She closed her eyes. I do so want him to love me. She wanted him to take her in his arms and tell her, yes I do love you, to kiss her fears away, but she knew he wasn't going to do that. Tommy was honest, and she knew that they had to begin with the truth between them, or what chance would they stand.

He caught her hands in his, 'Look at me Megan.'

She opened her eyes and suddenly she didn't care if he loved her or not - she had enough love for the two of them. She'd make him love her one day.

He looked deeply into her eyes, 'No, I don't love you Megan. I can't lie to you. I respect you and I'm very, very fond of you. Don't you think we could make a better life for both of us if we were married? My children need a mother, and I know how much you love them. I'll not pretend that's not a big part of why I'm asking you to marry me - but I need you too, Megan.'

Those last words gave Megan a glimmer of hope, *he said he needed her*.

'Yes Tommy. I'll marry you.'

He stood and pulled her gently to her feet still holding her hands, he drew her to him. She put her arms around his neck and he bent his head. His kiss was slow and tender. She felt his lips linger as she slowly pulled away.

Taking her face between his hands he said, 'Please Megan, let's not wait too long, make it soon.'

Over supper Tommy asked her why she'd looked so scared just before he'd proposed.

Megan flushed scarlet, 'Oh Tommy, I feel so silly now. I don't know whether to tell you or not.'

'Go on,' he urged.

'I thought you were going to tell me that you were going to get married again.'

'Well I was, sort of, wasn't I?'

'Not to me Tommy.'

'Well who, for goodness sake?'

'Liz Shelton. I know she fancies you.'

He burst out laughing, 'Megan give me credit! Who in their right mind would look at Liz with you around? She strikes me as being a real man eater.'

Megan wrote to Gareth and Thomasina, and the following day, Saturday, Tommy's day for visiting Amy, they set off for Swallowfield. They arrived to see Amy at the window looking out for Tommy.

Amelia was delighted, 'I'm so very happy for both of you,' she said hugging Megan, and turning to embrace Tommy too she said, 'I hope you realise just how blessed you are Thomas, and you be good to her, or you'll have me to deal with.'

'I certainly will Ma'am,' he twinkled. They were married quietly at the Registry Office in Reading a month later, with Georgie and Sylvia as witnesses. At Amelia's insistence they spent three nights at the Royal Hotel in Brighton. That was her wedding present while she looked after the children.

Chapter 20

Tommy stood by the window and lit a cigarette.

'If you'd like to use the bathroom first Megan.'

She emerged looking self-conscious in a long cream silk nightdress, with thin shoestring straps. The thin silk clung to her body showing the long line of her legs, her breasts, their nipples clearly visible through the flimsy material. He looked at her appreciatively.

He took his turn in the bathroom and came out wearing only pyjama bottoms, even in the depths of winter he never used the tops. He came and sat on the edge of the bed. He ran his hand lightly up her arm, sensing her nervousness, and bending his head he kissed her bare shoulder. Reaching out he switched off the light.

He felt her hand on his chest, he kissed her, lots of small kisses, her throat, her neck, and finally his lips found hers. She smelled of sandalwood.

She gave a shiver of anticipation as she whispered, 'Tommy, I've never...'

He silenced her, 'Ssh, I know Megan.'

He slipped the straps of her nightgown off her shoulders, pulling her gently against him. He caressed her breasts, he felt her nipples tighten and come erect at his touch. It took him every ounce of self-control to continue to go slowly.

He gently removed the nightgown and his pyjama bottoms as he slid into bed beside her. He stroked her body, and felt her tremble as he parted her thighs with his hand. She started to return his caresses, moaning softly. He lowered his mouth to hers once more and her lips parted under his.

She must have sensed his growing urgency as she whispered, 'Now Tommy.'

'Are you sure you're ready?' he asked in a low husky voice.

'Oh God! Yes, yes,' she urged.

He needed no further urging. She wrapped her legs around him as he plunged into her, bringing them both to a swift shuddering climax.

He heard the muffled sob, and sensed the silent tears. He felt her tremble, and he turned to her taking her in his arms, he gentled her the way he would a frightened horse, stroking her, whispering soothingly, softly until the trembling stopped.

'I'm sorry Tommy. I didn't mean to cry. You must be sadly disappointed in your wedding night. I tried to tell you I'd never...'

He kissed her, 'I know what you tried to tell me, that it was your first time. But I never thought I was so bad at it that I would actually bring a woman to tears. Possibly it should be you that's disappointed,' he smiled into the darkness.

She gave a nervous giggle, hearing the humour in his voice, 'I can't explain, but it was the opposite, that you were too good at it, I never dreamt it would feel so good. The tears just came, a kind of ecstatic release just washed over me. Was it really okay for you?'

'It was more than okay, but on second thoughts maybe you could do with a little more practice,' he suggested with a throaty chuckle.

‘Oh yes please Tommy, they do say that practice makes perfect,’ she said, and with that she rolled over trapping him beneath her.

He laughed delightedly, ‘Mrs Lawrence we’ve got all night to keep practising till we get it right.’

Long after she’d fallen asleep her head on his shoulder, did he whisper, ‘Megan please don’t love me too much.’

Tommy woke early the next morning, used the bathroom and let himself quietly out of the room. He walked along the seafront. It was a grey overcast day, a fine drizzle had already started.

He thought about last night, his new wife. Tommy had a strong sexual appetite and he knew Megan as an intensely shy person and had wondered how the intimate side of a marriage with her would be. After last night he knew he need have no fears, she’d been a willing partner. He’d been both surprised and delighted when she’d taken the initiative at one stage. Emma had once used the unkind phrase when referring to Megan as ‘a typical dried up spinster’ and nothing could be further from the truth.

He returned to the hotel to find a maid about to knock on their door with early morning tea.

‘Here, let me take that from you,’ he offered as he unlocked the door.

Megan lay stretched full length, the covers thrown back, every contour of her slender body accentuated through the cream silk. He stood looking down at her. She stretched and stirred, putting out a hand to his side of the bed, opening her eyes to discover him standing there. She reached for the bedding to cover herself. He caught at her hand as he sat beside her.

‘Don’t be shy Megan. You have a lovely body, don’t hide it.’ He was aware of her embarrassment as she blushed so he said lightly, ‘Can I pour you a cup of tea, Madam?’

'Yes please Tommy that would be very nice. You're all wet. Where have you been?'

'Just for a walk. It's miserable out, wet and cold,' he said handing her a cup of tea. 'What would you like to do today?'

'I don't know. Have you any ideas?'

'Looking at you in that very attractive nightdress I've got plenty,' he grinned, 'but I suppose seeing as we only have a couple of days, we should use it sightseeing. We can't very well go back and tell Amelia we only saw our bedroom ceiling. So how about we buy an umbrella and explore Brighton? My other ideas can wait for tonight,' he finished.

They went to the Pavilion, looked round the shops, stopping for lunch at a little cafe for fish and chips, washed down with scalding hot tea in a brown teapot reminiscent of Melchet Court days.

That evening over dinner Tommy asked Megan what she wanted to do with her cottage.

'I don't know Tommy. I honestly hadn't thought about it. What do you think?'

'It's up to you. You could try and rent it out if you want, or you can sell it and invest the money.'

'We've got two cars and we only need one, two lots of furniture as well. There are so many things we haven't thought of.'

'There's plenty of time to sort these things out Megan. If these are the biggest problems we're going to have to face, we'll be lucky.'

They returned to Amelia's on Sunday morning, leaving again just after lunch, taking an excited Amy with them, whose birthday it was the following week.

'Am I coming to live with you and Auntie Megan and Laura now Daddy?' she asked not fully understanding what was happening.

‘Yes baby, we’re going to be a family again,’ Tommy said hugging her, seeing the joy on her face.

‘Like when Mummy was here, before she went to heaven,’ she said innocently.

He looked at Megan across the top of Amy’s head. He hesitated then made the decision.

‘Yes darlin’ just like before, except now with Auntie Megan. It will be like having a new Mummy. Would you like that?’

‘Oh yes,’ she said matter of factly, ‘Cos now I can tell Maggie and Jenny that I’ve got a Mummy too. Will I call you Mummy now?’ she looked at Megan enquiringly.

Megan glanced at Tommy who nodded imperceptably.

‘Yes, if you’d like to Amy,’ Megan replied.

Later she questioned the wisdom of Amy calling her “Mummy”.

‘After all I’m not her mother, Tommy.’

‘Megan,’ he said patiently. ‘She’s a five year old child. Children are adaptable. She wants a mother. She wants to be the same as her cousins, and when she starts school in September she’ll want to be the same as all the other kids. She’s happy to accept you as her mother. She probably hardly remembers Emma anyway, after all it’s been eighteen months since she died. Other than a vague memory kept alive by us, what can she remember? When she’s older she can be told all about Emma, both of them can. For now,’ he went on, ‘let her be a child with a mummy and daddy like all the other kids.’

The war carried on, but the back of the German army had been broken in July that year. One of the biggest tank battles in history had occurred on the plain of Kursk in Russia.

In September Amy started school. She was excited and eager that first morning. Megan told Tommy she wished she’d had longer to get to know Amy. Between her and

Tommy marrying and Amy starting school, it had been barely six weeks.

Laura contracted whooping cough. She was so wracked with coughing at nights that Megan had taken to slipping from their bed and wrapping Laura in a blanket and would go downstairs to let Tommy get some sleep. Nearly a week of sleepless nights, with the prospect of another one ahead, she carried Laura down. She bathed the little girl with a damp cloth, changing her pyjamas which were soaked with sweat. She held her in her arms, but every time she attempted to lay her down on the settee, she'd cry. Eventually she fell asleep in Megan's arms. Megan went wearily to the settee and, still holding Laura, she sat down swinging her feet up she too fell asleep.

That was how Tommy found them as a milky dawn filtered through. He stood looking down at them, his wife and child. When Amy had been small and had had chicken pox and measles, it had been him, not Emma, that had heard her cry and had got up to comfort and nurse her. He knew Megan had been up for several nights with Laura, and she wasn't even her child. What kind of woman was she that he'd married?

Removing Laura gently from her arms he woke Megan.

'Is it morning yet?' she asked sleepily.

'Just about,' he replied. Come to bed. She's fast asleep.' He looked at the sleeping Laura in his arms. 'The worst is over.'

Once upstairs he laid Laura in her cot and walked back into their room. Megan was already asleep. He leant over and pulled the covers over her before going downstairs.

An hour later, the aroma of coffee filling the warm kitchen, Amy appeared rubbing the sleep from her eyes asking where Mummy was. Tommy smiled as he held out his arms.

'Good morning Amy, Mummy's asleep. It's Sunday, she's going to have a lie-in. Now what shall we have for our breakfast do you think?'

'Soft boiled eggs with smashed bread and butter like Mummy makes for me and Laura,' she said eagerly.

Tommy thought how fortunate they were, despite the rationing, eggs and butter were available to the lucky few living as they did in the country.

'Okay soft boiled eggs with smashed bread and butter it is, and you can help me get it.'

During Christmas nineteen forty three Amelia came to stay for two weeks, much to Amy's delight. She eagerly related her activities at school to her beloved Mielie.

Despite the war they had a joyful family Christmas, with all three adults delighting in seeing the two little girls playing happily together under the same roof, united as a family.

They saw in nineteen forty four just the three of them, wishing one another a good year ahead, and expressing the hope that the war would soon come to an end.

In April they received some bad news. Georgie let them know that Matthew's plane had been shot down somewhere over Germany. Tommy felt an unexpected sadness for the brother he'd never really known.

'It's strange Megan, but I didn't know Matthew. I last saw him when he was sixteen or so, just before I went to the Argentine. I don't know his wife or child,' he sighed. 'Georgie wants me to go to his funeral in Bournemouth. Please will you come with me?'

She nodded, 'Of course I will. I'll just have to see if I can organise for Blanche to look after the children. Is Sylvia going too?'

'Yes, when I spoke to Georgie on the telephone I told him we'd pick them up at Winchester Station, and we'll drive down together.'

They attended the funeral. There were two Air Force colleagues of Matthew's, and various relations of his wife. Tommy recognised Mrs. Metcalf, Alice's mother. After the service he spoke to Alice asking what her plans were. She said that she and the boy would move back to Swallowfield, where her mother could take care of him during the day, and she could get a job in Reading.

Tommy and Megan picked the girls up on their way home. Later, the children in bed Tommy suggested a drink.

'Yes please Tommy, I'll have a sherry.'

He poured Megan her sherry and himself a large brandy. They sat listening to a concert on the Home Service, during which he poured himself a second one. He wasn't particularly a drinking man but he felt emotionally drained, and in need of sustenance. Concert over, they went to bed.

Once ready for bed Tommy sat on his side of the bed, his head in his hands. He was thirty nine years old, still fit and lean with a flat stomach and well-muscled thighs from years in the saddle. The army had turned him down, and here was his brother at thirty five - dead. All chances of getting to know Matthew after the war was over, gone forever with his death. A tear slid down his face, but he brushed it away with the back of his hand.

Suddenly Megan was kneeling before him, putting her arms around his neck she said softly, 'Tommy don't torment yourself. You mustn't feel guilty. I know you wish you'd got to know him, but you've had enough to deal with in your own life, don't reproach yourself.'

He looked at her this woman who could read him so well, and who he realised, he hardly knew at all.

'But I do feel guilty Megan, I can't help it. I should have got in touch when I came home, seven years ago, and now it's too late.

She raised her face to kiss him. His arms went round her. He looked deeply into her green eyes and was filled with an aching desire, more powerful than anything he'd ever felt in his life.

His voice was thick with passion as he groaned, 'Oh God Megan, I want you.'

He removed her nightdress and started to caress her, within minutes they were both fully aroused as he laid her on the bed, slipping gently into her. He could feel her hands clawing at his back as their lovemaking intensified until finally she whimpered crying out, 'I love you Tommy.'

He too shivered with pleasure as he came into her.

Afterwards they lay their arms around each other with Tommy's one hand stroking her light brown curls. As they were drifting towards sleep she murmured, 'I love you Tommy.'

'Shush Megan, don't,' he mumbled as he leaned in closer kissing her, as if to silence her declaration of love.

Suddenly she was wide awake.

'Why Shush Megan? Is there something wrong with me loving you Tommy?'

He felt her body tense, 'Leave it Megan, let's be happy with what we have.'

'No Tommy. I can't leave it, and I am happy with what we have but don't treat me like a criminal because I tell you I love you. You're my husband. It's not a sin. You make me feel guilty for saying it.'

He sat up swinging his legs out of bed, 'I didn't mean to make you feel bad Megan, I'm sorry.' He went on, 'But I'm not ready to love again, don't you understand?'

'No, damn you Tommy Lawrence, I don't understand,' she said coldly. 'I knew when we married you didn't love me, and I'm not asking you to, but neither of us can help the way we feel. Doesn't what I want count for anything in this marriage?'

Before he had chance to reply, to try and explain further, Megan had got up and swiftly left the room closing the door quietly behind her. She went to the spare room where she spent the night.

Oh Lord, what was the matter with him? Why couldn't he just have accepted that she loved him? Why was he fighting against it? His experience with Catriona had not been a good one, it had left him wary and distrusting. During his marriage to Emma he'd sometimes felt burdened by her overwhelming need, her all-consuming love. Why was he thinking like that? Megan wasn't Catriona or Emma. She was a gentle loving person, putting both his, and his children's needs before her own.

Sleep was a long time coming that night.

Chapter 21

Megan lay in bed sleep eluding her, she couldn't stop thinking. Her mind was in turmoil. She loved Tommy desperately, but she'd never told him so until earlier when it had slipped out in the heat of lovemaking. She knew he didn't love her, and she vowed never again, not even during those most intimate of moments, would she ever tell him she loved him. One day Tommy Lawrence, you'll tell me you love me, she told herself. He denied it with his words, but his body told her differently. She had to believe that; it was the only way she could go on.

She was downstairs at six o' clock in her dressing gown, making sandwiches for Amy, for school, when Tommy came down. He came up behind her and put his arms around her waist, nuzzling her neck.

'I'm sorry Megan, I truly am,' he whispered. Please forgive me. I didn't mean to hurt you. I don't know what's wrong with me.'

Well you might not know, she thought, but I do, you're so afraid to commit yourself.

She turned her head slightly, 'It's okay Tommy.'

He rested his freshly shaved cheek against hers as she leaned back against him. His arms still clasped around her waist she could feel his growing arousal, as he kissed her neck murmuring how good she smelt.

Just then the door opened to reveal two little figures in their pyjamas.

Tommy groaned, 'Oh why couldn't they have stayed asleep just a little bit longer?'

Megan laughed as she moved away from the circle of his arms.

'I woke Laura up and brought her down for breakfast Mummy,' Amy's voice piped, sounding pleased with herself.

By the eighth of June the liberation of Western Europe had begun. It started on the fifth when endless convoys crossed the English Channel towards the French coast. Three million British, Americans and Canadians were prepared for the invasion. The papers called it the longest day. It really looked as if the war was going the Allies way at last.

Megan was in general content with her life with Tommy. He was a good husband, kind, thoughtful, and an exciting and imaginative lover. She loved Laura and Amy as if they were her own, in fact there were times, especially with Laura, that she forgot she wasn't. She'd cared for Laura from the age of six weeks, and although she'd only had Amy for the year that she and Tommy had been married, she was such a happy outgoing child she couldn't fail to love her too.

She wanted only two things to make her life complete. To be sure that Tommy loved her and a child of her own. The subject of children had never arisen between them. Megan had assumed that Tommy was content with the family he had, and she had no particular desire, until recently, for a child of her own. She hadn't bargained for a change of heart. Lately she thought constantly about a child, a child of her body, hers and Tommy's. Her shyness had so far held her back from broaching the subject, she knew she mustn't leave it too long. Tommy was already thirty nine and she would be thirty five in November, her birthday came and was gone,

Christmas nineteen forty four came and she still hadn't mentioned anything to Tommy.

Amelia came and spent Christmas with them. The world prayed for an end to the war. The Allies were slowly reconquering land controlled by Germany. Romania had capitulated in August, and Bulgaria had signed an armistice in October.

Megan's Christmas present to Tommy had been a new, heavy silver chain for his mother's ring which he still wore round his neck, nineteen years after her death. The old one had broken, luckily indoors, had it been outside he would probably have lost the ring. He'd been playing with Amy and Laura, a game they called 'Bears' which consisted of Tommy on hands and knees, making frightful roaring noises, which both terrified and delighted them. They'd shriek and squeal as he pretended to try and catch them, and consequently during one of these rough and tumbles, the chain, which had worn thin over the years, snapped.

Tommy had been touched by the thought that Megan had put into his gift.

'I know how much that ring means to you,' she said as she gave it to him, 'and it's quite exquisite. It would be a pity to lose it. What will you do with it eventually? Are you saving it for Amy, when she's grown up?'

He shook his head, 'No, not particularly. My mother gave it to me before she died saying she hoped I'd find someone I'd love enough to give it to. Somehow I've never been able to bring myself to part with it - silly really I suppose.'

Gareth had told Megan about Tommy's affair with Catriona, and there had been Emma. She wondered if there had been any specific reason why neither of them had been given the amethyst ring.

'Emma pestered the hell out of me to give it to her, several times. She used to make such a big thing about it,' he sighed. 'She accused me of not loving her when I refused one time.'

Amelia had been persuaded to stay with them till the end of January. The weather had turned bitterly cold and, as Megan had said, why go home to a cold empty house. By the time she left, there was something else to celebrate, Poland had been liberated.

Nineteen forty five was in its fifth month when, on the eighth of May in the French city of Reims, Germany signed an unconditional surrender. Three months later on the fifteenth of August, nine days after the bombing of Hiroshima, Emperor Hirohito announced his decision to surrender. The war was finally over.

Men returned to their wives, mothers welcomed their sons home, fathers returned to their children, some of whom they were seeing for the first time. Many didn't return at all.

Megan still hadn't mentioned her desire for a child. At times her longing had become unbearable, and she knew the time was fast approaching that if she didn't speak soon, it would be too late. Laura would be four in December, and Amy was already seven.

Amelia came to stay for the last two weeks of the school holidays. Megan thought she'd aged since they'd seen her last, and later that night, in the privacy of their bedroom, she commented on this to Tommy.

'Yes I suppose she has, but none of us is getting any younger Megan. You're the only one that doesn't look any different to when I first met you, d'you remember? When Gareth brought you here to look at houses, that was six years ago,' he added.

Megan knew she still retained that air of youthfulness, her body was still firm, he figure was as slender as it had always been. Was this perhaps the moment to bring up the subject of a child before it was too late?

'Thanks, I'm glad I don't look any different to you, you look pretty good yourself, but like you say, the years are passing. Tommy...' she hesitated, 'I wonder if...' she tailed off again.

'You wondered what Megan? Go on,' he encouraged.

'I want a child Tommy,' her voice was barely audible, 'before it's too late.'

He rolled over onto his elbow, and leaning over her, he studied her face in the half light of the summer night.

'Why Megan? What brought this on? We've got two children, isn't that enough?' he queried.

She felt rather than saw his penetrating gaze. She couldn't bring herself to answer, she just shook her head dumbly.

He kissed her gently on the lips, then asked again, 'Aren't our two enough?'

'Tommy they're not ours. You have two children, and no matter how much I love them, and I do, you know I do, they will never be mine. They're yours and Emma's,' she mumbled turning her face into the pillow.

Megan had never been jealous of Tommy's first marriage or of Emma. She'd accepted it as a fact, a part of his past, but now she wanted his child.

He cupped her face in his hand turning her gently back to face him.

'Oh Megan, I'm sorry. I never thought that you might want children. Maybe it's something we should have talked about before we got married.'

'You don't want any more children, do you?' she accused, a sob rising in her throat, despite her determination not to get overly emotional.

'No darlin', it's not that. Megan I'm forty years old,' he said. 'You don't think I'm too old to be starting over with babies again?'

'I don't know, you're a lovely father Tommy. You love your children, and they adore you, and I want a child so badly,' she pleaded, feeling him weaken.

'I don't know. If you were to have a baby, what if anything were to go wrong?'

'What do you mean, like what?' she asked, not understanding.

'Emma died when Laura was born. I don't want to risk losing you too Megan,' he said his voice full of emotion.

'Oh Tommy you won't be risking anything,' her heart leapt. 'Emma didn't die because Laura was born,' she paused waiting for this to sink in, before she went on. 'She died of pneumonia.'

He lay silent for a moment, 'This is very important to you isn't it Megan? You asked me once if what you wanted in this marriage counted for anything, well it does, and I suppose this is my chance to prove that whatever you want is important to me.'

'Can I take that as a "yes"?' she asked breathlessly.

'I must be crazy,' he whispered as he brought his lips down to hers once more.

She broke away saying, 'Oh Tommy you don't know what this means to me.'

'Well now we've decided, we'd better not waste any more time. Let's get started Mrs. Lawrence.'

His hands moved over her body flooding her with desire, whispers of pleasure teased her. A tongue of white hot fire licked through her as they made love slowly, tenderly with both of them reaching an earth shattering climax simultaneously.

Long after Tommy had fallen asleep she lay on her back with her knees drawn up - she'd read somewhere that it increased the chances of pregnancy to adopt that position after intercourse, a way to keep his seed within her. She didn't know if this was a fact, but it wouldn't do any harm to try.

Mrs. Stewart-Shenley had a telephone installed in Tommy's house. Things were changing now the war was over. Blanche's husband was among the first to be demobbed. They still had a land girl, and they had employed a young school leaver as a stable lad. Life had become a little easier for Tommy. He had more time to spend with Megan and the children.

The week before Amelia was due to return to Swallowfield, Tommy had just come in from work when the telephone rang. It was Mrs. Stewart-Shenley, she'd been returning from Winchester and, passing the part of the estate that included Cokers Wood, she'd seen some gypsies setting up camp. Would Tommy go and see them just to let them know that the estate was aware of their presence in the area. He didn't need to be harsh and move them on, but if he wouldn't mind keeping his eye on the situation.

'Dammit,' Tommy cursed, 'I'm not saddling up again. I'll drive along there. If she can see them from the road then I can obviously do the same. I won't be long Megan.'

'Can I come Daddy?' four year old Laura begged.

'Come on then Lolly,' he said sweeping her up into his arms.

She giggled, she loved it when he called her Lolly. He said it was short for Lollipop, because she was the sweetest of all. She idolised him. After supper, bathed and dressed in her pyjamas, she'd climb onto his lap saying, 'Snuggle me Daddy.' She'd invariably fall asleep there, Megan removing her and carrying her up to bed.

Supper will be an hour or so yet, Tommy,' Megan said as he set off with Laura to talk to the gypsies.

Chapter 22

Tommy drove out of the main gates taking the Winchester road, Laura sitting beside him clutching her favourite rag doll. He hadn't gone far when he saw them.

Five caravans in a clearing beside the road, the horses were tethered on the opposite side, where there was plenty of grazing.

Getting out of the car, he picked Laura up. He knew the inevitable dogs would appear as soon as he approached. He hadn't gone more than a few steps when an Irish wolfhound, grey and whiskery, rushed out from beneath the first caravan, closely followed by two lurchers and a fox terrier yapping excitedly round his heels.

Tommy had no fear of dogs and walked purposefully towards the camp. A couple of older women were sitting on the steps of one caravan contentedly smoking their pipes. Three younger women tended the children, and the cooking pots suspended over the fire.

The smell that emanated from the pots Tommy recognised as hare - a strong gamey smell, mixed with wild thyme and onions.

A vision from long ago flashed through his mind, of Miriam with her exotic looks, her dark tumbling curls, and her vivid coloured clothes.

He approached the two older women smiling pleasantly, 'Good evening. Your supper smells good.'

The one just stared at him suspiciously, the other answered civilly, 'Thank you, a man needs good food to fill his belly.'

She was like a fully blown rose, past it's best, but a trace of the beauty she had once been still remained. She wore a belt of gold coins around her waist which jangled as she rose from the steps. He noticed her necklace and earrings were of smaller gold coins.

'Is your man around by any chance?' Tommy asked, aware that it was probably the woman who answered him whose husband was the leader, judging by her authoritative manner and her adornments, although he knew, on the odd occasion, a matriarch led the tribe.

'The menfolk went to the village for baccy. They'll be back soon,' she replied.

It was highly unlikely that the gypsy men would have gone to the village en masse for tobacco - much more likely to be out in the woods setting snares. He decided to go along with her explanation and grinned wryly.

'Tell them I'll be along in the morning. I'm the estate manager. I just wanted a word with your man.' All the while he'd been there Laura had been trying to reach down murmuring, 'Nice doggie, nice doggies.'

The gypsy smiled - a slow smile, 'It's all right, you can set the babby down, the dogs won't hurt her.'

Tommy put Laura down and immediately the wolfhound put out an enormous pink tongue and licked her face. She laughed delightedly.

Tommy nodded at the woman, 'Enjoy your supper.' Taking Laura by the hand, he walked slowly back to the car feeling several pairs of eyes boring into his back.

He arrived home some ten minutes later to the smell of his own supper cooking.

'Did you find them all right?' Megan asked.

'Mmm,' he replied thoughtfully. 'I hate to say it, but I've got a feeling they could be trouble. Anyway never mind the gypsies, is supper nearly ready - I'm starving.'

'Me too Daddy,' Laura said in an effort to emulate him.

He hooted with laughter saying, 'Well go and find your big sister and tell her supper's ready.'

Amelia and Megan smiled indulgently at him. Tommy spoiled both of his children shamelessly, leaving all forms of discipline to Megan, who was never too strict, but always firm. Both of the girls understood perfectly just how far they could go, and rarely overstepped the mark.

Tommy returned to the camp early the next morning. He made an imposing figure as he approached on the better tempered grey.

The dogs didn't bark and the first one to notice him was the woman who'd sat glowering at him yesterday. She turned to one of the young women and spoke rapidly. The woman disappeared into the nearest caravan. The woman with the gold coins came down the steps saying. 'Billy Lee has been sent for.'

No sooner were the words out of her mouth when a man of roughly his age emerged from the caravan the young woman had gone into. His hair was long and greasy, a silver earring adorned one ear, his shifty glance swept swiftly over Tommy.

'Good morning to you,' Tommy began.

'You'll be the estate manager,' the man interrupted sullenly.

'Yes, that's right,' Tommy said keeping his tone pleasant.

At this juncture he was very aware that the woman who had spoken to him so civilly yesterday stood leaning in the doorway of her caravan, watching silently.

‘How long were you planning on staying in the area?’ Tommy asked.

‘Only a few days sir.’ The man’s sullen tone changed to one of whining, ‘I suppose you’ve come to move us on. We’re not doing any harm, and our women and horses need a rest for a couple of days, sir.’

‘No, I haven’t come to move you on,’ Tommy said steadily, ‘I’ve just come to find out how long you plan to stay in the area, and to warn you not to go straying onto the estate grounds. It’s private property.’

‘Oh no sir, we wouldn’t do that,’ Billy Lee grovelled.

Tommy saw the scar running from one corner of his mouth down to his chin, giving him a menacing look, a knife wound by the look of it.

The woman who had been watching throughout this exchange finally spoke, ‘We’ll be moving on the day after tomorrow. Will that be soon enough for you?’ she asked, her hand on her hip, her gaze, which he found slightly disconcerting, still steadily appraising him.

So she was the leader of the tribe. ‘Yes Ma’am,’ he smiled.

She smiled back showing small surprisingly white, even teeth. Tommy caught again a glimpse of what she must have been. There was something about her that he couldn’t quite put his finger on.

He rode away deep in thought. He’d be glad when the day after tomorrow came and the gypsies would be gone. He felt vaguely uneasy, he could sense trouble brewing like a fox smells a pack of hounds.

He was proved right. The following evening, riding home along the edge of Cokers Wood, he was thinking the gypsies would be gone tomorrow, when he heard the first scream. At first he thought it was a rabbit, caught in a snare, then it came again and he recognised it as the scream of a child in pain.

He urged Satan on, breaking into a canter coming into the encampment, where the noise had come from.

The sight that greeted him horrified and sickened him. A small boy of seven or eight was spread eagled, his wrists tied to the spokes of the caravan wheel to prevent him from running away. The gypsy. Billy Lee, stood with a horsewhip in his hand. Two welts an inch thick had already come up across the boy's naked back. As he raised his arm to inflict another blow, the gypsy woman - her gold belt jingling-grabbed at his arm. He thrust her off savagely.

Tommy threw himself from the saddle shouting, 'Hey you, stop that. D'you hear me, leave the kid alone.'

The gypsy spun round. 'Mind your own bloody business,' he snarled as he turned back to the boy.

Tommy lunged forward and catching the arm that held the whip in a vice like grip, he hissed, 'Drop it I said.'

The gypsy did, and as Tommy released his grip, he saw the flash of steel. Too late, the knife came down slashing his forearm, a long gaping wound, the blood pumping freely. He grabbed the gypsy's wrist again causing him to drop the knife. Tommy kicked it quickly out of reach, but he wasn't quick enough to dodge the man's fist as it smashed into his face.

He wasn't even aware of the pain, his breath came fast. He was filled with rage, a rage so violent it took over as he drove his fist first into the man's ribs, followed by another blow, and another into that shifty face. He didn't know how many times he hit him. He just rained blow after blow. He thought he heard someone shouting his name, screaming at him to stop, but that wasn't possible, no one knew his name.

The gypsy man finally slumped lifeless to the ground. Tommy wondered for an instant, had he killed him, and then he heard him groan. He stood there, his arm bleeding copiously. His lip was split and swelling rapidly. He was overcome with dizziness. He swayed on his feet, looking round wildly for Satan.

The gypsy woman with the gold took charge, rapping out orders.

'Bring him round and get him cleaned up,' she indicated to the half-conscious body of the gypsy man lying prone. 'And help this one into my van. You,' she said to another man, 'catch his horse.'

Tommy shook his head confused, 'No, I must go home,' as one of the men attempted to help him into the caravan.

'Yes, but first we must clean the wound, and stem the bleeding,' the woman said.

Hands helped him into the van and onto a bed with a gaily coloured quilt. The gypsy woman waved them away as she tended to his arm.

'It needs stitches,' she said. 'And thank you, you saved the boy from a terrible beating.'

He sat with his eyes closed feeling weak from the loss of blood while she bathed the wound.

As she sat beside him he could smell her perfume, a spicy smell, the smell of blackberries on a warm day, mingling with the faint aroma of wood smoke from the open fires.

He opened his eyes and looked at the woman, 'Is the boy yours?' he asked.

'Yes, and that's the last time he touches him,' she vowed, her mouth set in a determined line. 'They've caught your horse. There you are,' she said as she finished binding his arm up tightly.

'Thanks,' he said getting unsteadily to his feet. She rose and stood before him barring his way. Lifting her hand she stroked his cheek with her fingertips.

'Thank you again. Tommy,' she smiled.

His eyes widened, 'Miriam...?'

'Yes it's me. The years have been kind to you Tommy.' Her eyes burned into his, 'I told you I'd never forget you and I never did. I knew you straight away the other day. I never thought I'd see you again.' She rose on tiptoe and kissed him swiftly on the mouth, then just as quickly she was going down the steps calling out, 'Bring his horse over.'

The whole Lee tribe stood watching silently as he mounted Satan and rode from the camp.

He made it back to the stables, handing Satan over to the stable lad instead of seeing to him himself the way he normally did.

'What happened Mr. Lawrence? Are you all right?' the lad asked, his eyes like saucers.

He realised he must look a mess with his swollen face and blood-splattered shirt and riding breeches. The blood was already seeping through the makeshift bandage Miriam had applied.

'I'm all right Johnny, don't worry about me, you just see to Satan, make sure you give him a proper rub down.'

He made it the short distance to the house. His face was drained of colour beneath his tan.

'Oh Lord, Tommy what happened?' Megan gasped as he staggered in the back door.

'I've been stabbed Megan... the gypsies. It's okay. Get me to the doctor, it needs stitches.'

Amelia, followed by Amy and Laura, hearing Tommy's voice, came into the kitchen.

'I thought I heard your voice, Thomas...' Amelia turned ashen, bringing her hands up to her face. Laura took one look at Tommy and started to howl. Amy's lower lip trembled.

Megan took charge, 'That's enough now Laura, don't cry. Daddy's all right. I'm going to take him to the doctor.

You remember last week when I stitched up your teddy bear? Well the doctor will do the same for Daddy.'

She picked the little girl up giving her a kiss and a hug, she turned to Amy, 'Come Amy be a big girl for Mummy and take your sister out to play. Daddy's okay, he's just cut himself that's all.'

'Amelia, if you wouldn't mind keeping an eye on them for me, and finishing off the supper, it's nearly ready. We shouldn't be too long. Please fetch Tommy a towel from the airing cupboard and wrap it round that bandage while I get the car out.'

Later that night in bed. Tommy lay on his back, wide awake, his arm throbbing painfully. Megan lay quietly beside him, her arm flung across his waist, her head resting on the shoulder of his good arm.

'What happened Tommy?' she asked.

He told her starting with the beating of the gypsy boy, moving on to the painful memories of his own childhood beatings. Megan had never questioned his past, not his childhood, his strained relationship with his father, his close relationship with Amelia, and how it had come about. He'd never disclosed any of these things, not even to Gareth.

It was like a dam bursting its banks. Once started he couldn't stem the tide. That night Tommy bared his soul, as he'd never done to another human being, not even Amelia.

He told Megan of his gentle, but weak mother and of his love for her; he talked of his father and his black abusive rages, his father's scorn, his constant belittling of him as a child, continuing through to adulthood, of his father's ability to make him feel inferior, even now. He spoke of Amelia's many kindnesses to him as a very young child, of her love and support over the years, how on the death of his mother she'd told him he had a home with her whenever he wanted, or needed.

He told her of the final beating causing him to leave home, go to Melchet Court as a footman, to be trained as a butler. He told of those summer nights as an eighteen year old, he'd sneak out of the library window for his clandestine meeting with Miriam, the gypsy girl who'd introduced him to the delights of sex, while taking his virginity.

He talked of his love affair with the beautiful, selfish Catriona, who he'd wanted to marry, of his difficult early years of his marriage to Emma.

Tommy didn't know what made him reveal so much of himself to Megan. She'd listened as he talked, only interrupting once to ask, was there a connection between Miriam, and today's incident with the gypsies.

'Yes, she said she knew me as soon as she saw me, I didn't recognise her, but yes it was Miriam,' he replied.

He fell asleep that night feeling as if a weight had been lifted from his shoulders. His sleep was deep and peaceful.

Chapter 23

By September nineteen forty six, a year after the stabbing incident with the gypsy, despite a new closeness between Megan and Tommy, there was still no sign of the longed for child. It hurt Megan, she tried to hide her disappointment every month her bleeding started. Tommy would whisper that maybe next month she'd conceive. Twice recently he'd caught her in tears, he'd taken her in his arms, murmuring words of comfort.

But there was no comfort for her. Laura would be starting school after Christmas. She'd be alone all day, she knew Tommy worried about her, but what could he do? What could anyone do?

During September while Amelia was visiting, after lunch the two women were sitting in the garden, enjoying the warm autumn sunshine in the newly acquired deck chairs. Tommy having taken the girls with him to the stables to check on four new hunters that had been bought last week.

'Are you well Megan dear? You look very tired and you've lost weight.'

Megan smiled, 'Yes Amelia, I'm all right. Really I am. Has Tommy been talking to you?' her eyebrows raised.

'Oh dear, we're not very subtle, are we?' Amelia looked like a guilty child, with their hand caught in the cookie jar. 'He's very worried about you. You've been his anchor for a long time. Look at the way you took charge and saw him through Emma's death, and even last year that awful business with the gypsies. He relies so heavily on you, and you're so good together.'

'It's nothing Amelia. I should be ashamed of myself, because I have so much to be thankful for. I've got Tommy and the girls and now I'm crying for the moon.' As she finished a tear slid down her cheek. 'I'm sorry,' she whispered, her lower lip trembling, 'I try not to cry in front of Tommy. Am I being very silly Amelia?'

'It depends on why you're crying darling. Tell me, I hate to see you so upset Megan.'

'Oh Amelia I want a child so badly. We've been trying for a year, and it's not going to happen. I love Tommy so much, and I want to have his child. We've been married for over three years, and I don't even know if he loves me,' she sobbed.

Amelia looked shocked, 'Megan, how can you say such a thing. You silly girl, of course he loves you...'

'How do you know Amelia?' she sobbed wildly now. 'Has he told you he loves me, well, has he? Because if he has, I wish he'd tell me.'

'Megan child, I don't know what to say. Of course he hasn't told me he loves you. He doesn't have to. I can see it for myself, the way he looks at you - he adores you - and as for him telling you, well Thomas is not always very good at expressing his feelings,' she finished.

'Oh Amelia,' she laughed amidst the tears, 'I'm sorry, I shouldn't have said anything to you of all people, but,' she went on blowing her nose and wiping her eyes, 'it is making me very unhappy, the fact that I don't seem to be able to have a baby.'

'I once read somewhere that sometimes people try too hard to have children. Maybe you should relax a little more and forget about babies, just enjoy one another, and it just might happen.'

Megan smiled at her. Maybe she was right. Perhaps it wasn't meant to be.

A few days before her birthday in November she knew she was pregnant. Leaving Laura with Blanche, she'd visited the doctor who'd confirmed the pregnancy.

That evening sitting round the supper table, the eight year old Amy announced she'd been chosen to play Mary in the nativity play next month.

'Will you come and watch me?' she said excitedly.

'But of course we will,' Megan replied. 'Won't that be lovely Laura, seeing your big sister playing Mary?'

'Will you come too Daddy?' she cocked her head at Tommy.

He grinned, 'Wild horses couldn't keep me away. A budding actress in the family, you'll be famous Amy.'

'Oh Daddy! It's only a school play and Miss Chance said we mustn't get swollen heads if we were picked,' she said seriously.

'Well Miss Chance might be right about the swollen heads, but perhaps she wouldn't notice if mine swelled a bit for you,' he said conspiratorially.

'I'm going to school soon. Aren't I Daddy now I'm a big girl?' Laura chirped, not wanting to be left out of things.

'Yes Lolly, then we'll have no babies left...' he broke off suddenly as he ruffled Laura's hair, glancing at Megan over Laura's head. 'And what about you Mrs. Lawrence, what would you like to do for your birthday on Friday?' Tommy went on quickly changing the subject.

The girls giggled, they always thought it hilariously funny when Tommy called Megan, Mrs. Lawrence.

Megan joined in the laughter, answering, 'D'you know Mr. Lawrence we haven't been out to dinner and dancing for so long, that might be nice if I haven't forgotten how.'

Tommy looked surprised and the girls giggled even more. Megan usually made birthdays a family affair, cooking special suppers, celebrating quietly at home, arranging special treats like a pantomime or a trip to the circus, for the girls birthdays.

'Your wish is my command,' he smiled. 'How about we try that new place that's just opened up. Grange Manor, out near Alresford?'

She nodded, 'Sounds lovely Tommy.'

'Oh Mummy what about us if you and Daddy go dancing?' Amy pouted.

'Hey, what about you? Blanche will look after you. Mummy doesn't go out very often, and you two get plenty of treats. Oh okay we'll take you to Swallowfield on Saturday to see Mielie and your cousins,' he capitulated, seeing the look of disappointment on their faces.

Megan shook her head. He just grinned, 'Well that will be two birthday treats for you.'

Later in the bedroom Tommy said, 'Megan darling I'm sorry, I could have kicked myself for my unfortunate choice of words earlier when I said we'd have no babies left when Lolly goes to school.'

'Shush Tommy, it doesn't matter. Please don't feel you have to walk on eggshells around me when the subject of babies crops up.'

She saw the look of relief on Tommy's face, a look that said he was glad of her acceptance of the situation.

Megan could hardly wait for Friday. She was bursting to tell Tommy the news. Amelia had bought her some material in September saying it was an early birthday present. She must have used a year's clothing coupons to buy it. It was a beautiful sea green voile. She hadn't made it up yet, she had patterns and wondered if she could make herself a new blouse in time for Friday night. She didn't have much time.

She sewed frantically for two days, and by late Friday afternoon her new blouse hung in the wardrobe ready to wear.

By the time Blanche arrived to babysit. Tommy was already downstairs.

'Hello Blanche. Come in, how are you?' he asked. 'Megan, Blanche is here,' he called upstairs.

Megan came down wearing her mother's pearls and a small pair of matching earrings Tommy had given her last Christmas. She came into the room self-consciously just as Blanche was saying, 'My you do look handsome Tommy. I swear you get better looking as you get older. Not fair is it?' she sighed. 'We ladies just get older and fatter. Gracious me,' she said turning to Megan, 'You being the exception to the rule Megan, how do you stay so slim?'

'Oh Mummy, you look beautiful, doesn't she Daddy?' Amy sighed.

'She most certainly does Amy,' he agreed.

The evening was perfect. The atmosphere was intimate, the food superb, the music soft, and Tommy was at his most charming and attentive. After dinner he lit a cigarette offering one to Megan. She accepted and as he leaned over to light it for her he whispered, 'Amy was right, you do look beautiful Megan. What have I done to deserve you?'

She blushed and he smiled asking, 'Why are you blushing?'

'I can't help it Tommy when you look at me like that.'

'Like what?' he teased.

'You know,' she slapped his wrist playfully. 'Be serious Tommy, I've got something to tell you.'

'I'm very serious darlin',' He leaned forward kissing her briefly on the lips. 'Sorry, go on, what were you going to tell me? '

'We're going to have a baby Tommy,' she said shakily.

'Oh Megan,' he said huskily, closing his eyes for a moment.

'I still can't believe it Tommy. I'd given up hope. It's like a miracle,' she breathed, misty eyed.

'When Megan? Are you sure it's all right to be out dancing? We must look after you now.'

She laughed, 'Don't be silly Tommy. You've had two children. Women don't need to be wrapped up in cotton wool for nine months. As for when, early June. What would you like Tommy, a boy or a girl?'

Every man wants a son Megan, but I'll love it no matter what we have. What names do you fancy? The girls will have to share a room and we'll turn the other one into a nursery.'

His enthusiasm was infectious, a deep contentment swept over her, and the despair of the last year faded into oblivion.

'I thought you brought me out for dinner and dancing. So far you've wined and dined me, but we haven't got round to the dancing bit. I hope you're planning on asking me. I love this tune,' she said as the band struck up with "String of Pearls".

He rose to his feet and guided her to the dance floor, and taking her into his arms they danced the next three dances, his cheek resting against hers until finally he broke away and looked deep into her eyes, raising her hand to his lips he kissed her fingers.

'Tommy,' she murmured, 'people are staring.'

'Let them,' he smiled.

'You're doing it again,' she said, her cheeks flushing.

'Doing what?'

'Looking at me like that again.'

'I'm only looking at you the way any man looks at the woman he loves, and can't wait to take home and make love to,' he said softly, putting his arm around her waist as he led her back to the table signalling for the waiter to bring the bill.

Her heart sang as she looked at him and saw the love she'd craved for there in his eyes. She no longer had to wonder, she knew.

Less than an hour later in the privacy of their room. Tommy kissed her. Her lips parted beneath his and he undressed her swiftly, they made love slowly and lovingly. Later still they lay contentedly in one another's arms, Megan spoke at last.

'Please tell me again Tommy.'

She felt him smile in the darkness as he answered, 'I love you Megan Lawrence. You make me very happy. D'you know that?'

'If only you knew how much I've wanted you to love me, and I was beginning to be afraid you never would.'

'Oh Meggie,' he said using Gareth's pet name for her, 'I guess I've loved you for a very long time. I just didn't know it.'

'I love you so much Tommy. I've wanted to tell you so often, but after that one time I vowed I'd never tell you again until I was sure you loved me.'

'Please Megan, you can tell me every day, and you can be sure I'll always love you forever.'

Megan felt her eyes filling with tears, tears of joy. She had everything she'd ever wanted.

'Listen,' Tommy said, sitting up in bed and switching on the bedside light, 'Haven't you wondered why you haven't had a birthday present this year?'

'No, I hadn't thought about it.'

'And now, aren't you even a little bit curious as to why not.'

'Yes,' she smiled, 'Now you've aroused my curiosity.'

He took the silver chain from his neck and removed the amethyst ring. Taking her hand he slipped it onto her ring finger saying, 'When my mother gave me this ring she said she hoped I'd find someone one day that I would love enough to give it to. It's taken me half a lifetime to find you. I planned to give it to you earlier, but in all the excitement of your news, I forgot.'

'It's beautiful,' she breathed, 'Are you sure you want me to have it?'

'Positive. I never dreamed I'd ever love anyone the way I love you Megan.'

He kissed her once more as he leaned over and switched off the light. Tommy fell asleep instantly his hand resting on the growing curve of Megan's belly, as yet only a mere hint of a bump.

Megan lay awake a little longer basking in her new found happiness, blessing the day she'd decided to sell the family home, so glad she'd gone with her instincts, despite Gareth's efforts to dissuade her. Had she listened to her brother she would never have met Tommy. She wouldn't be lying here safe and secure beside the man she loved with every fibre of her being.

The following day they travelled to Swallowfield where they broke the news to Amelia and the children. Laura and Amy were so excited, and Amelia was overjoyed for them.

After lunch they visited Georgie and Sylvia, who added their congratulations. Georgie asked Tommy if he was going to visit their father.

'No, I wasn't planning on it,' he shrugged.

His visits to East Lodge had become more sporadic over the years, in fact he'd only taken Megan twice since their marriage, usually preferring to take the girls up on a Sunday morning, no more than three or four times a year at most.

'I think you should Tommy, and take Megan with you,' the normally quiet Sylvia said.

'You do! Why?' he asked.

'Because your Dad's not been so well lately, and he's getting on a bit, and he won't live forever Tommy,' she said bluntly.

'Mmm, perhaps next time we're up...'

'Yes let's go in the morning Tommy,' Megan cut in, 'Good idea Sylvia.'

Tommy looked surprised as he was well aware of Megan's dislike for his father. She felt him squeeze her hand.

The next morning they visited George and Maude as promised.

'Humph, s'pose we should consider ourselves honoured. T'isn't often you bring your wife here,' George muttered.

Megan tugged at Tommy's sleeve and shook her head as she saw his brows draw together.

'We've come to give you our good news,' she said pleasantly waiting for the derogatory comment to follow.

'That's wonderful news,' Maude said quickly. 'Congratulations both of you, you must be thrilled.'

They spent the next hour with the conversation kept going by Maude, Tommy and the children, Megan sitting quietly, and George sitting morosely in his chair. The visit passed with no further incidents.

Megan's pregnancy seemed to be an eye opener for Tommy. Megan had laughed as she pointed out he'd wrongly assumed because of his experience with Emma, that it was a bad time for all women. Megan assured him it was not, quite the opposite for her. She felt tranquil and at peace, delighting in every stage of her pregnancy, sharing each new experience with Tommy, who in turn shared her pleasure and her anticipation. In their bed at night he'd fall asleep with his hand resting on Megan's fast growing belly.

'Can you feel your son kicking? He's so lively. I'm sure it's a boy.'

Because of Megan's serenity during this time, the months flew by. June passed and still no baby. Tommy started to panic.

'The baby was due a couple of weeks back Megan, it's the first of July now. Are you sure everything's all right?'

She nodded. 'Everything's fine. He'll come when he's ready,' she reassured him.

On Sunday the third of July at eleven o'clock in the morning the pains started. Amy and Laura were unceremoniously bundled off to Blanche.

'Don't worry about them. They can stay here overnight. It won't hurt them to miss a day's school at their age. I'll expect you when I see you Tommy,' she said cheerfully. 'Give my love to Megan.'

Fourteen hours later Matthew James Lawrence came into the world by which time his father was a nervous wreck.

It had been a hard time for Megan and she lay utterly exhausted. Tommy finally got to see her at one thirty in the morning. Megan lay with the baby in her arms.

'Come and say hello to your son Tommy,' she smiled weakly.

'Oh Megan, thank God you're all right, and the baby, he's beautiful, thank you darling.'

Tommy sat on the bed and enveloped them in his arms until the sister came into the room.

'Good heavens, Mr. Lawrence, are you still here? It's time you went home,' she said briskly hovering in the doorway.

He turned to Megan and kissed her gently, and stroked the baby's cheek with one finger, 'I'll see you later.'

'Yes much later. Visiting hours are from three to four, and from seven till eight in the evening,' the sister informed him.

'Is my wife going to be all right?'

'Good gracious, of course she is. She's only had a baby. People do that every day. It's nothing special you know.'

Giving Megan a last quick peck on the cheek he whispered, 'It might be nothing special for her, but it is for us, something very special.'

The door closed softly behind him and Megan lay thinking, yes, it was something very special for both of them. How lucky she was that now, with this tiny bundle in her arms, her life was now complete.

Chapter 24

The new baby brought untold joy to the Lawrence household, Amy and Laura having endless arguments as to whose turn it was to hold him. Tommy doted on him, and was so glad to see Megan so fulfilled. He'd never felt so happy and relaxed with his life. Megan had recovered quickly from her ordeal of Mathew's birth.

Tommy looked forward to seeing Amelia's school holiday visit. He was always pleased to see her, his much loved friend. She'd always been there for him, helping him through a difficult childhood; consoling him on the death of his mother; the letters from his days at Melchet Court, through his twelve years in Argentina; welcoming him into her heart and home on his return to England; the unselfish gesture of taking Amy on Emma's death. Where would he have been in life without her?

'I've never seen you look so pleased with yourself Thomas,' she remarked one day during her stay.

'That's because I've got a lot to be pleased about Amelia. I never thought I'd ever be this happy. Does that sound silly?'

'No, of course not. All I ever wanted for you Thomas, and your mother too you know was for you to find peace and contentment, and I believe you've truly found it at last. I've often wanted to thank you for making me feel like I'm a part of your family.'

'Now that's being foolish Amelia,' he said, highly embarrassed by the turn in the conversation. 'I've done nothing, except return your many kindnesses to me over the years.'

'Oh but you have. No,' she held up her hand, 'please let me continue, I've been meaning to have this little chat with you for a while...'

The door opened and Megan came in with a tray of coffee.

Tommy coughed and took the tray from Megan saying, 'Where would you like me to put it Megan?' indicating the tray, relieved that her entrance had prevented the conversation from going any further.

One morning a couple of months later as Tommy was preparing to leave home, the letter box rattled and Amy raced to the front door picking up two letters from the mat.

'One for Mrs. Lawrence, and one for Mr. and Mrs. Lawrence,' she announced, handing them both to Megan.

'Who are they from?' Tommy asked, shrugging into his jacket.

Sylvia and Georgie, and Amelia by the looks of the handwriting.' she said glancing at the envelopes.

'What's Amelia writing for? She'll be here the week after next for Christmas holidays. There's nothing wrong is there?'

'No, there doesn't appear to be anything amiss,' Megan replied, scanning the letter quickly.

'That's good. C'mon girls, are you ready for school? You'd better hurry or you'll miss the bus. I'll see you later Megan, and you young man.' He went over to the pram where Matthew was gurgling happily, then turning to plant a swift kiss on Megan's lips, he hustled the girls, who were still struggling into their coats, out of the door, adjusting Laura's pixie hood as they left.

Tommy came home at lunchtime. 'Gosh it's turning hellish cold out there,' he said as he came in.

They sat down to a steaming bowl of homemade chicken soup, with bread, hot from the oven. After lunch Tommy went to the armchair to sit by the fire for half an hour before returning to work.

'What did Amelia have to say then?'

'Oh nothing much, just that she's looking forward to seeing us all over the Christmas.'

'And Georgie and Sylvia?'

'Much the same, looking forward to their trip down on Boxing Day. Now Georgie has finally been persuaded to buy a little car, it's so much easier than catching buses and trains.'

'You look a bit pale Megan, are you all right?'

She nodded, 'Yes I'm fine. I've just got a bit of a headache.'

He caught at her hand as she went to stoke up the fire, he pulled her gently onto his lap.

'Leave that Megan, I'll make up the fire before I go back to work. Are you sure that's all, just a headache?' He was concerned, Megan wasn't one for headaches.

'Yes of course,' she smiled, and putting her arms round his neck she gave him a long lingering kiss.

'Mmm,' he tightened his arms around her, his tongue gently probing. He slid one hand up under her skirt, stroking the inside of her thigh. Suddenly Matthew let out a long thin wail.

'Oh God! Not now Matthew,' she muttered as the wail died down while he filled his lungs with air ready for the next one.

He grinned ruefully, 'It's okay. See to him, and we'll just have to wait till tonight. Let's just be thankful he doesn't cry all night long, so we have all the time in the world to pursue our carnal pleasures.' He gave her an exaggerated leer. 'Meanwhile I'll make the fire up, and get off back to work.

'See you later.'

Tommy went to fetch Amelia the following weekend taking Amy and Laura with him, stopping briefly in Reading to see Annie and Frank, going on to Swallowfield.

They had a wonderful Christmas, with Georgie and Sylvia coming down on Boxing Day as promised. The house was crammed with people, the sounds of laughter reverberating throughout the house. By five o' clock Sylvia said they must be making a move.

Three hours later Tommy, Megan and Amelia sat in front of a crackling log fire, nursing a small brandy each.

'Would anyone like anything to eat?' Megan asked.

'Not for me Meggie, I couldn't,' Tommy answered.

'No thank you dear, me neither,' Amelia shook her head.

'I'm quite relieved about that, because now the kids are all tucked up in bed asleep. I'm really too comfortable to move until bedtime. Amelia, are you all right?' Megan asked.

'Yes of course dear,' she answered quickly. 'Just a touch of indigestion.'

In the middle of the final week of Amelia's visit she said one evening, 'I think I'd like to go home tomorrow Thomas. I realise you can't take me as you're working, but would you mind if Megan drove me up?'

Tommy looked up from the book he was reading and carefully closed it. 'Yes of course Amelia, but why? Is something the matter?' he asked, instantly attentive.

‘Well to tell you the truth Thomas, I haven’t felt so good these last couple of days, and I really don’t want to go and see a strange doctor. I think it would be better if I go and see my own,’ she finished.

‘Nothing serious I hope,’ he said.

‘Oh good gracious no,’ she assured him.

‘Well if you’re sure, yes of course Megan can take you home. Laura and Amy are already back to school. You don’t mind do you Megan?’

‘No of course not,’ Megan agreed.

The following morning Amelia joined the family at the breakfast table. She listened to Amy and Laura’s chatter of school, telling Amy how proud she was of her glowing end of year report, and told her to keep studying hard.

Tommy glanced at his watch. ‘I’d better go,’ he said rising from the table.

Amelia who had been toying with a small piece of toast rose too.

‘No don’t get up Amelia, finish your breakfast,’ he urged.

She took no notice saying, ‘I must say goodbye to the girls properly before they go to school.’

Megan was already helping Laura into her hat and coat.

‘Goodbye Amy darling, come and kiss me goodbye.’

Amy rushed over throwing her arms round her spontaneously. ‘Bye bye, Mielie. I love you. We’ll see you soon, won’t we?’

‘Me too,’ shrieked Laura, who was going through that noisy boisterous stage.

‘Yes, you too,’ Amelia bent to kiss her. Straightening up she turned to Tommy.

‘Thank you so much for a wonderful Christmas as usual Thomas. I do so look forward to my holidays with you.’

‘We enjoy having you Amelia. You’ll ring us and let us know how you get on at the doctor won’t you?’

‘Of course dear.’

He put his arms around her saying, ‘You’re very precious to us Amelia, so look after yourself, d’you hear me. If there’s anything you need, or that we can do, you will let us know won’t you, I mean it you know.’

He kissed her cheek, and she clung to him for a few seconds.

He kissed Megan goodbye, telling her to drive carefully, and set off down the path with Laura and Amy heading off to catch the school bus. He paused at the gate to looked back, to see Amelia standing at the window watching, he waved goodbye.

He couldn’t say why but he felt uneasy about Amelia. Was there something she was concealing from them? He’d thought that in general she hadn’t looked so well at all.

His fears were allayed on Saturday morning when he received a phone call from Amelia.

Megan had taken Laura and Amy to Winchester to buy them new shoes, leaving Tommy in charge of Matthew. On their return they rushed to show Tommy their purchases. They each received threepence a week pocket money, which was saved up, until they went to town.

‘Look Daddy, look. See what happens when you dip this in here and blow,’ Laura said. ‘I’m going to show Matthew.’

She’d bought a small tin of liquid soap, with a piece of wire with a loop on the end, which you dipped into the soap, and when held up and blown upon formed multi-coloured bubbles that floated through the air. Amy had bought a book.

‘And Mummy bought us new shoes, and the stickiest lardy cake Loman’s had for tea time. What have you been doing Daddy? Has Matthew been a good boy?’ Laura rarely waited for answers, she talked incessantly, and was already known as the class chatterbox.

'Amelia rang while you were gone Megan,' Tommy said, relieving her of some of her shopping.

'Oh did she, how is she, and how did she get on at the doctor?'

'She says she's fine now. She feels better already. Her doctor says she's got a tummy bug, and she's a little run down, so he's given her a tonic. She apologised for cutting her holiday short. I told her that wasn't important, and that she must stay an extra few days when she comes at Easter.'

Tommy's forty second birthday was celebrated by a trip to the pantomime "Puss in Boots" in Southampton.

He roared with laughter when Megan told him what she'd planned. 'Don't you think I'm a little bit too old for "Puss in Boots"?'

'Don't be silly Tommy,' she replied, 'You're never too old for pantomime, and the girls will love it, they're already looking forward to it. I'm surprised Laura hasn't told you, she's not very good at keeping secrets, and it's supposed to be a surprise for you. I've organised for Blanche to look after Matthew.'

On Friday night Tommy went upstairs to say goodnight to Laura and Amy as he normally did.

Laura wound her arms around his neck whispering, 'Daddy can you keep a secret?'

He nodded, 'I think so Lolly,' looking laughingly into a pair of smoky grey eyes, so like his own.

'Tomorrow we're going to take you to the pantomime, but you mustn't tell Mummy or Amy, because it's going to be a surprise,' she whispered confidentially.

He could smell her warm sweet breath on his neck, 'Okay Lolly, it'll be our secret,' he whispered back, 'and now c'mon, snuggle down.' He leaned over and kissed her, the smell of talcum powder filling his nostrils.

He went over to Amy's bed, and sitting on the edge, he asked, 'Would you like to read for a little while sweetheart?' He knew Amy was like he had been as a child, she loved books. She would be nine years old this year, and was turning into a studious little girl.

'Can I Daddy?' she asked eagerly.

'I think so, just for half an hour, after all there's no school tomorrow. Take your watch off,' this being a newly acquired Christmas present, 'and when it says half after eight you must put the light out and go to sleep, all right.'

'Thanks Daddy,' she said holding out her arms for her good night kiss.

Tommy's heart overflowed with love for these two children that he'd struggled to keep. They were his flesh and blood, and he knew that without Megan and Amelia it wouldn't have been possible. They, along with Megan and Matthew, were his world.

He closed the bedroom door softly behind him, and made his way downstairs.

Chapter 25

Megan thought of it as the day of *the letter*. Tommy had asked why Amelia was writing when she was coming for Christmas so soon.

She'd answered no, there was nothing wrong on scanning the letter briefly. After he'd left with Laura and Amy she'd sat down at the breakfast table, and unfolded Amelia's letter. The very first line had told her that something was very wrong.

Dear Megan,

Please don't tell Thomas as I don't want to worry him, but I'm afraid I have some bad news. A few months ago during the summer I saw a specialist in Reading, and I was diagnosed with cancer. I tried to talk to Thomas on my last visit, but it was just too difficult. I saw the specialist again last week, and he's given me two to three months to live. I have come to terms with it, but I wanted you to know by this letter that my last will and testament is lodged with a firm of solicitors, Jacobs & Hartmann of Reading. Thomas is my sole beneficiary, but why I'm really telling you this, my dear Megan, is so that at least one of you is prepared for my death.

I know it is a great burden I'm putting upon you, but you are his strength, the best thing that ever happened in his life, and I know that you will support him in his hour of need.

When I arrive next week I shall not want to discuss this any further. I just felt that you my dear child, should be forewarned.

I look forward to seeing you all.

Fondest love Amelia.

Megan was shattered. She put her head in her hands, the tears trickling through her fingers, until Matthew's whimpering brought her back to the present.

By the time Tommy returned at lunchtime, she'd composed herself, and put the letter into her handbag. When he asked casually what Amelia had to say, she managed to lie quite calmly. On the Saturday when Tommy took the girls to go and fetch Amelia for the Christmas visit, Megan was left at home with Matthew and her thoughts. They were in turmoil, she dreaded facing Amelia. Could she pretend nothing was wrong? Would she look terribly ill? Would Tommy notice? A hundred questions buzzed round her brain. She ran through her greetings: "Hello Amelia how are you?" "Hello Amelia, you look well"… that might be totally inappropriate. "Hello Amelia, nice to see you"… that sounded fairly safe and normal for someone who was terminally ill. She was still wondering how she was going to cope with the next three weeks, when she heard the car pull up.

She ran her fingers through her hair nervously as she went to greet them.

'Hello Megan, how are you?' Amelia greeted her.

'I'm fine Amelia,' she answered, 'and you?'

'Oh I mustn't grumble darling, getting older by the day, but then aren't we all?' she said brightly.

Megan was taken aback. She'd expected a drastic change in Amelia's appearance, but this wasn't someone that looked on the verge of death. She looked a little older, a little wearier, but not someone with a matter of months left. Could the specialist have been mistaken Megan wondered? As a doctor's daughter she knew they weren't infallible, they made their mistakes too.

Christmas day went off without a hitch. They woke to a beautiful crisp white frost, sparkling in the winter's sunshine. They walked to church with Amelia insisting on accompanying them. The children opened their presents on their return, the adults deriving as much pleasure from watching them, as the children got from opening them.

Boxing Day followed, a day full of fun, with Georgie, Sylvia, Maggie and Jenny joining them. The small house was bursting at the seams with ten of them. They played games after lunch, until Sylvia said at around five thirty that it was time they were making tracks.

Later that evening, visitors departed, children in bed, the three of them relaxed, each of them with a small brandy, Megan offered refreshment, and expressed her relief when both Tommy and Amelia declined her offer.

She saw the spasm of pain cross Amelia's face, as she asked a little too sharply, 'Amelia are you all right?'

The words were out before she could stop herself. She vowed she wouldn't fuss, but over the following days she watched Amelia as discreetly as she could. Several times she saw the pain in her eyes, but she refrained from asking was she all right. It was obvious to Megan that Amelia wanted to keep up appearances, and she continued to be cheerful.

Megan respected her wishes and remained silent, but it hurt her to have to hide it from Tommy. They shared everything, no secrets between them. She felt guilty, but she couldn't bring herself to betray Amelia's confidences.

The morning of Amelia's early departure she'd joined the family for breakfast, and having said her goodbyes to Tommy and the children, she stood at the window, Megan thought her heart would break as she watched a tear roll down Amelia's cheek as Tommy turned and waved goodbye, she heard her whisper, "Goodbye Thomas". Amelia's whole stance portrayed defeat.

Megan touched her gently on the arm, 'Are you absolutely certain this is the way you want it to be Amelia? Tommy wouldn't want you to be alone. Neither of us want that for you.'

'I know Megan, I really do. But first of all Thomas was with his mother when she died in his arms of cancer. I don't want to put him through that again because of me; and secondly, a purely selfish motive, I would like to retain as much dignity as I can,' she finished.

Megan put her arms round this very courageous lady, and held her close for several minutes before finally saying, 'Are you ready to go home Amelia?'

'Yes dear, I'm quite ready.'

They drove to Swallowfield, and Amelia talked. She spoke mainly of Tommy, as a child, then of a young man, of his many kindnesses to her, of their lifelong friendship. 'He's been like a son to me,' she mused, 'I've been so very fortunate.'

Megan listened her only comment being, 'He loves you very much Amelia.'

'I know dear, but I'm doing the right thing. A month or so back the pain had eased slightly, the doctors said it would,' she paused. 'They've given me pills for when it gets worse again, as they warned me it would. The specialist said it wouldn't be long once the pain resumed. 'I've tried to prepare myself,' she gave an almost inaudible sob. 'I'm sorry Megan, I'm afraid I'm not being terribly brave.' She closed her eyes and dozed fitfully for the rest of the journey.

Megan took Amelia's case in for her asking, 'Is there anything else I can do for you Amelia, before I leave?'

'No thank you darling. I'll just have a last look at your beautiful son before you go.'

Matthew had been fast asleep in his carrycot on the back seat. Megan opened the car door and was about to lift him out when Amelia stopped her, 'No Megan, leave him sleeping.' She kissed the tip of her finger and touched it gently to his cheek. 'You'd better start back, you've a family to care for, and I think I'd like to lie down for a while, I'm very tired.' She held out her arms, 'Please look after him Megan, God bless you. Goodbye,' she said kissing her swiftly, 'I'll call you.'

'Promise?'

She smiled, 'I promise.'

Megan sat in the car, the tears rained unheeded down her face. She sat for a moment, the tears temporarily blinding her. Finally composing herself, she wiped her eyes with the back of her hand, and slowly pulled away.

On Saturday on her return from a shopping trip to Winchester, Tommy told her Amelia had rung. She asked how she was, trying to sound casual, hoping she'd hidden her anxiety.

After that Megan would ring Amelia every few days, while Tommy was at work and the children at school. They would talk, although it was mainly Amelia talking, with Megan a willing listener.

'It does me so much good to be able to talk to someone who understands my situation,' Amelia told Megan each time before they'd hang up.

Amelia rang in early February. She sounded cheerful enough and she wanted to talk to Tommy after which she asked to be put back to Megan.

‘I know you’re worried about me darling, but you mustn’t be. I have a nurse calling in. I’m really all right you know, and I’m quite ready when the time comes.’

The time came quickly. On the fifteenth of February Georgie rang to say Amelia had passed away.

Tommy was numb with shock. The funeral was well attended as Amelia had lived in the village all her life, and had taught so many children, many of whom came to pay their respects. Amy insisted on accompanying Tommy and Megan. At first Tommy resisted.

‘Amy sweetheart, you’re too young. A funeral is a very sad occasion. I think you should stay with Matthew and Laura, they’re going to Blanche’s.’

‘No Daddy, please let me come,’ she pleaded. ‘Mummy says it’s your last chance to say goodbye to people before they go to heaven, and I want to say goodbye to Mielie, please Daddy?’

‘Tommy please let her come,’ Megan put in.

So it was that the three of them went to Swallowfield. Jacobs & Hartmann had already contacted Tommy. The will was to be read immediately after the funeral at Rose Cottage. It came as no surprise to Megan, who already knew the contents. The sole beneficiary being my good friend, Thomas Robert Lawrence, I leave Rose Cottage and all its contents, plus the sum of fifteen thousand pounds.

There was a letter Amelia had sent to the solicitors just before she died addressed to Tommy. He put the envelope into his pocket without opening it. He locked the door of Rose Cottage, and giving Georgie and Sylvia a spare key, he said he’d be ready to face the house at a later date.

They went back to Georgie’s for some refreshment before going home. Georgie would look after the garden, and Sylvia would make sure the house was aired, until such time as Tommy wanted to come and sort things out.

'She was a lovely woman,' Georgie said. 'She taught both of us as kids, and Matthew, and she was still teaching when our Maggie and Jenny started school. I find it hard to believe she's gone, she seemed fine at your place on Boxing Day. It's so sudden.

'I know,' Tommy replied. 'I can't believe it either, why didn't she tell me she was ill?'

'You loved her very much didn't you Tommy?' Sylvia said, 'so you must be thankful that she wasn't ill for a long time, and hope that she didn't suffer too much.'

That evening at home Megan and Tommy sat cuddled up together on the settee in front of a roaring fire, with steaming hot cups of coffee.

'Have you read your letter yet Tommy?' she asked.

He shook his head, 'No, I'd forgotten about it. It's in my jacket pocket. I'll get it.'

Returning minutes later he said, 'Megan I've got something to ask you. You didn't seem surprised when we got the news of Amelia's death. Did you know something I didn't know? Something that perhaps you kept from me?'

'Yes Tommy, I did know Amelia was ill. I hated keeping it from you, but she didn't want you to know. I couldn't go against her wishes. Read the letter.'

He read aloud:

My dear Thomas,

I have loved you dearly from when, as a six year old you stood at my desk, with a bunch of primroses asking me, 'Miss, do you like flowers?'

This is just to tell you that my illness has been of a short duration. Please don't be upset that I didn't tell you, but I didn't want to burden you with it, although Megan thought you should be told. I made her promise not to tell you, and she reluctantly agreed. She has been wonderfully supportive to me over these last difficult weeks, telephoning me every few days, giving me someone to share my thoughts and feelings with. You are a very lucky man.

I can assure you I have suffered very little and will die happy and content in the knowledge that you are settled and happy with a loving family, and I thank you for always making me feel a part of it.

This is goodbye and bless you,

Your loving friend Amelia Nelson.

That night in the solitude of their bedroom, Megan held him in her arms as he finally broke into heartrending sobs of grief for the woman that had taken the place of his mother.

Chapter 26

It took Tommy till Easter before he was willing to return to Rose Cottage. Suddenly the week before Easter he made the decision.

'Megan it's time for us to go and sort out Amelia's things, and put the cottage on the market. I thought perhaps we could go up over Easter and stay for a few days,' he suggested.

'Yes of course Tommy, good idea if you feel you're ready.'

He nodded, 'Yes I'm okay. I just couldn't face it at the time. While we're there for a few days I shall have to take the girls to see Annie and Frank. They haven't seen them since when I fetched Amelia for Christmas. I feel a bit guilty, but I just don't seem to have had time. And I suppose we'd better visit Maude and the old man too.'

Now it was Megan's turn to nod, 'Sylvie said in her last letter your Dad's very frail, and Maude's really having to look after him now.'

'Poor old Maude. She's not a bad old stick, and she's been good to the old man. I suppose in a way she's kept an uneasy peace between us for years now,' he mused.

They arrived at Rose Cottage on Thursday afternoon. Megan threw all the windows open wide. Georgie had looked after the garden planting daffodils, creating a riot of bloom leading from the gate to the front door with its familiar lion's head brass knocker. The girls rushed straight off to their cousins' house to play leaving Tommy, Megan and Matthew at the cottage. Matthew had fallen asleep on the journey, and as it was nearly time for his afternoon nap, Megan just lay him on the bed in the spare room.

Tommy looked around him at the all too familiar things. It felt strange to be there without Amelia. Megan came downstairs.

'I was just thinking it feels funny to be here without Amelia and I do miss her Megan. I really did love her. I wonder if she knew that.'

'Of course she did,' Megan replied, 'She understood you very well.'

Megan went across to where Tommy stood, his fingers caressing the old oak table polished to a high gloss over the years. He'd sat at that table many a time as a small boy, with a glass of milk and biscuits, while Amelia would find another book for him to borrow. Megan touched his forearm bringing him back to the present, and he turned towards her a smile playing on his lips.

'I was just remembering, there's only one woman that's ever known me better than Amelia and that's you Meggie. I love you Megan,' he whispered, his arm going round her shoulders. She leaned against him as his arm tightened round her.

'Where shall we start, or shall we wait till morning?' he asked.

'Wait till morning. Meanwhile what shall we do? The girls won't be back for a while. Shall I make us some coffee?' she suggested.

'No, I've got a better idea. The girls are at Georgie's, Matthew's asleep, why don't you and I slip upstairs and I'll show you just how much I love you,' he said huskily, his mouth against her ear.

She blushed. He loved the way she still did that and she took his hand and led the way upstairs.

The following morning they started to go through Amelia's things. Megan sorted clothes, making neat piles, which they decided they would give to an old age home in Reading. Tommy opened the first drawer of a chest in the corner of the room to find bundles of letters tied up neatly. He glanced at the top envelope recognising his own handwriting as he read the faded postmark, Blandford. The drawer was full of letters, all from Tommy, well thumbed, dating back to nineteen twenty. Right through his Melchet Court days, through to his final letter dated March nineteen thirty seven telling her he would be returning to England in May that year. Seventeen years of letters.

'I just can't believe she'd keep them for all those years Megan. Why?' he asked incredulous.

'Because she loved you Tommy. You were the son she never had,' Megan said simply.

The next drawer amazed Tommy even more. It contained almost every gift he'd ever bought her, a slim volume of poetry, boxes of handkerchiefs, fancy soaps, he recognised a soft pale lemon angora bed jacket still wrapped in its tissue paper, and various small pieces of inexpensive jewellery he'd bought her over the years. He shook his head.

'I guess this was Amelia's treasure chest,' Megan said softly, kneeling beside him.

It took them all day to clear all the cupboards, deciding what to do with things. Friday evening they went to Georgie and Sylvia for supper. Later they sat chatting, while the four girls played Monopoly. Matthew who was now ten months old and starting to pull himself up on the furniture, sat at Tommy's feet playing contentedly with two gaily painted wooden lorries. He was a happy child who cried little, slept through every night, and was spoilt by both Tommy and his sisters.

‘What are you doing tomorrow Megan? More sorting out still?’ Sylvia asked.

‘No, I think we’ve finished. Tommy wants to take the girls to see Annie and Frank, and we’ll drop Amelia’s things off at the old age home.’

‘Are you going to keep any of Amelia’s furniture Tommy?’ Georgie asked.

‘Yes, a few pieces,’ he nodded. ‘The rest can be sold with the cottage. Megan’s the expert.’

‘Well I don’t know about expert. I know what I like. When my father died, I kept the old oak Welsh dresser, and the Chesterfield. That’s probably why our house is overflowing now. I only want to keep Amelia’s lovely Victorian single ended chaise lounge. I always fancied myself reclining gracefully on one of those, you know like Cleopatra. And I have to keep her old mahogany bureaux with the bombe front, and then just the Victorian walnut washstand with the white marble top.’

‘I think she’ll have me moving out in a minute to make room for all she wants to keep,’ Tommy laughed. ‘Haven’t you forgotten something?’

Megan looked puzzled, ‘Like what?’

‘Plus, can you believe, a funny old oak cradle that looks as if it came out of the ark and, I might add,’ he said giving her a mock glare, ‘I’ve already warned her she can forget any thoughts she may have of filling it again because,’ he rose and, bending down picking Matthew up, he continued, ‘this young man will be the last for this branch of the Lawrence family.’

‘Come along girls,’ Megan called through to the kitchen, ‘Time to go home.’

‘By the way,’ Tommy turned round to Georgie and Sylvia, ‘is there anything you would like from Rose Cottage? Because you know you’re very welcome. It’s a help for me to know that the place is being looked after and kept tidy, because that's another thing I have to do tomorrow in Reading, see the estate agent and put it on the market.'

'Oh Tommy, do you really mean it? I'd love the oak table and chairs. We've had ours since we were married, and it was only cheap when we bought it.' Sylvia said.

'Please, after this weekend, it's yours,' he said generously, 'and wouldn't you like that mantel clock from Amelia's sitting room? You don't have a clock in here.'

'Thanks Tommy. You're sure you don't want it Megan?'

'Oh no, I forgot to mention Meggie's keeping the walnut grandfather clock. At this rate we'll need a new house for the bits and pieces Megan wants to keep,' he teased. 'Talking about a new house, there is something I want to talk to both of you about. Tomorrow we're going to Reading and Sunday we'll go and see the old man. How about Easter Monday come and have lunch with us?' He turned to Megan, 'That'll be okay won't it?'

She nodded. 'Of course. We'll see you Monday. Thanks for a lovely supper Sylvie,' she said kissing her goodnight.

It took another ten minutes to round up a protesting Laura and Amy, who weren't ready to go home yet.

On the way back to Rose Cottage, with Tommy carrying a sleepy Matthew, Megan asked quietly, 'Are you going to tell them about Argentina, Tommy?'

'I think I should darlin', don't you? After all he is my brother. That was why I asked them to come to us on Monday.'

They'd received a couple of letters from Gareth in recent months suggesting that they think about his idea of the two families going in together on the purchase of some land. Tommy had promised to give it some thought. Megan had the money from the sale of her cottage, and he'd always been thrifty. With what he had accumulated and now the windfall from Amelia, they were financially secure with a substantial sum to invest or to start a new life with.

Maude welcomed them on Sunday and drawing Tommy to one side she said, 'Tommy I know it's never been your fault, but please try and be patient with your father. Dr. Jones came last week and said he mustn't get upset or over excited.'

He nodded, 'Okay Maude, I take it he's not doing so well.'

'Well that depends on how you look at it. He's nearly seventy six you know. That's a good age. He's had a good innings by anybody's standard.'

'What'll you do Maude, when anything happens to the old man?'

'Oh don't worry about me Tommy. I've got a widowed sister that lives in Malmesbury. I shall go and live with her. It's kind of you to ask though, you're a good boy.'

He smiled fondly at her. A good boy! He was forty three years old, twice married with three children, and Maude still thought of him as a good boy.

He went into the sitting room. His father was in his armchair holding Matthew on his knee, under Megan's watchful eye. His body was now frail and stooped, but his mind was still alert.

'There's only two male Lawrences to carry on the line, Matthew here, and Matthew's son John. Too many girls, four of 'em,' he mumbled.

'We don't get a choice Dad. We have to take what comes and be grateful.'

Laura went to sit beside Maude confiding, 'Do you know Nana Maude? We might be going away soon to Argentina where Daddy used to live.'

You could have heard a pin drop. Tommy looked from Maude to his father. Oh Lord! Maybe the old man hadn't heard it, but he could see that Maude had by the look of dismay that crossed her face.

'Laura,' Megan said gently, 'nothing has been decided yet Maude. We're still thinking about it.'

'First we've heard on it,' George muttered darkly.

'Dad, like Megan says, we haven't decided yet,' Tommy said looking apologetically at Maude.

'What would you want to go back there for?' his father asked.

'It's a beautiful country Dad. Still a land of opportunity if you're prepared to work hard. It's vast and unspoiled. A man can own a lot of land. I've got a bit of money and was wondering about an *estancia*, a farm of our own. Megan's brother is keen for us to go back there.'

Tommy waited for a scathing comment he felt sure would come, but when his father spoke it was totally unexpected.

'You've not done badly for yourself Thomas,' he said gruffly. 'Your mother would have been proud of you.'

Tommy just stared at him. It had been twenty three years since Martha's death. In all that time George had never once made any reference to her. It had been as if she'd never existed.

Tommy said softly, 'And you Dad? Are you proud of me?'

'Humph, I s'pose you haven't done badly for yourself,' he answered grudgingly.

Tommy caught Megan's eye. His lips twitched in the semblance of a smile. Maude nodded her approval.

'Thanks. Anyway we'll let you know when we've made a decision.'

Later that evening, the children all in bed. Tommy said to Megan, 'I wish Amelia was here to see this day, because that's the closest to praise I'm ever going to get. It's ridiculous Megan, all these years I looked for, and worked for, a sign of his approval, and now I've got it, it doesn't mean a thing. It's not important anymore.' He shook his head. 'I wonder what that cost him, and why now?' he mused.

'Maybe he knows he's nearing the end of his life Tommy. Perhaps he has regrets.'

He kissed her on the cheek, letting his lips linger as he murmured, 'Darling Meggie, Amelia was right about you.'

'What do you mean? In what respect?'

'She told me after you and Gareth had stayed with her, that she thought you were a lovely girl, and she said she hoped I wouldn't take it amiss when she said she wished I'd met you as soon as I came back from the Argentine. She reckoned you were worth your weight in gold. When I asked her what she meant, she went on to say, she didn't mean any offence to Emma, but she thought you would have made me a perfect wife. Of course Emma never really liked Amelia, she was jealous of her. Emma and I had words more than once regarding Amelia. She tried after Amy was born, but they were never really close. But Amelia was right, you have made me the perfect wife.'

Monday they broke the news to Georgie and Sylvia of the possibility of their return to the Argentine. They were disappointed as Georgie said, but they were also excited for them. As Sylvia put it, 'If it's what you want, that's the most important thing.'

Rose Cottage sold four months later and the following week Tommy arrived home one lunchtime to find a letter postmarked Ushuaia, Argentina on the mantelpiece.

'Looks very official. I wonder who it's from.'

She smiled, 'Well I suggest you open it and put us both out of our misery, I've been wondering all morning what it was about. I'll just take the pasties out of the oven.'

He sat down at the table and, opening the letter began to read. Megan busied herself with lunch. She looked up as she heard his sharp intake of breath.

'Not bad news I hope,' she queried.

He didn't reply, but carried on reading, drawing his brows together in a frown, trying to absorb the contents.

'Tommy what is it?' she asked anxiously.

He finished reading and silently passed her the letter, which was from a firm of solicitors in Ushuaia. There was actually two letters, one being a copy of a letter dated November nineteen thirty seven written by Catriona Sanchez nee Ramirez of the Estancia Montalban informing him of the birth of his son, Emelio. This information was to be passed on to him only in the unlikely event of herself, and her husband, Eduardo Sanchez's death should they occur simultaneously, before Emelio reached the age of twenty one.

Megan looked at Tommy as she sat down abruptly, 'Oh Tommy, my legs feel like jelly. I can't read any more. I've got as far as *you should be told in the event of her and her husband's death.*'

Tommy took the letter from her and read on.

On the marriage of Catriona Ramirez to Eduardo Sanchez, the two estancias *would be run as separate entities. If there were any offspring from the union the Sanchez* estancia *would go to them, the Ramirez property would go to Thomas Lawrence to be passed on to Emelio on his father's death. In the event that there were no children from their union then both of the adjoining* estancias *would eventually go to Emelio.*

The solicitors letter stated much the same, on the proviso that Tommy were to take up permanent residence on the *estancia*, as the owner, and as Emelio's publicly acknowledged father. In the interim the *estancia* would be run by a manager, under the guidance of an appointed board of trustees until such time as Tommy had informed them of his decision.

'It's all so complicated Tommy,' Megan whispered. 'I don't fully understand. Are they saying the *estancia* is yours as long as you go and live on it, and be a father to the child, and from you it passes down to Emelio?'

'I think that's the gist of it.'

'Did you know about the boy?'

'No Megan. I promise you I had no idea, but I've got a strange feeling your brother had an inkling at least.'

'Gareth? Why d'you say that?'

'Just the way he was asking questions about had I ever heard from Catriona. I don't know - something I can't put my finger on. Oh God, Megan! Can you forgive me for bringing this on you?'

'Hush Tommy. It happened long before you knew me. It's part of your past. Right now you must decide what you're going to do about it.'

'She was sixteen years old Megan when she made a play for me. I was twenty eight, old enough on reflection to know better. It was when Gareth came home in nineteen thirty one,' he went on, 'and I had the accident. I've often wondered if I hadn't had the accident, if Gareth had been there, maybe it wouldn't have happened. Lack of opportunity, circumstances, I tried to break it off several times, but she was beautiful, passionate and forbidden. I was so besotted with her, and she knew it. Eventually I realised we were going nowhere, and that's when I left Argentina and came home.'

‘Listen Tommy, go back to work. Let it sink in. Think about it. We’ll talk some more tonight.’

He felt his whole world had just fallen apart. Their lunch sat untouched. The situation was a nightmare, but he knew it wasn’t one that he’d wake up from to find it had only been a dream.

Megan rose, and taking some greaseproof paper she wrapped a pasty up.

‘Here Tommy, take this and go back to work. You know whatever you decide my darling, I’m with you all the way.’

Taking her hand, he raised it to his lips, kissing her palm, he said simply, ‘I’m sorry.’

He left knowing he had a few hours’ breathing space, but he knew it was only a reprieve, a decision would have to be made, and soon.

Chapter 27

Megan agonised the whole afternoon. What would Tommy decide? She thought of the boy, eleven years old and alone. His mother, and the man he'd known as his father killed in a freak accident. A car crash, they had been returning overnight from a trip to Buenos Aires on a straight stretch of road. There was no visible cause, no other vehicle involved, Eduardo had been driving, possibly he had fallen asleep at the wheel. No one could say for sure, there had been no witnesses. A verdict of accidental death was recorded. She didn't want to influence Tommy; it had to be his decision. He'd never been a man to shirk his responsibilities. She'd seen his face go deathly pale as he read the letter, and she felt for him, but she could do no more than be there for him. She prayed silently that he'd make the right choice, for whatever he decided would ultimately affect their whole family.

They were already seriously considering the possibility of going to Argentina. Tommy hadn't been totally sold on the idea of going in with Gareth. This way the question wouldn't even arise.

The Estancia Montalban had been left to Tommy, with the stipulated conditions. It would be a huge undertaking, a responsibility that she wasn't sure he'd want to assume. She knew that when Tommy had talked of buying land he'd been thinking of something on a much smaller scale that he could run with a little hired help.

Evening came, and Megan noticed during supper Tommy was distracted, not concentrating on what was going on around him, until finally Laura catching at his sleeve got his attention.

'Daddy, please will you come? You will won't you?' she pleaded.

'Sorry Lolly, come where?' he asked.

''Daddy! To school tomorrow night. It's open night and you can come and see our work.'

'Yes Lolly, I expect so,' he replied absent-mindedly.

'Mummee...'

'Shush Laura. Have you finished your supper? Then you can take Matthew into the garden and play for a while,' Megan said.

The corner of Laura's mouth turned down.

'Laura,' Megan warned.

'Laura, you heard your mother. Now stop your nonsense and do as you're told!' Tommy snapped.

Laura's eyes filled with tears at the unaccustomed harshness of his tone. Her chin started to quiver. Amy took her by the hand, 'C'mon Lolly, Matthew, and I'll give you both a nice push on the swing.'

Laura cast a reproachful backward look at Tommy as she left the room.

Rising from his chair, he lit a cigarette as he paced restlessly. 'Sorry Megan, would you like one?' he offered.

Megan who rarely smoked nodded. 'Yes I think I would Tommy, and how about we have a drink too,' she suggested.

'Good idea. Oh God Megan,' he said pouring them both a brandy, 'This has been an awful shock for you. I'm so sorry, I really am.'

'I'm sure it's been a worse shock for you. Have you thought about what you're going to do yet?'

'I've thought of nothing else all afternoon, and I still don't know. Do I really have a choice? The child is mine without doubt. No one in their right mind is going to leave me an estate of that size with those conditions unless they knew for certain I was his father. Are they now?'

'No, I suppose not,' she said thoughtfully, 'If you decide to refuse, then what would we do? Would we still go to Argentina anyway, or would we stay here?'

'I'd sort of got my heart set on going back anyway Megan, but an *estancia* of that size... It's a hell of a responsibility but,' he hesitated.

'But what Tommy?'

'Have I got the right to refuse? The boy's eleven years old and I'm his father, whether I like it or not. I'm going to have to accept.'

Just then Amy came hurtling through the back door to the sounds of Laura screaming, 'Mummy, come quick! Laura's fallen off the swing and she's bleeding.'

In three strides Tommy was across the room and out into the garden. Megan could hear Laura bawling as she rushed after him. Tommy had picked her up, she was more frightened than hurt. Her knees were grazed and bleeding. She clung to him sobbing.

'It's all right,' he assured Megan, 'No serious damage. Amy darling pick Matthew out of the flower bed, I think he's trying to eat the flowers.' It meant the end of their discussion for the time being. 'Hush Lolly, it's okay. Let's go in and get you cleaned up,' he soothed.

It wasn't till much later while they were preparing for bed that they resumed where they had left off.

'You do understand, don't you Megan? It's something I have to do. I feel terrible about the whole thing. You've loved me and my children selflessly. Before I met you I would never let myself love anyone heart and soul because I thought if I did it would give them the power to hurt me. In so many ways you gave me back my life after Emma died, and this is how I repay you. Can you forgive me Meggie?' he begged full of remorse.

For an answer she raised her face to him, she put up her hand and lightly traced his lips with her fingers. He held her close and she kissed him, his lips were firm against hers.

'Oh Megan, I'm sorry,' he muttered hoarsely.

She unbuttoned his shirt, her hands caressing his body. 'It's all right, it's all right,' she soothed, her lips brushing his. She felt his arms tighten around her, and sensed the urgency of his returned kiss. She moaned softly as she could feel his desire mounting. He picked her up and carried her to the bed where they made love slowly and sweetly.

The decision was made. He wrote a letter to the solicitors accepting their conditions. The passage was booked for October. It seemed like a lifetime away, but in reality it was two short months away. They must ship what few belongings they wanted to take, which consisted of Megan's Welsh dresser, her Chesterfield and Royal Worcester dinner service that had also belonged to her parents, plus the few things of Amelia's.

When it came to the cradle Tommy had laughed, 'You don't really want to cart that thing half way across the world do you? '

She nodded determinedly, 'Yes I do Tommy.'

'Okay, whatever you say darling.'

Tommy, with Megan's help, had written to Emelio. Laura and Amy were excited at the prospect of a journey by ship, a farm and a new big brother at the end of it all. Tommy had given Mrs. Stewart-Shenley notice as soon as he'd made his decision, and they were hoping to have his replacement starting by the beginning of September, giving him a month working with Tommy before they sailed on the third of October. Megan knew Tommy was sad to leave, as he'd been there since his return from the Argentine. Mrs. Stewart-Shenley expressed her regret at Tommy's leaving, and had gone on to say that she was surprised he'd stayed so long, a man of his obvious capabilities could, she was sure, have gone much further. She'd wished him well in his new venture.

As the time came nearer Megan became nervous and apprehensive.

'Oh Tommy, it's such a big step. What if we're making a mistake? Will Emelio like us, and will the girls and Matthew settle all right?'

'Don't worry Megan darlin' we'll all be fine, children are adaptable. You're all going to love it. You'll learn to ride, and you're going to see your brother again and meet his family. Aren't you excited?' he asked trying to allay her fears.

Megan laughed, 'Yes I am. Really I am. I'm being silly aren't I?'

'No my love,' he shook his head. 'It's natural. I know exactly how you feel - all the same thoughts and fears I had when I went the first time, except I was alone, twenty years old, but you've got me and the children. There's nothing to keep us here Megan.'

She looked at him, this beloved husband of hers, and she knew she'd go to the ends of the earth with him if he'd asked her.

The few weekends they had left were spent visiting family. Annie and Frank had long since retired from The Greyhound to a small house in Reading. Annie had been most indignant when Tommy broke the news of their impending departure.

'You must be mad Tommy, taking our Emma's girls to some God forsaken country at the other ends of the earth. How can you even think of it?' she exploded.

'Annie,' he said gently, 'Have you stopped to think that if Emma had been alive, we still might have decided to emigrate?'

'Nonsense! Our Emma would never have agreed to have gone off to foreign parts. For goodness sake,' she said turning to Megan, 'can't you talk some sense into him?'

'It's what Tommy wants Annie,' she replied.

Megan had never seen eye to eye with Annie. She found her proprietary attitude towards Amy and Laura most annoying. After all Emma had only been their niece. What rights did Annie have to voice her opinions on their general upbringing, and she had on several occasions.

It had always riled Annie in turn that Emma's children should address Megan as Mummy, and she actually raised the subject once with Tommy, who'd told her in no uncertain terms, that it was none of her business, going on to point out that Megan had been a wonderful mother to them. He was actually so angry that he went so far as to say that Megan was a better mother to them than Emma was. This was something Annie had never forgiven him for, although she knew it to be the truth.

'Humph, and what about you Megan, are you happy to tag along with everything he wants. Don't you have a mind of your own?' she asked scornfully.

'Yes, indeed I do,' Megan retorted sharply, 'but Tommy and I are in complete accord. We're all looking forward to it as a great adventure.'

'Great adventure!' Annie snorted.

'That's enough Annie,' Tommy interrupted, 'I know you'll miss the children, but it's our life, and our choice - not yours.'

‘Well don’t forget to write to us Amy,’ Frank said.

‘Don’t worry Frank, I shall write too and tell you how the girls progress, and we can send you photos so you can see how they’ve grown,’ Megan assured him.

‘Well I suppose we shall have to be satisfied with that then, shan’t we?’ Annie said.

‘Yes Annie I’m afraid you will,’ Tommy replied.

Farewell to Maude and Tommy’s father was a little more emotional. Maude’s plump chins wobbled, her eyes bright with unshed tears as she hugged the children to her ample bosom.

‘We shall miss you all,’ she said, ‘I hope you’ll find time to write to us. ‘

‘Of course we will Maude,’ Tommy said patting her shoulder. He turned to his father who held out his hand. Tommy clasped it in both of his.

‘Goodbye Dad. Look after yourself.’

Megan noticed there was only the slightest tremor in his voice that betrayed his emotions.

‘You too, Thomas. Safe journey,’ his father said gruffly.

Later Tommy confided to Megan how hard he’d found it.

‘I know Tommy, I know you’ve never been close to your father, but he is your flesh and blood after all.’

‘I try not to look back Megan, but when I shook the old man’s hand I realised that the last physical contact with Dad had been the beating I’d taken when I was fifteen years old. There’s been a lot of water under the bridge since then. I didn’t expect to feel anything, but it felt strange to think I might never see him again.’

Georgie and Sylvia were the worst - Sylvia in tears and Megan visibly upset, but trying to comfort her.

‘Oh dear Megan, Tommy we’re going to miss you, and the girls too, and you my precious,’ Sylvia finished picking Matthew up and burying her face in his light brown curls so like his mother’s.

Megan touched Tommy’s arm, a gentle reminder that it was time to leave.

Georgie held out his hand and Tommy clasped it in a firm grip, reluctant to let go. There was a moment’s silence.

Eventually Georgie managed to say brokenly, ‘I don’t suppose we’ll see you again will we our Tommy?’

‘Oh yes you will Georgie, I promise you.’ Letting go of his brother’s hand, he put his arms around him. ‘Believe me, give us two or three years and we’ll come back for a holiday, really,’ he finished seeing the look of disbelief on their faces. It was beyond Georgie and Sylvia’s imagination, anyone crossing half the world for a holiday.

The day finally arrived and as the ship pulled slowly away from the dockside they stood at the rail, a tight little family group, the children waving along with everyone else. As they watched the people grow smaller and smaller, only Megan and Tommy knew that they had no one there to wave to. A tear slid down Megan’s cheek. She wasn’t sure why. She supposed it was because she was leaving behind the only world she had ever known.

Two weeks out to sea and Megan had been nauseous, even though the crossing had been relatively calm so far. One evening, the children having eaten at the earlier sitting, Megan and Tommy went down to dinner leaving them in the care of a stewardess.

‘You look lovely Megan, quite radiant. Would you like to go dancing tonight, if you feel up to it?’ he asked.

‘I’d love to Tommy, but what about the children, have you forgotten them?’

‘No, he shook his head, ‘I asked Tina our stewardess, if she’d look after them for the whole evening, just in case.’

‘Oh lovely, Matthew’s getting to be a real terror. Thank goodness I bought him that set of leather reins otherwise I swear we’d have lost him overboard by now,’ she laughed.

Matthew was becoming a real handful, fourteen months old and into everything, and already showing signs of a temper. His plump little face would turn red with frustration if things didn’t go the way he wanted. Tommy and the girls would laugh, but Megan would firmly chastise him. Small as he was she could see trouble ahead.

‘He’s only a baby Meggie,’ Tommy would say. ‘He’ll grow out of tantrums. Don’t worry.’

But she did worry. He was a hyperactive child, keeping her on the run all day.

‘Right that’s settled then, a night off for you. You can forget the kids for a whole evening and concentrate all your attentions on me,’ he grinned.

‘Have you been feeling a bit neglected lately then?’

‘A little, you’ve been so busy packing, visiting and tearing around behind our son, we don’t seem to have had much time to ourselves lately. I thought we could finish off the evening with a nice romantic stroll in the moonlight.’

She smiled at him, ‘You wouldn’t by any chance be trying to seduce me with soft words and music would you?’

‘I most certainly would, but first let’s dance.’

They danced till almost eleven when Tommy suggested they go up on deck for their stroll, before turning in.

The sea was choppy and the moonlight turned the wave caps silver. They stood at the rail. Tommy behind Megan, his arms around her waist. A fierce gust of wind whipped Megan’s skirts round both their legs.

‘I love the elements, wind, rain even snow,’ Megan said. ‘It must be the Welsh in me.’

He tightened his arms around her, ‘I love you Meggie,’ he whispered as he nuzzled her neck.

‘I love you too Tommy. You can be so romantic,’ she replied squirming round in his arms, winding her arms round his neck as she kissed him.

He grinned as he broke away, ‘It’s all part of the grand seduction scene, this romantic bit. But seriously Megan, I’m glad you’re feeling better. I did want you to enjoy the voyage. It would have been a shame if the seasickness would have ruined it for you.’

She laughed, ‘Oh Tommy.’

‘What’s amusing you?’

‘Two things actually. I was just remembering how you laughed at me for keeping that funny old oak cradle and, secondly, for a man of the world you can be so naive. I haven’t been seasick darling, seasickness is not restricted to early mornings only.’

‘What!’ he looked into her sparkling green eyes till he too started to laugh. ‘Oh Lord! Megan, you’re not...?’

‘I’m afraid so. What would you like this time, a boy or a girl?’

‘I don’t really care this time. I just think it sounds perfect: a new baby, a new country and a new life. The future is ours Meggie. What more could a man ask for?’ he whispered as he held her close.